**"A DAGGER OF TH[...]
WIELDED BY AN A[...]
COURT. . . ."**

Mrs. Ruth glared down at the offending blade for a moment. "Obviously an Adept of the Dark Court has come through the barrier to our world."

"Can they do that?" Roland asked.

"Listen up, bubba," Mrs. Ruth advised, "I just said they did. Of course, it takes a lot of power and the Dark isn't known for doing things without a reason. It's my guess that something big is coming down."

"Something big?"

"To put it bluntly, you've got a whole heap of shit to deal with."

"Deal with?" Roland groaned.

"Deal with. . . . Ignore. . . . It's your choice. You can always let the world and every living soul on it plummet into eternal Darkness. Or you can ask for help, ask an Adept of the Light into our world."

"And just how do we do that."

"I suggest you send a message with the dead," Mrs. Ruth said.

"Oh," Rebecca said. "I could do that. I know a ghost. . . ."

The Finest in Fiction and Fantasy by
TANYA HUFF
available from DAW Books:

*forthcoming from DAW Books

The Finest in Fiction and Fantasy by
TANYA HUFF
Gate of Darkness, Circle of Light

GATE OF DARKNESS
CIRCLE
OF LIGHT
TANYA HUFF

DAW BOOKS, INC.
DONALD A. WOLLHEIM, FOUNDER
375 Hudson Street, New York, NY 10014

ELIZABETH R. WOLLHEIM
SHEILA E. GILBERT
PUBLISHERS

First Printing, November 1989
4   5   6   7   8   9

DAW TRADEMARK REGISTERED
U.S. PAT. OFF. AND FOREIGN COUNTRIES
—MARCA REGISTRADA
HECHO EN U.S.A.

PRINTED IN THE U.S.A.

DEDICATION:

For Kate.

For the future.

ACKNOWLEDGMENTS:

I'd like to thank Hania Wojtowicz, the Metropolitan Toronto Police Department, the University of Toronto Archives, and Dr. Douglas Richardson at University College for their help and their patience.

I'd also like to thank Mercedes Lackey for generously allowing me to use both *The Bait* and *Wind's Four Quarters.*

Chapter ONE

"Rebecca!"

Rebecca paused, one hand on the kitchen door.

"Did you put your tins away neatly?"

"Yes, Lena."

"Have you got your uniform to wash?"

Rebecca smiled but otherwise remained frozen in the motion of leaving. Her food services uniform was folded neatly in the bottom of her bright red tote bag. "Yes, Lena."

"Do you have your muffins for the weekend?"

"Yes, Lena." The muffins, carefully wrapped, were packed safely on top of her soiled uniform. She waited for the next line of the litany.

"Now, don't forget to eat while you're home."

Rebecca nodded so vigorously her brown curls danced. "I'll remember, Lena." One more.

"I'll see you Monday, puss."

"See you Monday, Lena." Freed by the speaking of the last words, Rebecca pushed open the door and bounded out and up the stairs.

Lena watched her go, then turned and went back into her office.

"And you go through this every Friday, Mrs. Pementel?"

"Every Friday," Lena agreed, settling down into her chair with a sigh. "For almost a year now."

Her visitor shook his head. "I'm surprised she's allowed to wander around unsupervised."

Lena snorted and dug around in her desk for her cigarettes. "Oh, she's safe enough. The Lord protects

his own. Damn lighter.'' She shook it, slammed it
against the desk, and was rewarded by a feeble flame.
''I know what you're thinking,'' she said, as she
sucked in smoke. ''But she does her job better than
some with a lot more on the ball. You're not going to
save any of the taxpayers' money by getting rid of
her.''

The man from accounting frowned. ''Actually, I was
wondering how anyone could continue smoking given
the evidence. Those things'll kill you, you know.''

''Well that's my choice, isn't it? Come on,'' she
rested her elbows on the desk and exhaled slowly
through her nose, waving the glowing end of the cigarette at his closed briefcase. ''Let's get on with it . . .''

''They cut emeralds from the heart of summer.''

The grubby young man, who'd been approaching
with the intention of begging a couple of bucks, hesitated.

''And sapphires drop out of the sky, just before it
gets dark.'' Rebecca lifted her forehead from the
pawnshop window and turned to smile at him. ''I know
the names of all the jewels,'' she said proudly. ''And
I make my own diamonds in the refrigerator at home.''

Ducking his head away from her smile, the young
man decided he had enough on his plate, he didn't
need a crazy, too. He kept moving, both hands shoved
deep in the torn pockets of his jean jacket.

Rebecca shrugged, and went back to studying the
trays of rings. She loved pretty things and every afternoon on the way home from the government building
where she worked, she lingered in front of the window
displays.

Behind her, the bells of Saint James Cathedral began to call the hour.

''Time to go,'' she told her reflection in the glass
and smiled when it nodded in agreement. As she
walked north, Saint James handed her over to Saint
Michael's. The bells, like the cathedrals, had frightened her when she'd first heard them, but now they
were old friends. The bells, that is, not the cathedrals.

Such huge imposing buildings, so solemn and so brooding, she felt couldn't be friends with anyone. Mostly, they made her sad.

Rebecca hurried along the east side of Church Street, carefully not seeing or hearing the crowds and the traffic. Mrs. Ruth had taught her that, how to go inside herself where it was quiet, so all the bits and pieces swirling around didn't make her into bits and pieces, too. She wished she could feel something besides sidewalk through the rubber soles of her thongs.

At Dundas Street, while waiting for the light, a bit of black, fluttering along a windowsill on the third floor of the Sears building, caught her eye.

"No, careful wait!" she yelled, scrambling the sentence in her excitement.

Most of the other people at the intersection ignored her. A few looked up, following her gaze, but seeing only what appeared to be a piece of carbon paper blowing in the wind, they lost interest. One or two tapped their heads knowingly.

When the light changed, Rebecca bounded forward, ignoring the horn of a low-slung, red car that was running the end of the yellow light

"Don't!"

Too late. The black bit dove off the window ledge, twisted once in the air, became a very small squirrel, and just managed to get its legs under it before it hit the ground. It remained still for only a second, then darted to the curb. A truck roared by. It flipped over and started back to the building, was almost stepped on and turned again to the curb, blind panic obvious in every motion. It tried to climb a hydro pole, but its claws could get no purchase on the smooth cement.

"Hey." Rebecca knelt and held out her hand.

The squirrel, cowering up against the base of the pole, sniffed the offered fingers.

"It's okay." She winced as the tiny animal swarmed up her bare arm, scrambled through her hair, and perched trembling on the top of her head. Gently she scooped it off. "Silly baby," she said, stroking one finger down its back. The trembling stopped, but she could still feel its heart beating against her palm. Continuing to soothe it, Rebecca stood and moved slowly back to the intersection. As the squirrel was too young to find its way home, she'd have to find a home for it, and the Ryerson Quad was the closest sanctuary.

The Quad was one of Rebecca's favorite places. Completely enclosed by Kerr Hall, it was quiet and green; a private little park in the midst of the city. Very few people outside the Ryerson student body knew it existed, which, Rebecca felt, was for the best. She knew where all the green growing places hid. This afternoon, with classes finished for the summer, the Quad was deserted.

She reached up and gently placed the squirrel on the lowest branch of a maple. It paused, one tiny front paw lifted, then it whisked out of sight.

"You're welcome," she told it, gave the maple a friendly pat, and continued home.

A huge chestnut tree dominated the small patch of ground between the sidewalk and Rebecca's building, towering over the three stories of red brick. Rebecca often wondered if the front apartments got any light at all but supposed the illusion of living in a tree would make up for it if they didn't. Stepping onto the path, she tipped back her head and peered into the leaves for a glimpse of the tree's one permanent inhabitant.

She spotted him at last, tucked up high on a sturdy branch, legs swinging and head bent over the work in his hands; which, as usual, she couldn't identify. All she could see of his face were his eyebrows which stuck out a full, bushy, red inch under the front edge of his bright red cap.

"Good evening, Orten."

" 'Tain't evening yet, still afternoon. And my name ain't Orten, neither."

Rebecca sighed and crossed another name off her mental list. Rumplestiltskin had been the first name she'd tried, but the little man had merely laughed so hard he'd had to grab onto a branch.

"Well, hello, Becca." The large-blonde-lady-from-down-the-hall stepped through the front door, thighs rubbing in polyester pants.

Rebecca sighed. Nobody called her Becca, but she couldn't get the large-blonde-lady-from-down-the-hall to stop. "My name is Rebecca."

"That's right, dear, and you live here at 55 Carlton Street." Her voice was loud and she pronounced each word deliberately, a verbal pat on the head. "Who were you talking to?"

"Norman," Rebecca ventured, pointing up into the tree.

"Not likely," snorted the little man.

The large-blonde-lady-from-down-the-hall pursed fuchsia lips. "How sweet, you've named the birds. I don't know how you can tell them apart."

"I don't talk to birds," Rebecca protested. "Birds never listen."

Neither did the large-blonde-lady-from-down-the-hall.

"I'm going out now, Becca, but if you need anything later don't you hesitate to come and get me." She brushed past the girl, beaming at this opportunity to show herself a good neighbor. *That Becca may not be right in the head,* she'd often told her sister, *but she's so much better mannered than most young people. Why, she never takes her eyes off me when I speak.*

For almost a year now, Rebecca had been trying to decide if the white slabs of teeth between heavily painted lips were real. She still couldn't make up her mind, the volume of the words kept distracting her.

"Maybe she thinks I can't hear?" she'd asked the little man once.

His answer had been typical.

"Maybe she doesn't think."

She fished her keys out of her pocket—her keys always went in the right front pocket of her jeans, so she always knew where they were—and put them in the lock. Then she thought of a new name and, leaving the keys dangling, went back to the tree.

"Percy?" she asked.

"You wish," came the response.

She shrugged philosophically and went inside.

Friday night she did-the-laundry and had beef-vegetable-soup-for-supper, just as she was supposed to according to the list Daru, her social worker, had drawn up. Saturday, she spent at Allen Gardens helping her friend George transplant ferns. That took all day because the ferns didn't want to be transplanted. Saturday night, Rebecca went to make tea and found she was out of milk. Milk was one of the things Daru called odds and ends groceries and she was allowed to buy it herself. Taking a dollar and a quarter out of the handleless space shuttle mug, she let herself out of the apartment and walked down Mutual Street to the corner store. She didn't stop to talk to the little man, nor to even look up into the tree. Daru had said over and over she had to be careful with money and she didn't want to hold on to it any longer than she had to.

Hurrying back, she wondered why the evening had grown so quiet and why the poorly lit street suddenly seemed so filled with shadows she didn't recognize.

"Mortimer?" she called when she reached the tree, knowing he would answer whether she guessed his name or not.

A drop of rain hit her cheek.

Warm rain.

She put up her hand and it came away red.

Another drop crinkled the paper bag around the milk.

Blood.

Rebecca recognized blood. She had bleeding once a month. And Daru had said that any other time but then blood meant something was wrong and she was to call her no matter when, but Daru wouldn't see the little man and he was the one bleeding, Rebecca knew it, but she didn't know what to do. Daru had said she must never climb trees in the city.

But her friend was bleeding and bleeding was wrong.

Rules, Mrs. Ruth had often said, exist to be broken. Putting down the milk, she jumped for the bottom branch of the chestnut. Bark pulled off under her hands, but she tightened her grip—people were always surprised at how strong she was—and swung herself up, kicking off her thongs. Men in orange vests had tried to take that branch off earlier in the spring, but she'd talked to them until they forgot why they were there and they'd never come back. Rebecca didn't approve of cutting at trees with noisy machines.

She climbed higher, heading for the little man's favorite perch. The dusk and the shifting leaves made it hard to see, throwing unexpected patterns of shadow in her way. When her hand closed over a wet and sticky spot, she knew she was close. Then she saw a pair of dangling boots, the upturned toes no longer cocky as blood dripped off first one and then the other.

He had been wedged into the angle formed by two branches and the main trunk. His eyes were closed, his hat was askew, and a black knife protruded from his chest.

Carefully, Rebecca lifted him and cradled him against her. He murmured something in a language she didn't understand but otherwise lay completely motionless. He weighed next to nothing and she could carry him easily in one arm as she descended, his legs kicking limply against her hips, his head lolling in the crook of her neck.

When she reached the bottom branch, she sat, wrapped her other arm about her wounded friend, and pushed off. The landing knocked her to her knees. She whimpered, then got up and staggered for the safety of her apartment.

Once inside, she went straight to the bed alcove and laid the little man upon the double bed. Around the knife his small chest still rose and fell so she knew he lived, but she didn't know what she should do now. Should she call Daru? No. Daru wouldn't See so Daru couldn't help.

"She'll think I'm slipping again," Rebecca confided to the unconscious little man. "Like she did when I told her about you at first." She paced up and down, chewing on the nails of her left hand. She needed someone who was clever, but who wouldn't refuse to See. Someone who would know what-to-do.

Roland.

He hadn't ever actually said he could See. He'd hardly ever said anything to her at all, but he spoke with his music and the music said he'd help. And he was clever. Roland would know what-to-do.

She sat down on the edge of the bed and pulled on her running shoes, then turned and patted the little man on the knee.

"Don't worry," she told him. "I'm going for help."

Grabbing up her sweater, she stepped out into the hallway and paused. Would he be safe in there all alone?

"Tom?"

The large gray tabby, moving with stately dignity down the hall, stopped and turned to face her.

"The little man from the tree has been hurt."

Tom licked at the spotless white of his ruff, waiting to be told something he didn't know.

"Can you stay with him? I'm going for help."

He considered it while inspecting one forepaw. Rebecca bounced as she waited, but she knew there was no use in trying to hurry a cat. Finally he stood and came forward to brush against her legs, his head bumping into the hollows of her knees.

"Thank you." She reached behind her and pushed open the door. Tom went in, snapping his tail out of the way as she closed it behind him.

Heading for the stairs, she broke into a run.

Roland scowled at the scattering of money in his open guitar case. It hadn't been a good evening. In fact, for a Saturday at Yonge and Queen, it had been pitiful. A breeze lifted one of the few bills and he grabbed for it. His uncle was pretty understanding about waiting for the rent on his basement room but point-blank refused to feed him. *A twenty-eight year old man*, his uncle often said, *should have a real job*.

A teen-age girl, almost wearing a pair of pale blue shorts, came up from the subway and Roland watched

appreciatively as she passed by him and stood waiting
for the light.

He'd had real jobs, off and on, but he always came
back to music and music always brought him back to
the street where he could play what he liked when he
liked. Occasionally, he filled in when local groups
needed a guitarist at the last minute. He was supposed
to be filling in tonight, but this afternoon he'd gotten
a call saying both the drummer and the keyboard player
had picked up the same bug as the man he was to
replace and the gig had been called off. He checked
his watch. Eight forty-five. Both Simpsons and the Eat-
ton Centre would be closing in fifteen minutes and
business might pick up on the street.

Drifting up from the passage that ran under Queen
Street, connecting Simpsons to both the Centre and
the subway, came something Roland thought he recognized as a Beatles song. The Beatles probably
wouldn't have recognized it, but in the six days this
guy had been down there Roland had gotten used to
his peculiar interpretations. The guys who sang in the
subway made more money, but they had to pay a hundred bucks a year to the Toronto Transit Commission
for a licensing fee and move from station to station
according to a schedule that came down from the head
office. Roland refused to even consider it; licensing
busking was an obscenity as far as he was concerned.

He checked his watch again. Eight forty-seven. Time
flies. He scanned the few people on the street and
from slogans on T-shirts—*the right to arm bears?*—
assumed they were American tourists. Probably from
Buffalo or Rochester. Sometimes it seemed like half
of upper New York State came into Toronto on the
weekends. He sighed and flipped a mental coin. John
Denver came up and he launched into "Rocky Mountain High." So much for artistic integrity.

By the second verse, the satisfyingly solid thunk of
the new dollar coins hitting his case had put him in a
better frame of mind and he was able to smile at Rebecca when he noticed her standing in front of him.
The part of his mind not occupied with going home to

a place he'd never been before wondered what she was
doing out so late. He usually saw her in the early afternoon when she spent her lunch break sitting listening to him play and he never saw her on the weekends.
He suspected she wasn't allowed out at this hour but
didn't take it for granted; he'd learned not to take much
about Rebecca for granted.

"I'm not retarded," she'd told him that first afternoon, prompted by his condescending voice and manner. *"I'm mentally disadvantaged."* Her pronunciation
of the long words was slow, but perfect.

"Oh?" he'd said. *"Who told you that?"*

*"Daru, my social worker. But I like what Mrs. Ruth
says I am better."*

"And what's that?"

"Simple."

"Uh, do you know what that means?"

"Yes. It means I have less pieces than most people."

"Oh." There wasn't much else he could think of to
reply.

She'd grinned at him. *"And that means I'm solider
than most people."*

And the funny thing, Roland mused, was that while
undeniably retarded, in a number of ways Rebecca *was*
solider than most people. She knew who and what she
was. *Which puts her two up on me,* he added with a
mental snort. And sometimes she'd say the damnedest
things, right out of the blue, that made perfect sense.
With some surprise, he realized he actually enjoyed
talking to her and looked forward to spotting her smile
amidst the harried lunch hour scowls.

As Roland moved into the last chorus, he saw she
was bouncing, rising up on her toes and back, up on
her toes and back, the way she did when she had something important to tell him. The last something important had been the hideous orange sweater she now
had tied around her waist. (*"I bought it myself at
Goodwill for only two dollars."*) He thought she'd been
overcharged, but she'd been so proud of her purchase
he couldn't say anything. It looked worse than usual
tonight against her purple tank top and her jeans.

He finished the song, smiled his thanks as a fortyish man in a loud Hawaiian shirt dropped a handful of loose change into the case, and turned to Rebecca.

"Hey, kiddo, what's up?"

Rebecca stopped bouncing and stepped toward him. "You have to help, Roland. I got him in my bed, but I don't know what to do now. Or how to make the bleeding stop."

"WHAT!"

She took a startled step back. There were too many built things around, too many cars, too many people; she could feel all the pieces pushing in at her. She could feel the outside nibbling at her edges but she knew she couldn't go to the quiet inside place if she wanted to save her friend. Moving forward she clutched at Roland's arm. "Help. Please," she pleaded.

Roland considered himself a good judge of emotions—a necessary skill for survival on the street—and Rebecca was definitely frightened. Awkwardly, he patted her hand. "Yeah, don't worry. I'll come. Just let me pack up."

Rebecca nodded, a jerky motion which Roland knew meant she wasn't far from panic for her movements were normally slow and deliberate. *Where the hell is her social worker?* he asked himself, scooping change into a small leather bag. *She's supposed to be riding to the rescue, not me.* He laid the guitar down, tucked the bag along the neck, and closed the lid. *And what the hell happened? Can't stop what bleeding? Oh, Jesus, just what I need; Simple Simon stabs a pieman, film at eleven.*

He straightened up, shrugged into his corduroy jacket—wearing it was easier than carrying it, even if it was still hotter than blazes out—picked up the guitar case, and held out his hand.

"Okay," he said in what he hoped was a reassuring tone, "let's go."

She grabbed the offered hand and pulled him forward, across Yonge and east along Queen.

The light was green; fortunately, because Rebecca didn't look and Roland didn't think he could stop her.

He suspected that if he tried to pull his hand free she'd crush his fingers without even noticing it. He hadn't realized she was so strong.

Wait a minute! She got him in her bed?

"Rebecca, did a man attack you?"

"Not me." She continued to pull.

He had a feeling she didn't understand the question and with no idea whether she knew what rape meant, he didn't know how to rephrase it. Trouble was, while her mind might be no more than twelve at best, her body was that of a young woman; a well padded young woman, pretty in a comfortable sort of a way. Roland could remember being disappointed himself when he caught sight of the expression that went with the curves but he knew that wouldn't discourage a lot of men and would, in fact, encourage a few. *The world,* he sighed silently, *has a fuck of a lot of shitheads in it and a distressingly large number of them are men.* It wasn't that Rebecca was innocent, she had too much unconscious sensuality for the word to apply, it was more that she *had* an innocence—though, if pressed, Roland knew he couldn't define the difference. He twisted away from the subject. The whole concept made him sweat.

One thing Roland had come to know about Rebecca: she never told lies. Occasionally her version of the truth was a little skewed, but if she said that someone was bleeding in her bed, she truly believed someone was. *Of course,* he watched the curls bob on the back of her neck, *she also believes that a troll lives under the Bloor Viaduct.* He couldn't decide whether he should get upset or wait until he was sure that there was something to get upset about.

At Church Street, Rebecca began to calm down. She walked this route every day and the familiarity of it soothed her.

It's nine o'clock, Saint Michael's told her as they passed. *Nine, nine, nine. Hurry, hurry, hurry. Late, late, late.*

She let go of Roland's hand and ran a little ahead, unable to keep herself to his pace any longer.

Roland flexed his fingers, feeling circulation return. He couldn't help but smile as he watched her run forward, then back to make sure he still followed, then forward again. It reminded him of an old Lassie movie. He hoped he'd have nothing more complicated to deal with than little Timmy trapped in a flooding river. He hoped. But he doubted it.

When they reached her apartment building, Rebecca darted up the path and snatched up a brown paper bag leaning up against the foot of the tree. She looked inside, nodded in satisfaction, and held it out for Roland's inspection.

"My milk. I left it here earlier."

"It'll be warm, kiddo."

Touching the side of the cardboard carton, she shook her head. "No. It's still cool." Then she turned the bag and pointed at a reddish-brown stain. "See."

Roland leaned forward. It looked like . . . "Oh my god, that's blood!" Someone was bleeding in her bed . . . Jesus! And here he was, dashing to the rescue. He should've called a cop the moment she showed up.

Handing him the milk—he held it gingerly, hardly able to take his eyes off the stain—Rebecca unlocked the entrance and led the way upstairs.

"I left Tom with him," she explained, pausing in front of her apartment. She gave the door a push and it swung silently open.

Roland stared into a scene of utter chaos and felt his jaw drop. One piece of curtain hung crazily askew, swinging in the breeze from the open window. The other appeared to have been shredded and flung about the room. A kitchen chair lay on its back, dripping with water and garlanded with cut flowers, the broken vase on the floor beside it. Plants and dirt were everywhere.

In the center of the mess, sat a large tabby cat, placidly grooming the white tip of his tail. An ugly scratch showed red against the pink of his nose and one ear had acquired a fresh notch.

"Tom!" Rebecca stepped over a pile of green fur

Roland assumed had been a rug before puss and his
playmate had gotten to it. "Are you all right?"

Tom curled his tail around his toes and stared up at
her with gold, unblinking eyes; then he noticed Roland
and hissed.

"It's okay," Rebecca explained. "I brought him to
see. He'll know what to do."

Tom looked Roland up and down, then twisted
around to wash the base of his spine, a gesture of
obvious disbelief.

"Yeah? Well, same to you, buddy," Roland growled
as they headed past him into the bed alcove. He hated
cats, the sanctimonious little hairballs. "Okay, Rebecca, where's this . . ."

The question remained unfinished. Rebecca sat on
the edge of her bed holding the hand of a little man,
no more than a foot high. Although he wore trousers
of green and an almost fluorescent yellow shirt, the
color red dominated the scene. His hair, eyebrows,
and beard looked almost orange beneath the bright red
cap which matched the scarlet bubbles appearing between his lips with every breath. But it was the crimson stain beneath the handle of the black knife in his
chest that drew the eye.

His eyes opened, focused on Rebecca, and the ghost
of a smile drifted over his face. His hand tightening
on hers, he tried to speak.

She leaned closer.

"Alex . . . ander," he gasped.

"Alexander? But I guessed that months ago!"

"I know." He fought for one last breath. "I lied."
The ghost of the smile returned and the little man died.
Slowly, the body faded away until only the black knife
and the red stains remained.

Chapter TWO

Without the little man's body wrapped about it, the black knife looked smaller but no less deadly. The triangular blade, no more than three inches long, tapered down to a wicked point and the edges were honed to razor sharpness. The grip had been wrapped in black leather that now glistened with blood.

"I don't believe it," Roland muttered. "This isn't happening."

Rebecca looked up from the knife, her head cocked to one side, "But you saw," she pointed out.

"Yeah, I know I saw. But that doesn't mean anything. I've seen a lot of things I didn't believe in."

"Like what?"

"Well, like . . . like . . ." He threw his hands up in the air and backed out of the bed alcove. "Well, things. Get out of my way, cat!"

Tom moved free of Roland's legs, his expression clearly stating that even such as Roland should know cats had the right of way. Jumping up on the bed, he circled the knife, his bristling fur making him appear at least twice his normal size. He growled and slapped at Rebecca's hand as it reached into the perimeter of his pacing.

"I wasn't going to touch it," she protested.

He sat, tail wrapped around toes, just at the edge of the blood, and stared at the dagger.

Rebecca watched him for a moment, but he neither moved nor blinked so she went into the other room to see what Roland was doing.

Roland was cleaning up. Torn curtains, spilled plants, and scattered cushions, he could deal with. Murdered figments of Rebecca's imagination were giving him just a little more trouble. Had the dagger and the blood disappeared with the body he could've convinced himself, with very little effort, that nothing had happened. But it hadn't. And he couldn't. And he didn't know what, if anything, he should do about it.

He scooped dirt back into an empty margarine container, resettled the geranium—one of two indoor plants he could recognize and he hoped Rebecca wasn't growing the other—and put the whole thing back on the wide shelf that ran under the window. Brushing them clean, he settled the sofa cushions where they belonged and reached for a large pad of poster paper that lay crumpled in a corner.

Crumpled. Like the little man had been against the pillows.

He'd *have* to think about it sometime. Later.

The poster paper had two holes punched into its narrower edge and was obviously meant to hang on the wall opposite the window. He heaved it onto the hooks—the two-foot by three-foot pad was heavy—and smoothed down the top sheet.

Friday, it said, and the date. Then, *supper: beef vegetable soup and crackers.* And, *Do laundry: cold water, one cup of detergent, warm dry with softener sheet.* The words had been printed in block letters and stirred vague memories in Roland of primary school activity lists. He peered at the next sheet down.

Saturday, it said, and the date. *Don't forget to eat. Wear shoes.*

"Rebecca," he asked as he read the instructions for Sunday and Monday—*Be in bed by ten. Take your clean uniforms to work.* "What is this?"

"My lists. Daru and I write them on Monday after we go and get groceries." She crawled out from under the tiny kitchen table, a plastic saltshaker clutched in one hand. "And I do what they say. They remember things for me so I can think of other stuff. Except I forgot to take Friday's list down. You can if you want to."

Do laundry. Don't forget to eat. Wear shoes.

Roland wasn't sure why the lists bothered him, but they did. They seemed so horribly binding; which was ridiculous for his mother had often left *much* more explicit lists for his father. "What would happen if you didn't follow them?"

"They said I'd go back to the group home." She pulled on her lower lip. "And I don't want to go back."

"Why?" he asked gently. "Were they mean to you?"

"No." Rebecca sighed, more in weariness it seemed to Roland than anything else and just for an instant she wore an expression he couldn't recognize. "They just never let me be alone." She set the saltshaker down on the table. "Now what do we do, Roland?"

"Well, we . . . uh . . ." He waved a vague hand around at the mess. "I, uh, guess we report this."

Rebecca looked worried. "Report what?"

"That someone broke into your apartment . . ."

"Oh. That." She smiled indulgently and shook her head. "That was just someone trying to get to Alexander, 'cause they knew he wasn't dead yet. Tom took care of it."

"Rebecca, Tom is a cat."

"Yes." She waited for a moment and when Roland seemed to have nothing more to offer repeated, "Now what do we do, Roland?"

He took a deep breath and let it out slowly. He didn't have the faintest idea.

"Daru would believe me if you told her, too."

Briefly, Roland considered telling Daru that he'd seen nothing at all. If the woman had worked with Rebecca for any length of time, she'd know the girl told the most fantastic fables believing them to be the truth—although, given what had happened tonight, perhaps the world held too narrow a view of just what truth was. That aside, Daru would thank him for supporting Rebecca in her panic and his involvement in all this dangerous weirdness would end.

Then he looked into Rebecca's eyes and discovered that, amidst all the strange and magical things she believed in, she also believed in him.

"Call Daru," he said, surrendering to the moment

and surprised at how good it felt. "I'll back up anything you tell her." He couldn't remember if anyone
had ever believed in him before.

Rebecca nodded, pulled an old phone out from under the sofa, and plugged it into the jack. "I don't like
the noise when it rings," she explained to Roland's
raised eyebrows. "I unplug it and it doesn't."

He could see a strip of white adhesive tape along
the back of the receiver, the numbers printed on it
visible from across the room. Daru's number, he assumed and Rebecca did seem to be dialing it. Hooking
a chair with one foot, he pulled it under himself, sat,
and reached for the clasps on his guitar case. He always thought better when he was playing. Without his
willing it, his fingers slipped into "Red River Valley,"
the first recognizable piece of music he'd ever learned.
From this valley they say you are going . . . He
watched Rebecca on the phone and wondered why that
was the only line he could remember.

Rebecca frowned, took a deep breath, and began
speaking in a high, tight voice. "My name is Rebecca
Partridge and it's Saturday night and his name was
Alexander and he lied to me, but then he died. We
still have the knife, but we don't know what to do, so
please tell us." She paused, wet her lips, and added,
"Thank you." Then she hung up.

"Answering machine?" Roland guessed.

"Un-huh." She unplugged the phone and shoved it
back under the couch.

"What if Daru calls?"

"She won't be back all weekend. The machine said
so. What do we do *now*, Roland?"

A very good question, Roland thought, picking out
a minor scale. They couldn't exactly report the death
to the police, not without a body. Come to think of it,
reporting this death, even *with* a body might not be
such a good idea. He marveled at how calmly he was
taking this—"this" including having his entire world
view overturned—and decided a major case of hysteria
was on the shelf until the time was right. "I guess we
wait for Daru to call."

"But I want to do something now," Rebecca protested. "Alexander was my friend and someone killed him."

. . . and someone killed him . . .

Roland's brain made the final connection; the little man didn't just die, he'd been killed, murdered, offed, terminated with extreme prejudice. With an effort, Roland got a grip on his thought processes. "I guess we should find out who did it." But how?

As if she'd been following his line of reasoning, Rebecca stood and said, "We'll go see Mrs. Ruth. She'll know. She knows everything."

"Then why didn't you go to her first?" Roland asked, putting his guitar away.

" 'Cause she wouldn't have come back with me and Alexander wasn't dead then."

"Well," Roland stood and stretched the kinks out of his back, "if Mrs. Ruth knows everything, by all means, let us go to Mrs. Ruth. We'd better take the knife. It's our only clue." Even playing private investigator beat staying here with that accusatory stain on the bed. If Mrs. Ruth had answers, he was all for her. So far the night had been made up too entirely of questions. He checked his watch. It wasn't quite ten o'clock.

Rebecca got a flowered towel from her tiny bathroom and managed to wrap the knife without touching it. "Are you taking your guitar?" she asked, dropping the bundle into her red bag.

"Where I go, it goes. Can your cat go out?"

"He's not my cat," Rebecca told him, getting a bowl of red pistachio nuts out of the cupboard and putting it on the table. "He's his own cat."

Tom ignored them both and sat staring at the door. When it was opened, he squeezed out and padded away on business of his own.

"Good-bye to bad news," Roland muttered after him and stepped aside to let Rebecca lock up.

The walk to Bloor Street and Mrs. Ruth was an eye-opener for Roland in more ways than one. Rebecca led him through quiet residential neighborhoods that he'd never suspected existed so close to the noisy heart of the city. And Rebecca spoke to creatures he'd never suspected existed—period. The trees and shrubs along the way were home to more than squirrels and the red and golden eyes peering up through sewer grates did not belong to rats and cockroaches.

He ducked the clutching hands of something vaguely human perched on the lowest branch of a crab apple tree overhanging the sidewalk. "Where did all these things come from?" he wondered, staring at the creatures who were not moths fluttering around a streetlight.

"The littles? They've always been here."

"Oh, yeah? Then why haven't I ever seen them?"

Rebecca considered it for a moment. "Have you ever looked?" she asked.

"Looked?" He waved a hand at the shadows. "Why would I look for things I don't believe in."

"Then that's why you never saw them."

"But I see them now."

She smiled. "Now you're looking."

"No I'm not, I . . ." After the undeniable reality of the dead little man, how could he help but look? How could he help but believe? "I . . . What the hell is causing that?" He pointed to where a larger than average front lawn undulated up and down, up and down, like some sort of turf-covered waterbed.

Rebecca stopped and studied it, head to one side, squinting a little in the uncertain light. "I don't know," she said at last. "Should we find out?"

"No!" Grabbing her arm, he pulled her quickly along. "I don't think we should find out. I don't think we should have anything to do with it." He hung on until the disturbance was two blocks and a corner behind them, and then he let her go. She had a funny expression on her face and Roland hoped she wasn't angry.

"Penny for your thoughts?" he asked gently.

"Okay."

He waited.

"You offered me a penny," she pointed out.

"That's just a . . . oh, never mind." He pulled a handful of change out of his pants' pocket, separated a penny, and placed it in her hand. It seemed easier than explaining.

"I was just thinking that we haven't seen a little since that lawn moved."

Roland took her arm again. "Is that bad?"

"I don't know."

"Right." He picked up their pace. "How much farther to this Mrs. Ruth?"

"Not far. We're almost at Spadina. See?"

She pointed and Roland could, indeed, see the busy thoroughfare at the end of the quiet little street they traveled and he got the impression as they moved out into the light and the noise that they were stepping out into another world.

At least these dangers I understand. He herded Rebecca out to the road, then had to pull her from the path of a speeding truck.

"Rebecca? Oh, damn . . ," The girl's eyes were wide, whites showing all around the irises, and her head whipped back and forth so quickly he was afraid she'd dislocate it. A car swerved to miss them and she froze, her hand closing about his arm.

"Jesus!" His arm felt like it had been caught in a vise. "Rebecca, let go!" He couldn't shake free of her. The Spadina bus went by and she wailed, a high-pitched keen that made the hair on the back of his neck stand up. "Rebecca! I won't let anything happen to you, but we've got to get across the street." He began to drag her forward; if he couldn't get her to let go, he might as well get some use out of that deadly grip.

Spadina would have to be four fucking lanes wide, he thought when they at last reached the opposite curb. His arm, below the tourniquet of her hand, was starting to go numb.

She didn't begin to calm until he got her a little way down the dark side street. Sagging against a tree, she released his arm and the wild look went out of her eyes.

"What do you do when you're alone?" he asked,

watching the marks left by her fingers turn from white
to red. If she went that crazy crossing a street, how
could this Daru person let her wander about?

"I go down to the stop lights . . ."

Roland dimly remembered a set of lights a block
south of where they'd crossed.

". . . and I cross on the green. I never try to race
the yellow. Then I walk back to this street on the sidewalk." She stared at him gravely, still breathing a little quickly. "You're not supposed to cross without the
green light."

Her panic, he realized suddenly, had been partially
about the speeding cars and partially about breaking
what she perceived as the rules. This bothered him the
same way the lists back in the apartment had. Rebecca
lived a very fettered life although, he had to admit,
probably a safe one if she always crossed on the green.
Safer than his own, anyway.

"Are you ready to go on?"

Rebecca nodded. "We're really close," she said as
she straightened. "Just down here and then turn and
go to Bloor."

"Can't we stay out where it's light?" Spadina would
get them to Bloor just as easily.

Out on Spadina, two Jeeps and a BMW roared by
and Rebecca winced, her expression speaking her
preference very strongly.

"It's okay," Roland patted her shoulder, "we'll go
your way."

Her smile made it worth the risk. He looked down
the street to where the great bulks of chestnut trees
seemed to soak up the streetlights. Almost.

The traffic sounds faded quickly as they walked and
the silence grew. Roland began to get a very good idea
of why the phrase, "It's too quiet," had become a
cliché of old horror movies. Even the noise of his guitar case brushing against his jeans was curiously
muted. The lit windows of the houses they passed
seemed farther from the sidewalk than he knew they
could possibly be. They saw no littles and, by now,
Roland was definitely looking. He could feel sweat

soaking into his T-shirt and it had nothing to do with the heat.

Rebecca pressed up against his side, her expression more wary than frightened.

"Don't worry, kiddo," he said in what he hoped was a reassuring tone, "it's only . . ."

And then the lawn they were passing attacked them.

Except it wasn't a lawn anymore. Roughly humanoid, it swatted Roland aside with one massive arm and lunged for Rebecca.

She stood her ground, the red bag holding the dagger clutched tightly under her elbow.

The thing touched her, jerked back, and crumbled formless to the ground; a harmless pile of man-shaped earth.

Roland scrubbed dirt out of his eyes and stood. He'd scraped an elbow raw hitting the pavement, but other than that and a bruise or two he wasn't hurt.

"What the hell was that?" he demanded, his voice rising in a nervous shriek.

"A nasty thought," Rebecca said seriously. She looked him over, nodded, knelt, and began to shovel handfuls of dirt off the sidewalk and back where it belonged.

"Say what?" He detected a distinct note of panic and forced himself to calm down. After all, no one had been hurt. By a lawn. Attacking. "I don't think I want any more to do with all this," he murmured, though he suspected it was far too late—that it had been too late when he'd let Rebecca drag him off.

"A nasty thought," Rebecca repeated, continuing to lift double handfuls of dirt off the concrete.

"Right." He checked his guitar case, thankful now that he'd spent the extra money on a good one. "What was it doing?"

Rebecca frowned. "I don't know. But Mrs. Ruth will."

"Then let's go see her, shall we?" His voice still sounded strained. He marveled that someone who couldn't cross a street without falling into little pieces

could take something like this so completely in her
stride.

"In a minute." She brushed the remaining soil into
a pile and placed it carefully back on the ruin of the
lawn. The little space for growing things left in the
city needed to be taken care of. Frowning, she righted
a small piece of sod. Only a very nasty thought would
rip grass out of its home. "Maybe we should tell the
person who lives here about this. So he can replant
things."

"Uh, no."

"No?" She stood, wiping her hands on her jeans.

"No. He wouldn't believe us. He'd think we did it."

"But I'd never do something like that."

Even in the darkness, Roland could see how hurt
she looked. "I know, kiddo." He patted her awkwardly on the shoulder. "How about we keep going?
It's getting late and we don't want to catch Mrs. Ruth
in bed."

"We won't." Rebecca sighed and began walking
again. "He really wouldn't believe me?"

"No." Roland rubbed his chest where he suspected
bruises were rising to join the mark of Rebecca's hand
on his arm. Believing in something, he was forced to
conclude, had nothing to do with its reality.

It turned out Rebecca had good reason to be so certain they wouldn't catch Mrs. Ruth in bed; she didn't
have a bed. Mrs. Ruth lived under the lilacs at Trinity
United Church.

What now? Roland wondered, as Rebecca beckoned
him into a leafy tunnel. Then he shrugged and dropped
to his knees, crawling past two heavily laden bundle
buggies, sliding his guitar case along the grass. *Well,
it isn't Delphi, but it is centrally located.*

One of the exterior church lights shone directly
above the small triangular area between the lilacs and
the building, making it the best lit place Roland had
been in since they'd left Rebecca's apartment. That
was about all it had going for it as it stank of urine
and unwashed bodies. Roland breathed shallowly
through his mouth and got only as close as necessity

dictated to Mrs. Ruth, who sat with her back against
the limestone of the church.

A bag lady oracle. Why not? He hoped his expression remained noncommittal. *It's no weirder than anything else that's happened tonight. In fact, it's
considerably less weird than being attacked by a lawn.*

Mrs. Ruth appeared to be in her late forties or early
fifties although Roland knew she could be younger;
life on the streets tended to strip youth away in record
time. The stringy hair that escaped from under her red
kerchief was about fifty/fifty brown and gray and her
eyes were a washed out hazel between pink lids. Rolls
of fat kept her face from wrinkles and she had almost
no eyebrows. In spite of the heat, her round little body
hid beneath layers and layers of grimy clothing.

"So? So?" Her accent hovered somewhere in East-
ern Europe. "What is it this time that you bother an
old lady, bringing strangers to her home?"

"This isn't strangers, Mrs. Ruth," Rebecca told her
earnestly. "This is Roland."

"Roland?" Her brow furrowed and she dropped the
accent. "Oh, yeah, the Bard."

"Musician," Roland corrected.

"Look, bubba," her washed out old eyes focused
on him and he had the strangest impression of being
transparent, "you want my advice or not?"

"Well, yeah, I guess . . ."

"Then you can stop contradicting everything I say."
She pointed a grimy finger at him. "I say you're a
Bard, you're a Bard. I say you're a wienie, you're a
wienie. And," she added, "I strongly suspect you're
a wienie."

"Oh, no, Mrs. Ruth, he isn't. He Sees."

Mrs. Ruth sighed, her breath smelling of mint gum.
"You're not listening again, Rebecca. I just said he
was a Bard and *all* Bards have the Sight, so *he* must.
Q.E.D., whatever that means. Now then, get to the
point, why are you here? Not that I don't enjoy your
company, but I have things to do."

*Probably missing the midnight madness sale at the
local dumpster,* Roland speculated as Rebecca opened

her bag and dumped the rolled towel out on the grass. Carefully she flipped back the ends, shaking her head sadly at the bloodstains on the cloth.

Mrs. Ruth sucked breath through yellow teeth. "Where did you find that?"

"In Alexander."

"Who is?"

"Was. He was the little man in the tree outside my apartment building. Someone killed him."

"And you think I know who did it?"

"Do you?" asked Roland.

"Sort of. It's a long story." She reached out, snapped off a dead branch, and poked at the dagger with it. "This weapon belongs to an Adept of the Dark Court." Her mouth twisted into something close to a smile. "Should I start at the beginning?"

"Please," Rebecca said. And Roland found himself nodding.

"Our world is a neutral area, a sort of buffer zone, between the Dark Court and the Light. Back in the bright beginning, creatures from both Courts wandered freely through it, fighting when they met. When life indigenous to the area developed, barriers were raised around it in order to give that life a chance to grow without interference." Mrs. Ruth snorted. "Both Dark and Light, by their nature, love to interfere. Only the gray folk, the creatures with no alliance to either court were permitted to pass back and forth through the barriers at will.

"Unfortunately, both the Dark and Light still want in, seeking to use our world to strengthen themselves. The Dark chips away at the barriers and slips nasty bits through . . ."

"A nasty thought attacked us," Rebecca interrupted, "on our way here."

Mrs. Ruth tapped the knife. "This attracts them. How did it attack?"

"It made a body out of dirt."

"Dirt?" She snorted again. "Stupid."

"Wait a minute," Roland protested. "Do you mean

to tell me we were actually attacked by *a nasty thought wrapped in dirt?*"

Mrs. Ruth shrugged. "You tell me. You were there."

"Well, it . . . I mean, I . . ."

"Look, bubba, let's just say you were attacked by a bit of unformed Darkness and leave it at that. Okay? Now," she looked pointedly at him, "if there are no further stupid questions, I'll go on. The Dark slithers in when and where it can, but the Light waits to be invited. Actually," her expression softened, "you'd be surprised by the number of people who ask for a little bit of Light to enter their lives. The balance stays pretty even. The Light gains strength by conversion, free choice being part of its nature. The Dark couldn't care less how it builds followers and finds terror the easiest tool.

"A dagger of this kind," Mrs. Ruth glared down at it, "can only be wielded by an Adept of the Dark Court. Obviously, an Adept of the Dark Court has come through."

"Can they do that?" Roland asked.

"Listen up, bubba," Mrs. Ruth advised, "I just said they did." She rubbed her chin, leaving a smear of dirt on the sweaty skin, and frowned. "Of course, it takes a lot of power and the Dark isn't known for doing things without a reason, so it's my guess that something big is coming down."

"Something big?"

"Something that'll let them recoup the power they lost and then some. Something that the death of your little friend was just the barest beginning of. Or to put it bluntly, you've got a whole heap of shit to deal with."

"Deal with?" Roland groaned.

"Deal with . . . Ignore . . ." Mrs. Ruth shrugged. "Your choice. You can always let the world and every living soul on it plummet down into eternal Darkness. Let anger and fear and uncaring rule. Don't get involved."

Rebecca turned to him, eyes wide, and he saw again

the little man bleeding out the last of his life on her bed. Saw the headlines in the newspapers he'd stopped reading because war and pain and hunger held no thrills for him. Sighed. "Why me?"

"Beats me, bubba. You wouldn't be my first choice."

"What do we do?" Rebecca wanted to know, leaning forward eagerly.

"You start by asking for help. This whole mess has knocked the balance of Dark and Light enough out of kilter that an equivalent Adept of the Light should be able to get through the barriers if invited."

An Adept of the Light? Roland repeated to himself. *Oh, wonderful, more weirdness.* "Why do we need help?"

A cracked, yellow nail tapped on the towel just beside the dagger's blade. "You know how to deal with this?"

"No," he admitted.

"Then call someone who can."

"Call someone? Right. I suppose they're in the book?"

"Yes," Mrs. Ruth told him, "they're in The Book." The capital letters were very apparent in her voice. "But you'll never get your hands on a copy. Use the gray folk. Have them carry a message."

"But Alexander was the only little I actually spent time with," Rebecca protested. She paused. "Except the troll, but he never travels. And you know how long it takes before a little trusts you."

Mrs. Ruth sighed and patted Rebecca's knee. "No, I don't. I've never heard of a gray one trusting anyone but you. As you've no time now to make new friends, I suggest you send a message with the dead."

To Roland's surprise, Rebecca nodded thoughtfully and said, "I could do that."

He poked her shoulder. "With the dead?"

"Uh-huh." She smiled. "I know a ghost."

"Great." He began to back out of the bushes. "I guess that's it, then." Trouble was, he had no trouble at all believing Rebecca did, indeed, know a ghost.

"I wouldn't worry about ghosts, bubba," Mrs. Ruth chuckled, correctly interpreting the expression on his face. "If they're the worst you have to deal with before this is over, you're luckier than you deserve to be."

"Oh, that's really bloody encouraging," Roland muttered, not caring if the old lady heard.

Rebecca scooped up the dagger with the towel and stuffed it back in her bag. "We'd better keep this. We can give it to the Light when he comes."

"Couldn't we . . ." Roland began.

"A very good idea," Mrs. Ruth interrupted him sternly.

Rebecca beamed and began to follow Roland out. "Sometimes I have one."

Free of the bushes, Roland straightened and took a deep breath. Even the car fumes that lay over Bloor Street like a blanket were an improvement. He figured he'd carry Mrs. Ruth's distinctive perfume with him for the rest of the night.

"Hey, Bard!" Her red kerchief was a splash of contrast amidst the dark green leaves. "Two things!"

He turned.

"First, don't get cocky. You've barely finished your first fourteen years. You're still in training."

He waited and wondered if the second thing would make as little sense.

"Second, you got a buck for a cup of coffee?"

Chapter THREE

Walking back the way they'd come, down dark, tree-lined residential streets which now seemed threatening rather than quiet, Roland considered the nature of good and evil. He'd never really thought much about the subject before, but then he'd never had a night like this before. Somehow, the mythic tale of Light and Dark made sense coming from Mrs. Ruth. The bag lady—

like Rebecca, he realized—was just too real to doubt.
And about Light and Dark once roaming the world?
Well, it made as much sense as any other creation
myth. Mrs. Ruth hadn't said at what speed indigenous
life developed, so that took care of Darwin and—
Rebecca's bag bumped against his thigh and he could
feel the weight of the black dagger—some pretty solid
evidence seemed to be piling up on her side.

Spotting the dark on dark shadows of the destroyed
lawn, he took hold of Rebecca's arm and tried to steer
her out onto the empty road.

"But, Roland," she twisted free, "walking on the
road is dangerous!"

"So is being attacked by landscaping," he pointed
out.

"But the nasty thought has left." Rebecca turned
slowly about, scanning the neighborhood. "I think."

"Let's not take any chances, okay?" She looked
unconvinced, so he added, "Too much depends on
us."

"Oh." She thought about it for a moment. "We
could go back to the corner and cross?"

"Yeah, fine." They could go back to Bloor Street
and take the subway for all he cared, he just had no
intention of passing that lawn. "You lead, I'll follow."

And that, he added to himself, *about sums it up.* He
didn't really need to believe any of this. He'd deal with
it the way he'd dealt with almost everything else life
had thrown at him over the years—by not dealing with
it at all, letting it carry him willy-nilly where it would.
He doubted he'd even get around to having the hysterics any normal person would feel entitled to. *Someday,*
he thought as Rebecca turned them south, *I've got to
develop a backbone.*

A wild and overgrown rosebush reached past the
fence intended to confine it, hooked into the shoulder
of Roland's T-shirt, and hung on. He tugged, it stuck.

"Wait a sec, Rebecca, I don't want to tear . . ." He
turned his head and came face to face with a tiny little
person, sexless as far as he could tell, clinging to his

T-shirt with both miniature hands, its green-brown legs wrapped around the branch of the bush. It grinned maliciously at him as he tried to twitch free. The rose-bush whipped back and forth, but the creature lost neither hold.

Rebecca peered up at it. "You let go right now," she commanded.

It stuck out a surprisingly pink tongue.

"This man is a Bard," she warned, "and if you don't let go, he'll write a song about what you do with bugs."

The creature looked indignant and let go. Its fingers, Roland saw, ended in claws almost as long again as the fingers themselves. One of those fingers snapped up in a rude gesture, then it scampered down the branch and out of sight.

"What does it do with bugs?" Roland asked as they walked on.

"I don't know." Rebecca shrugged, then stared at him very seriously. "You mustn't let the littles get away with things, 'cause the more things they get away with, the more things they do. Pretty soon you wouldn't have any quiet. None at all."

Roland had a sudden vision of his apartment crawl-ing with tiny little men and women, each with tiny little brains, and tiny little opposable thumbs. *And I thought roaches were a problem. . . .*

They came out on Harbord Street, a block from Spa-dina, and headed for the lights.

"Rebecca, where are we going?"

"To see the ghost."

"No, I mean where in the city."

"Oh." She took a deep breath and pronounced each syllable carefully, her usual habit with words of more than two, "To the university."

The University of Toronto took up a large area in the center of the city, its old, ivy covered buildings an interesting contrast to its young, denim covered stu-dents. They'd cut across a corner of it on their way to see Mrs. Ruth. Now, they headed into its heart.

"I didn't know there was a ghost at the university."

"You didn't?"

The streetlight illuminated her expression of disbelief very clearly and Roland felt like he'd just admitted he didn't know in what direction the sun rose in the morning.

"But he's famous. He's been on television."

"The ghost was on television?"

She thought about that while they waited for the light to change. "No," she admitted. "But they told his story." She thought a moment longer. "But they didn't tell it very well. They got lots of stuff wrong. I don't think they talked to Ivan at all."

"Ivan? That's his name?"

"Uh-huh." The light changed and she took his hand. "Come on."

This crossing of Spadina differed drastically from their first. Rebecca walked quickly, but she stayed calm and Roland marveled at the difference.

"Rebecca?"

"Yes?" She kept her eyes on the walk sign they were approaching.

"What do you do if there aren't any lights. At all."

"Then I cross at the corner and I look both ways and I don't run 'cause then I could fall. 'Cept I wouldn't, but Daru says I might. Or I use a magic crossing."

"A magic crossing?"

"You know." They stepped up on the curb and she turned to smile at him. "With the big yellow lights and the lines on the road where you stick out your finger and the cars stop."

Crosswalks, Roland realized she meant, although magic crossings were as good a name for them. Personally, he was afraid every time he stuck his finger out he was going to lose it; that some jerk in a Firebird would roar by and take it off.

"Uh, Rebecca, this ghost of yours . . ."

"He's not my ghost. He's the university's ghost."

"Whatever . . . he's not, uh . . ." Roland searched for the word. A number of movie ghosts, with gaping wounds and grayish-yellow skulls visible beneath decaying flesh paraded across his mind. Finally he pulled the word from Rebecca's vocabulary. ". . . icky?"

Rebecca understood and shook her head. "Oh, no. He's a little misty sometimes, but he's not icky. It's a really sad story."

"If I'm going to meet him . . ." And Roland was not thrilled about that, he had problems with dead people that didn't stay decently dead in fiction. He didn't know how he was going to react in real life. ". . . perhaps you'd better tell me."

"I'll remember better if I sit down, 'cause then I won't have to think about walking, too."

They were on the campus now and Roland graciously waved her to the grass surrounding the university library. Between the streetlights and the floodlights on the building, shadows didn't stand a chance and the brittle brown lawn looked about as threatening as a bowl of shredded wheat. With most students home for the summer, the area was deserted.

Rebecca sat down, putting the bag with the knife on the ground beside her. She waited patiently until Roland got settled, and then she began.

"His name is Ivan Reznikoff and he's a stonemason. That means he makes buildings and stuff out of stone. Well, he doesn't anymore, but he used to." She paused, Roland nodded, and she went on. "He was born in Russia, but he's been in Canada so long that he's a Canadian now. He's been a ghost for over a hundred years."

"But how did he become a ghost?" Roland prompted.

"He died."

She isn't doing it on purpose, Roland reminded himself and he kept his voice calm as he asked, "How did he die?"

"His friend stabbed him and threw him down the stairs and his body fell into an air shaft and no one knew it was there and no one looked 'cause he was just some poor dumb Russian and no one cared."

Roland heard the stonemason's voice in the last few words.

"See, his friend made a gargoyle thing that looked like him and Ivan got mad and started to make one like his friend. Actually," she confided, "it doesn't look at all like him so I guess he had a reason to get mad. Anyway, he saw his friend, 'cept they weren't real friends now, with his girlfriend—her name was Susie and he talks about her a lot—and he ground his teeth and she said, *What's that sound?* and the friend said, *It's only the wind* just like in the story with Sister Anne."

She'd lost Roland at that point, but he nodded anyway.

"And then he attacked his friend with an ax. He says he was drinking or he wouldn't have done it and he's pretty sorry about it now. His friend ran inside and the ax hit the door—I can show you the door—and then they chased each other up to the top of the tower and Ivan got stabbed and pushed down the stairs and he died. And now he's a ghost."

"What happened to Ivan's ex-friend?" Roland asked, fascinated in spite of himself.

"Nothing. See, they didn't find the body for years and years, not until after the big fire. The tower wasn't finished and Ivan's friend . . ." She frowned. "I wish I could remember his name 'cause he wasn't Ivan's friend anymore. Anyway, this person put the body deep in an unfinished part, then I guess he finished it and no one found it, then they had this big fire and they found him. Maybe the person and Susie got married and lived happily ever after." Sweeping her fingers lightly over the grass, she added, "I don't think we should say that to Ivan."

"Uh, right. No point in hurting his feelings," Roland agreed. Putting aside for the moment the question, "Do ghosts have feelings and if so, can they be hurt?" he stared at Rebecca. There had been, for an instant, another Rebecca superimposed over the one he knew. It had looked, Roland thought, both more and less like the Rebecca he knew. Had looked like the Rebecca that should have been. . . .

"What are you staring at, Roland?"

He started and forced a nervous smile. "Nothing." For nothing remained but the memory. *A trick of the light,* he decided, although given the night he'd had he wouldn't be at all surprised to find he was seeing things. Things that weren't there as opposed to things that were there but he didn't believe in even though he could See them. *Life was a lot less complicated yesterday.*

"Can I keep going, Roland?"

"Yeah, please, keep going."

"Okay. Anyway, when they found Ivan they buried him in the square place, 'cept back then it wasn't square because the new part made it square and that's where we're going to find him now."

"At his grave?"

"Uh huh."

"On the university campus?"

"Uh-huh."

"Rebecca, I don't think that's legal." The story had sounded pretty plausible until she'd gotten to the burial. Now Roland was beginning to think the whole thing existed only in Rebecca's head. "You can't just bury people in the closest bit of unoccupied dirt."

"He wasn't people by then. Just bones."

"Still . . . Who told you all this?"

"Ivan."

Roland sighed. Ivan was an authority hard to argue with. He got to his feet and held out a hand to Rebecca. "Let's go, then." His watch said it was twenty to eleven and a lifetime of horror books and movies told him he didn't want to meet this guy—giving the story the benefit of the doubt—at midnight.

Rebecca slung her bag over her shoulder and stood. Where the bag had rested, the grass appeared scorched. Rebecca looked down at it and shook her head sadly.

"Grass doesn't have a lot of protection," she sighed.

"Yeah, right. Are you sure you should be carrying that thing?" He shifted to put a little more space between himself and the bag.

"You mean the dagger?" She patted his arm comfortingly. "It's okay. I'm stronger than grass."

Roland allowed himself to be hustled along, glancing back only when they got to the corner and had to wait for a green light. The scorch was a clearly visible puddle of darkness against the dull yellow grass. He blinked and looked again. Beside it, arcing out in a gentle curve about six inches wide and four feet long, grew a swath of new green grass. In his memory's eye, Roland saw Rebecca absently stroking the lawn in front of her as she talked.

I'm stronger than grass.

Does she even know she did it? he wondered, staring down at the top of her head and remembering the other face that had briefly masked hers.

The light changed and they stepped off the curb. Roland, his eyes still on Rebecca, tripped over his guitar case.

Rebecca caught him, steadied him until he found his feet, and then propelled him across the intersection. "You have to be more careful crossing the street," she chastised.

Roland twisted around and took one last look at the two marks on the lawn. "Yeah, right," was all he could find to say.

They turned south, down behind a block of residences, onto one of the many footpaths that crossed the campus. Every twenty feet or so, an old-fashioned lamppost stood in a circle of light and Roland got the impression that they hurried from one island of safety to another with the darkness between wrapping about them, trying to get to the dagger. He peered down at Rebecca, but she seemed unconcerned so he tried to take his cue from her. It didn't quite work.

"So Ivan hangs around the university, eh?"

"Uh-huh. When people who don't See see him, the university is in danger."

"Does he ever haunt the place where he died?"

"No. He didn't die until he got to the bottom of the stairs and it's in a cupboard in the principal's bathroom now. If he haunted that, no one would ever see him.''

''How do you know all that?''

''Ivan told me. He watches them fix things up, do reni . . . reni . . .''

''Renovations?''

She beamed, becoming for a moment one more circle of light. ''That's it. He likes to keep an eye on things.''

They reached a small open area and Rebecca pointed down a fire access to a wrought iron gate set in the space between two buildings, one of new yellow brick, the other old and gray.

''We'll go in through there.''

''Isn't that a private section?'' In his experience, gates meant keep out.

''No, it's a green part,'' Rebecca explained, ''and green parts belong to everyone.''

Roland hoped campus security felt the same way. He didn't really feel up to explaining this evening to anyone else, particularly to someone in a uniform, trying to charge them with trespassing.

A closer inspection showed that half the gate was angled slightly open and they both squeezed through.

Ghost or no ghost, Roland decided, as they walked into the court, *this is spooky.* He clutched the handle of his guitar case tighter, taking reassurance from the sweaty plastic.

The court wasn't large, but trees broke the light from the buildings into patches of flickering shadow, now concealing, now revealing at the whim of the wind. With his back to the new addition, Roland had no trouble believing himself in the cloisters of a medieval monastery. Across the central bit of open grass—which he would not cross for love or money; he couldn't imagine being more exposed—he could see the rear of what had to be a chapel, the stained glass windows cut into eerie patterns by the trees. The only sounds were the whisper of leaves and the soft pad of Rebecca's running shoes as she walked along the raised flagstone path to the northeast corner.

Shadow patterns, dark and light,
Keep the secrets of the night.
Silence shrouds the empty . . .

"Roland! Come on!"

Jerking himself out of the song lyrics, shoving them away where he could work on them later, Roland hurried to where Rebecca waited at the edge of the grass. Her voice sounded unnaturally loud, as if it had bounced back off the old stones. The skin along his spine crawled as he realized that even the leaves had ceased to rustle and the whole place had taken on an air of expectant listening.

"What now?" he asked in a nervous whisper.

"Now we talk to Ivan." She stepped down onto the grass and walked a little way out from the buildings.

"Uh, Rebecca, Ivan can't be buried where you're standing."

Rebecca looked down at her feet and then up at Roland. "Why not?"

He pointed. "Because you're right beside a sewer grate. If he was ever there, they'd have dug him up when they put it in."

"It's okay." She dismissed the sewer grate with a wave of one hand. "He's still here."

Roland sighed. Then he blinked. Then he felt his eyes widen and his jaw drop and his heart start thudding like a jackhammer.

Something drifted up from the ground about a foot from Rebecca. It looked like a wisp of smoke, or a weirdly contained patch of fog, but as it swirled and grew, Roland caught glimpses of deep-set eyes, tendrils that could be long curly hair, and a pair of large, workman's hands.

Suddenly, he knew what it meant to gibber in terror because he desperately wanted to do it, and he was barely able to wrestle down the urge to run screaming all the way home. The eyes were the worst; they didn't just exist, they stared.

The final form was a column of mist, vaguely man shaped, a little over six feet high. It was so thin in places that Roland could see Rebecca through it. His heart began to slow to a more normal speed as he realized he had no really good reason to be frightened.

Rebecca put her hands on her hips and glowered. "How can I talk to you if you keep shifting around. You get solid, Ivan!"

"No. I don't want to." The voice, thickly accented, sounded as wispy as the form appeared and sulky at the same time.

"Why not?" She crossed her fingers and hoped he wasn't in one of his moods.

He was.

"Because. Go away. I don't want to talk to you. Nobody cares about me. Everyone ignores me." A deep sigh came from the center of the mist. "Go away," he repeated. "I want to rest in peace. Not that anyone cares."

He began to sink downward, back into the earth, but Rebecca lunged forward.

"Ivan, don't!"

He stopped sinking and twisted to avoid her grasp. "You don't care. No one cares."

This guy sounds more like the ghost of a little old lady than a Russian stonemason, Roland thought as the mist rose a little in the air and sped toward the west wall.

"Come on," Rebecca called and dashed off in pursuit.

Roland hesitated. He really didn't want to step away from the shelter of the buildings and cross that open area.

"Come *on!*" Rebecca called again.

He shrugged and started after her. It wasn't as bad as he'd feared, but he still had the impression of watching eyes. *I wonder what Ivan shares his last resting place with?* Shadows shifted by the chapel wall. *On second thought, I don't want to know.* He put on a burst of speed and caught up to Rebecca.

Together they pounded back up onto the flagstone path and down the arched passage that led through the west wall. The column of mist floated before them, almost disappearing as it passed under one of the old-fashioned lamps. It paused, streaked upward, and vanished behind the ivy that wrapped around the circular extension on the southwest corner of the building. The gargoyle that was peering out over the ivy came suddenly to life.

"Holy shit," Roland rocked to a halt, staring.

The first gargoyle settled back into stone and the second snarled down at him.

"Come on." Rebecca tugged on his arm. "I know where Ivan's going."

She headed around to the front of the building with Roland close behind, his running hampered by his total oblivion to where he put his feet. He couldn't take his eyes off the gargoyles animating one after the other, paralleling their course. He let Rebecca guide him around a small flower bed and up onto the lawn and he narrowly avoided slamming into her as she stopped.

Directly in front of them were two gargoyles, close together and tucked low in a corner. The one on the left slowly came to life.

"Okay, Ivan," Rebecca had reached the end of her patience, "stop playing games. We chased you so you know it's important. Now, listen."

"I'm listening," the gargoyle sighed.

The bits of broken carving that filled the gargoyle's mouth in combination with the Russian accent made its speech practically incomprehensible. Yet Rebecca seemed to understand.

"Mrs. Ruth says there's an Adept of the Dark here and we need you to take our . . ." She turned to Roland, looking for the word.

"Invitation?" Roland suggested.

"Yes, that's it. We need you to take our invitation to the Light so an Adept of the Light can come through and fight him."

"No."

"But Alexander died!"

"So." The gargoyle shrugged stone shoulders. "Death isn't so bad. You get used to it. Why should I travel far from my home, such as it is."

"But . . . you . . . oh!" Rebecca stamped her foot and the gargoyle smiled.

Roland noticed that some of the pieces of broken carving had once been teeth, teeth that had probably protruded a fair amount. "Look," he said, stepping forward and thereby surprising himself almost as much as Ivan, who hadn't appeared to notice him before, "you're supposed to appear when the university is in danger, right?"

"Right," the gargoyle agreed suspiciously.

"Well, if the Adept of the Dark gains the upper hand, the university, along with everything else, will be in a lot of danger. Shouldn't you do something about that?"

Ivan thought for a moment and Rebecca bestowed a smile of such benediction on Roland that he suddenly, inexplicably, wished he could do more for her; climb mountains, fight dragons, drive away the Darkness with his own two hands . . . *Uh, never mind.* He stomped hard on the last thought.

"No," the gargoyle said at last, "I just appear. I don't do things." It pointed one skinny, deformed arm at the guitar case. "You got something to drink in that?"

"No. Just a guitar."

"A guitar?" The gargoyle sighed. "I haven't heard music in so long . . . Play me a song."

Roland opened his mouth to tell the ghost just what he could do with that request, then closed it again. If music indeed had charms . . . He laid the case on the lawn and took out his old Yamaha. When he'd bought her, more than a dozen years ago, she'd been the best he could afford, but still a long way from a top of the line guitar. Through seasons on the street, folk festivals small and large, and smoke-filled rooms beyond counting, she'd never let him down, her voice as sweet and clear as the day he'd bought her. When he talked to her, he called her Patience, although he never let anyone know he did either.

He slipped the strap over his head and sat on the lowest step of a small, stone flight of stairs. Beneath

his butt, as he tuned, he could feel the dip worn in the
rock by thousands of climbing feet.

Both Rebecca and the gargoyle that was Ivan waited
expectantly.

> *"Across the steppes the wind is blowing*
> *Bringing songs and scents of home*
> *Can you feel it? Do you know it?*
> *How far, how far, how far it blows."*

The music he had for the old Russian folk song had
actually been written for the bandura so Roland had to
adapt it as he played, leaving him little leisure to observe his audience. Fortunately, melody and lyrics
were simple and Roland soon lost himself in the song.

> *"Now your travels have all ended*
> *Lay your head upon her breast.*
> *Let the wind blow on without you.*
> *It blows, it blows, but you may rest."*

The last notes drifted away and Roland rode them
out of the music.

Slowly, mist seeped out of the gargoyle and spun
itself into a tall, broad featured man dressed all in
black with long curly hair topped by a conical hat.
Around his waist he wore a stonemason's apron. A
single tear trickled down his cheek, catching the light
of a nearby lamp.

He spread large hands, scarred with the marks of
stone and tools. "I would embrace you if I could. You
took me back to my mother Russia as I have not been
in over a hundred years. Ask, and I will do your bid-
ding."

"We need you to take our invitation to the Light.
That's all."

Ivan nodded. "This I will do. You have wakened
such feeling in my heart."

"Was that you playing?"

Rebecca gave a little shriek and Roland whipped
around. An officer of the Campus Security Police stood

at the edge of the lawn. Roland suddenly noticed how exposed they were, sitting on the front steps of the oldest building in the university with nothing between them and anyone passing on the sidewalk, the road, or crossing the grassy common. And he'd been playing old Russian ballads to a ghost.

"Is there some kind of problem, officer?"

"Hell, no." The security officer smiled broadly. "I was just doing my rounds and I heard you and I thought I'd come over and say how pretty it sounded. It's nice to hear a song that isn't all random noise."

"Uh, thanks."

"This time of night you're not going to be disturbing anyone, residences are at the back of the college— not that there's many in them at this time of the year. No, you guys can—" he broke off, squinted, and shook his head. "That's funny, I could've sworn I saw three of you as I came across here. Great big fellow with a funny hat . . ."

"That was Ivan," Rebecca told him seriously.

"Reznikoff? The ghost?" He chuckled. "Sure it was. Maybe you'd better be moving along after all if you're seeing ghosts."

Roland leaned over and set the guitar in its case. "We were just going anyway."

"I will not fail you, singer. Your message will go to the Light." Ivan tipped his hat to Rebecca and faded away.

The security officer was not so easily gotten rid of. He walked them around King's College Circle, proving to Roland that he knew the title and first four lines of every Beatles song ever written.

"I like the yeah, yeah, yeah one best," Rebecca put in as they passed Convocation Hall.

"Why?" Roland asked.

"Because I can remember almost all the words."

Over her head, the security officer tapped a finger against his temple. Roland shot him a vicious look in response which he missed, caught up in professional concern about a group of shadows crossing the common, the bright ends of lit cigarettes red punctuations amid the black.

"I gotta go; those kids could burn this whole place down; that grass is too dry to smoke on it. Specially if what they're smoking is grass if you know what I mean. Been nice talking to you." And he bounded away.

"Roland?"

"Yeah?"

"You did a really good thing with Ivan."

"Thanks, kiddo." It took him a little by surprise that her words meant so much. They walked in quiet companionship down to the corner.

At College Street, a well lit artery that would take them straight to Rebecca's apartment, Roland looked back the way they'd come; up the short straight bit of King's College Road, across the Circle and the dark common to where a chipped and crumbling gargoyle hung in the night. He'd just spent time talking to a stonemason who'd been dead for over a hundred years. He'd received mystical advice from a bag lady. He'd seen an imaginary little man die. It had been quite a night. Now they'd asked for help and their job was over. He hoped that all the wonder so suddenly visible in the world would not disappear with equal suddenness.

Headlights on the far side of the Circle caught his eye and despite the distance he could hear the roar of an engine. Sports car, he decided and, along with Rebecca, carefully looked both ways before they crossed the street.

The roar grew louder as the headlights raced around the Circle and sped straight for them.

Roland dove forward but Rebecca froze, pinned in the glare.

The world slowed as he turned and knew he couldn't reach her in time.

. . . and then she was thrown into his arms and they were both rolling on the pavement as the brilliant red fender brushed ever so lightly against the bottom of her shoe.

Tires squealing, the car turned onto College Street, fishtailed slightly and accelerated away. Something squat and faintly luminescent clinging to the rear bumper, flashed them a cheery salute and began to rip its way into the trunk, stuffing great handfuls of metal into its mouth.

Roland helped Rebecca to her feet and pulled her the rest of the way across the road. She didn't seem panicky, merely shaken. He supposed it was because this time she'd followed the rules and so wasn't at fault.

"Are you okay?" he asked, looking her over critically.

"Yes," she nodded. "Are you?"

"I think so." He popped open the guitar case to see how Patience had survived. "Yeah, I'm fine."

Rebecca pointed to a manhole cover lying slightly ajar in the middle of the street. "The little came up out of that and pushed me out of the way."

Roland noticed that the pointing finger was unmoving in the air. *His* hands were shaking like leaves in a high wind.

She turned to face him. "Did you notice, the car had no driver?"

He swallowed. "No. I didn't."

"Should we tell the police? Daru says bad drivers should be taken off the road."

Roland could just imagine explaining this to the police. "No. No, police. If it didn't have a driver, who could they take off the road?"

"Oh." She sighed. "Roland, let's go home."

"Good idea, kiddo."

They started walking east, just as the clocks in the city's towers started to ring midnight. When the bells quieted, Rebecca touched Roland gently on the arm.

"You have lines on your forehead. What are you thinking about?" she asked.

He laughed, but the sound had little humor in it. "That it isn't over until the fat lady sings."

Rebecca considered that for a moment.

"Roland?"

"Yeah, kiddo?"

"Sometimes you don't make any sense."

Chapter FOUR

Roland stopped just inside the door to Rebecca's apartment and stared. The minor bit of tidying they'd done before going to consult Mrs. Ruth had left the apartment only marginally less chaotic than it had been when they'd first arrived. Now, it was spotless. All the dirt had been swept off the floor and the floor had been not only scrubbed but waxed and buffed to a warm glow. The plants stood in a neat and leafy row on their shelf in front of the window. The tattered shreds of the curtains had been . . . He leaned his guitar case against the wall, crossed the room, and peered more closely at the fabric. Tiny stitches joined each piece in nearly invisible seams.

"That's impossible," he murmured, more for form's sake than anything; if nothing else, this night had proven to him that impossible was a word that seldom applied. He turned, watched Rebecca scoop up the bowl of empty pistachio shells from the table, and followed her into the tiny kitchen. It gleamed.

"What happened here?" he asked, backing out again. The room was too small for two people and a conversation.

"The apartment got cleaned," Rebecca told him, dumping the shells in the garbage.

"Yeah, I noticed that." He took a deep breath. It even smelled clean. Not like cleansers or detergents, just clean. "But who or what did it?"

"I don't know." Her voice came muffled from behind the refrigerator door. "Does it matter?"

He looked round the spotless room, sighed, and shrugged. "I guess not," he admitted. The way things had been going tonight a magical maid service seemed comparatively normal. He gave himself a mental pat on the back for taking one more bit of strangeness in stride. And then he remembered the bloodstain on the bed.

The double doors that separated the bed alcove and the bathroom from the rest of the apartment were almost closed. The left, Roland noticed, had been dogged down. The right, he tentatively pulled open.

All he could be sure of in the spill of light from the living room was that Rebecca's double bed remained in place. He moved carefully down the narrow space between it and the wall, groping for the half remembered chain of an old-fashioned wall light. It took him a moment, running his hand up and down the wall in near darkness, but his fingers finally closed on the chain and he pulled.

The pale green blanket—the same pale green blanket he was sure—looked new. Nothing marked it to show that a little man named Alexander had died on it earlier in the evening and Roland was willing to bet the sheets below it were similarly unmarked.

Tom lifted his head from his paws and glared at the light.

"I thought you'd gone out," Roland muttered.

Tom yawned, pink tongue curling up delicately, clearly not giving a damn what Roland thought. He settled back into his hollow between the pillows with the air of a cat who plans to stay the night. Only by the quivering white tip to his tail did he give any indication that Roland still existed.

Quashing the urge to give the furry flag a tweak, Roland made a quick trip to the bathroom—immaculate as expected—and headed back out to the main room.

"If you want the light off," he said to the cat as he passed, "you get up and turn it off."

Rebecca was leaning halfway out the window.

"What are you doing?"

She straightened and tossed her curls back off her face. "Putting out a bowl of milk for the littles."

"What?"

Patiently, she repeated herself.

"Okay. Why?"

"Because they like it."

He took a deep breath. Why not? He was just going to have to get used to an absence of explanation in his life from now on.

"You're sure that the Adept of the Light will come here?" he asked.

"Yes. Even if Ivan doesn't say who sent him and give my address—which I don't think he knows so he can't—we have the dagger and that should attract him."

That made sense. In fact, upon reflection, it made a great deal of sense and up until tonight Roland had thought sense and Rebecca were mutually exclusive. Either she was smarter than previous observation indicated or he wasn't handling things as well as he thought.

Or a bit of both, fairness forced him to admit.

The bag, still zippered shut, lay in the middle of the floor. Roland pushed it under the table with the toe of one desert boot. No sense leaving it lying out in the open where it might attract more than the Light. He shot a suspicious glance at the dirt in the flowerpots.

Rebecca yawned and Roland suddenly felt exhausted.

"I'm going to bed now," she told him. "The Light can wake me up when it gets here."

They both seemed to take it for granted that Roland was spending the night.

"Do you want to sleep with me?"

Roland closed his mouth, took a deep breath, and told himself sternly to clean up his gutter mind. Her face was as innocent and guileless as a child's, open and trusting, the faint sprinkling of freckles across her nose and cheeks adding a wholesomeness that was almost cliché. But her body . . . Her breasts were heavy, the nipples denting through both bra and tank top, with more freckles scattered lightly across their upper curves. Below a remarkably tiny waist, her hips flared then tucked down into muscular thighs. A little plump in this age of anorexia, but the flesh was firm and the form most definitely woman. *When the kid says sleep, she means sleep, you pervert. Nothing more.*

"No. Thanks. I'll sleep on the couch."

"Okay." Rebecca yawned again and headed for her bed. "Good night, Roland."

"Good night, kiddo, pleasant dreams."

"I always have pleasant dreams."

Roland grinned. In that calm assurance, he found the Rebecca he knew again and could banish the ripe form of the other from his mind. He checked that the door was locked, lifted Patience from her case, and flicked off the light. Settling down on the couch, a huge old piece of furniture at least as long as his six feet, he began to pick out a quiet melody. He hadn't needed light to play for years.

He heard the mattress creak as Rebecca got into bed and then he heard her murmur peevishly; "Move over, Tom, you're hogging all the space."

Good thing I didn't take her up on her offer. All I need to finish off the evening is a cat fight.

His hands continued making music without him and after a few moments he realized he was playing an old Irish Rovers' hit.

Oh, no, he chided himself, moving his fingers away from that particular tune, *that's just a little too close.*

"It's dark down here tonight."

Police Constable Patton peered through the open window of the patrol car and frowned. "It's always dark down here," she pointed out acerbically. "Too god-damned many trees."

It was, in fact, easy to forget they were driving through the heart of a major city. Rosedale Valley Road followed the bottom of one of Toronto's many ravines and on either side huge trees crowded the pavement, looming out over this slash through their domain, intimidating the infrequent streetlights, and generally making Man aware in no uncertain terms that, down here at least, he was an intruder.

"Rally lights," PC Patton muttered. "That's what we need, rally lights."

"You worry too much."

"You don't worry enough." She turned from the window to face her partner. The litany was a familiar one, guaranteed to take place once a shift. Maybe she did worry too much, but surely that was better for a cop than never worrying at all. "Don't forget to slow down right before we get to the bridge."

PC Jack Brooks smiled, the expression hidden in his heavy moustache. "You figure they'll come back?"

The young woman shrugged. "Beats me. Who can tell with transients? All I know is it's too damn dry for them to be lighting any fires down here."

"Can't argue with that, Mary Margaret."

She rolled her eyes at her given names. The son of a bitch insisted on using them together, refusing to call her Marge like everyone else did. "And why can't you argue with it?" she asked. "You argue with everything else I sa . . . Holy shit!" She grabbed at the dashboard as Brooks swerved to avoid the glowing white shape that darted out from among the trees. But it was too close. And they'd been moving too fast.

There was a jar as the fender hit it, then a double bump as it went under front and back wheels.

Brooks fought the car to a stop, his curses accompanying the scream of rubber on asphalt. Both officers grabbed for hats and sticks and scrambled out onto the road. They could see what they'd hit about fifteen feet away, the night making it no more than a pale, crumpled shape against the pavement. They paused for an instant, knowing there was no way it could still be alive.

"Someone's big white dog?" Brooks offered.

"Maybe." She took a deep breath; dead people had always been easier for her to deal with than dead animals. "Come on."

Brooks reached it first, knelt down, and froze. Away from the car, his vision had adjusted quickly to the lack of light and he could clearly see what they'd hit. It couldn't have been more than three feet high at the shoulder, each slender leg ending in a tiny, cloven hoof. Its head was as delicate as a flower and from its brow grew a spiraled crystal horn. An onyx eye gazed up at him, bright with pain, and he realized that it still lived, although as he watched the brightness began to dim.

"Jack, what is . . . Mary, Mother of God . . ." *This isn't possible. This can't be possible.* She knelt as well and, while her right hand sketched the sign of the cross, her left reached out and gently stroked the long white hair. It flowed soft and warm under her trembling fingers, as real and as insubstantial as a summer breeze.

The unicorn sighed, one long drawn out breath that carried the scent of moonlit pastures, shuddered, and died.

The road was empty between them.

Tears running down his cheeks, Brooks reached out and touched the spot where it had lain. "I'm sorry," he whispered. "I'm so sorry."

"Jack!"

His head snapped up at the urgency, at the fear, in his partner's voice. She was on her feet, her nightstick angled across her body, the knuckles of both hands white. A rustling in the underbrush drew his gaze to the side of the road.

Black on black. And a fetid smell that made him choke.

Slowly, he rose from his knees, fighting against a fear that threatened to paralyze him. An ancient fear, of the dark and of the unknown things that dwell in it. *Run*, screamed a voice in his head, *RUN!* But training held, and carefully, they backed up to the car. Where they sat, hearts pounding, palms damp with sweat, although no threat had followed them.

"That thing . . ." The words cracked into a myriad of pieces so she tried again. "That thing," marginally better, "drove it out onto the road."

"Yeah." He didn't trust his voice for more.

They sat a while longer until the headlights of an oncoming car snapped them back into the real world.

In the harsh glare of the passing vehicle, which had slowed considerably upon spotting the patrol car, PC

Patton shot an anxious glance at her partner. His face looked drawn and tired, but he seemed okay. She gave thanks to all the saints that she hadn't been driving.

"We didn't see anything," she said at last.

"No," he sighed, the sound a faint echo of the unicorn's dying breath, "we didn't."

He started the engine and they continued their patrol.

A single white hair blew off the car fender and was lost in the night.

Roland, always a light sleeper, came fully awake at the first knock. He shook his head to clear the last remnants of a dream—Mrs. Ruth dancing naked in the moonlight was a dream bordering on nightmare—and tried to swing his legs off the couch.

A warm and furry weight held them right where they were.

In the dim light, for no city apartment is ever completely dark, Roland could see the faint golden gleam of eyes. He kicked.

"Ouch! Damn it, cat . . ."

The second knock got lost in the brief scuffle that followed.

"Roland, what's wrong?"

He squinted against the sudden glare. Rebecca stood by the light switch, a fuzzy blue dressing gown belted around her, her hair an even more unruly mass of curls than usual. He pointed at Tom who sat washing one shoulder with sublime indifference.

"That cat bit me!"

"Why?"

"Well . . ." He had the grace to look sheepish. "I, I kicked him."

"Why?"

"Because he was sleeping on my feet."

The third knock diverted Rebecca's attention. "There's someone at the door," she said with a happy smile. "It must be the Light."

"Yeah, maybe." Roland's bare feet made no sound on the smooth wooden boards as he padded around the end of the couch. "But the odds are just as good it's the Dark."

Rebecca looked thoughtful. "I don't think the Dark would knock."

The fourth knock sounded a bit impatient.

"Okay, okay, we're coming." The chain lock clattered against the wall. "Stay behind me, kiddo."

"Why?"

"For protection."

"Against the Light?"

Roland sighed as he worked the deadbolt. "We don't know that it's the . . ."

A young man in his late teens or early twenties stood framed in the open door. His eyes were a stormy mix of blue and gray and Roland's gaze dropped before them, seeking stability in the speckled brown pattern of the hall carpet. When the world had stopped spinning and he thought he had his pulse under control again, he took a deep breath and began working his way back up, taking inventory as his vision climbed: black boots; tight and faded jeans; a red bandanna knotted just above one knee; three belts, thick with studs surrounding slim waist and hips; one arm circled halfway from wrist to elbow with a jangle of silver bracelets in all sizes; a blinding white T-shirt with the sleeves ripped out sporting a single, tiny button . . . a happy face, white on black.

Roland paused for a moment at the long, golden line of the throat, then snapped his eyes up before he chickened out. The point of the young man's chin just missed being delicate and his face missed being pretty by the same small margin. A large silver hoop pierced one ear and his heavy sweep of hair darkened gradually from white blond at the tips to golden blond at the roots. Roland didn't think it was dyed.

Then he smiled and Roland forgot everything he'd just seen in the sweet sensuality of the expression.

"Jesus Christ."

The smile quirked into an equally fascinating grin. "Not quite." His voice caressed the words like verbal velvet. "Can I come in?"

"Uh, yeah." Forcing his gaze to one side, Roland stepped back. He felt dizzy. He felt other things as well, but he refused to acknowledge them, pushing them down with panicked force. *Forget that. I'm too old for a major lifestyle change. I don't care how pretty he is.* When he turned, the young man was bending over Rebecca's hand.

It should've looked ludicrous—a heavy metal wet dream genuflecting before a tousle-haired, vacant-eyed young woman in a fuzzy blue bathrobe—but it didn't. It looked right. It looked more right than anything that had happened to Roland since his mother had died four years ago. He could see the song in it, hear the music, feel the power.

"You have called, the Light has come. Lady, my name is Evantarin."

His silver bracelets chimed as he lifted her hand to his lips.

Rebecca looked momentarily puzzled until she figured out what he was doing, and then she grinned. "Hello Evantarin, my name is Rebecca."

"Perhaps," he said, and Roland added the twinkle in those stormy eyes to the music he heard, "but I will call you Lady, and you will call me Evan. Evantarin is for those who do not know me well."

"Okay." She nodded, satisfied with his explanation although it made no sense to Roland at all. In trying to work it out, he lost the threads of his song.

"No." The word came out almost as a moan. It had been the most perfect song. . . .

"Don't worry," Evan reached back and touched Roland's arm. "There will be many more songs before this is over. And you will find that one again, I promise."

Roland's eyes widened.

"What else could have caused you such pain?" Evan answered the unasked question. "You are a Bard; or will be." He spread his hands in a fluid gesture that spoke eloquently of understanding. "Such pain could only be the loss of a song." Then he started and the stormy eyes snapped down. "Small furred one, you surprised me."

Tom sniffed the offered fingers, then butted his head against Evan's hand, a deep rumble beginning in his throat.

"I'm going to make tea," Rebecca told them, including Tom in the declaration. "Everyone sit down."

I don't believe this, Roland thought a few moments later. *It's ten after three in the morning and I'm sitting drinking herbal tea with an Adept of the Light.* At the other end of the couch, the Adept yelped as Tom's kneading claws dug through his jeans. *I don't even like herbal tea.* Every time he looked at Evan he could hear the broken pieces of the music, but they came and went as they would; he could no longer hold them.

He cleared his throat and Rebecca looked expectantly up at him from where she sat cross-legged on the floor.

"The first thing we have to determine,"—*Good lord, I sound like Uncle Tony at his most pompous*—"is just who exactly you are." The expression on Rebecca's face stopped him for a second, but he took a deep breath and continued. These were words that had to be said, even if Rebecca thought he'd lost his mind. "I mean, we've been assuming you're from the Light and for all we know you could be a trick of the Dark."

"Oh, Roland." Rebecca frowned. "Can't you See?"

Roland opened his mouth to defend himself, but Evan broke in.

"He does not See as well as you, Lady, and the Dark can appear to be very fair. Our foe is strong, and will use any tool he can to achieve his ends." Rebecca nodded thoughtfully and Evan turned to meet Roland's eyes. "But if you do not See, surely you Hear."

And the song burst forth again, whole for an instant.

"Yeah, okay," Roland muttered, his tone brusque to distract the others from the tears in his eyes, "but I had to ask. I mean, you look like . . ." Words failed him.

Evan looked worried. He glanced down at himself

then up at Roland. "Is it not suitable? As I crossed the barrier, I let the power form me as it would." He tossed his hair back off his face and frowned. "I like it, but maybe . . ."

"No, no!" Roland broke in, stifling the ridiculous urge to reach out and brush the frown away. "You look great."

"Do you really think so?" Evan ducked his head a little sheepishly. "It's foolish, I know, but I have always been vain. If my appearance . . ."

"Your appearance is fine, I really think so. In fact, I think . . ." *I think I'm in over my head. I mean he's . . . And I . . . Oh, shit.* Roland could tell by Evan's expression that the Adept knew exactly what thoughts were chasing themselves around in his head. He felt his face grow hot.

"Roland, all good people wish to become closer to the Light. When the Light has physical form," Evan shrugged, a graceful movement that involved his whole body, "that desire is physical, as well." Then the grin returned and one silken eyebrow rose. "I don't mind."

His tone hovered between acceptance and invitation.

Roland forced himself to hear it as the former.

Rebecca poked at the toe of Evan's boot. "I like the way you look."

The grin softened. "And I like the way you look, Lady."

"Becca!" BANG. BANG. BANG.

Rebecca's fingers tightened around her mug. "It's the large-blonde-lady-from-down-the-hall."

"Becca, I know you've got a man in there!" BANG. BANG. BANG.

"Old news," Roland muttered, irrationally peeved that Evan got this reaction and he didn't seem to count.

"I'm not going away until you open this door!"

"Does that mean she'll go away when I open it?" Rebecca sounded completely confused. "Why does she want me to open the door if she'll just go away?"

"Never mind, kiddo." Roland began preparing his best scathing glare. "I'll get it."

"No." Evan lifted Tom, who had gone boneless in contentment, off his lap. "Let me."

"Be my guest." Roland waved a gracious hand but got to his feet anyway. He wanted to be in a position to see the reaction when Evan opened the door. He'd feel a lot better if he knew that the Light Adept carbonated hormones as a matter of course.

"Becca! Don't make me call your social wo . . . Oh." The large-blonde-lady-from-down-the-hall froze, one dimpled set of knuckles raised. "Oh," she said again, and the hand came down to stroke her peach muu-muu smooth over her hips.

"Is there a problem?" Evan asked.

"Becca," she wet her lips and appeared to be struggling for breath, "has a man in her apartment."

"Yes." From her new expression, eyes half closed and cheeks bright pink, Roland assumed Evan had smiled. "Is there a problem with that?"

"Oh, no."

She swayed and Roland hoped she wasn't going to faint, overcome with desire. He didn't think the three of them could lift her.

"There's no problem with . . ." Her sway moved her line of sight past Evan and onto Roland. "Two men. Two men! Oh. Oh. Oh . . ." Her mouth worked soundlessly for a moment before she could get the words out. "How dare you take advantage of that poor helpless child." She tried to push by Evan but he was a rock. "Becca! Becca, you come here."

"Why?" Rebecca asked calmly.

"They can't hurt you when I'm here. You come to me and we'll call the police!"

She glared up at Evan and Roland suddenly realized the emotion behind the new outburst. One man; Rebecca had obviously been misbehaving. Two men; they had to be forcing themselves on a helpless simpleton. After all, how could Rebecca have two men while she had none.

Evan sighed. "We haven't got time to unravel this."

Where Evan had stood rose a column of light wrapped about a figure of blinding beauty.

"Go back to your bed," said the figure.

The large-blonde-lady-from-down-the-hall pressed one hand to her mouth, the other to her chest.

"Things will be better in the morning." The figure raised a hand in benediction and petulant lines relaxed into an expression of peace.

She nodded, half smiled, and left.

Just for an instant, through eyes squinted almost shut, Roland thought he saw great white wings arching up to brush the ceiling. All his senses gave a sudden jump as he tried to understand; then Evan stepped back and closed the door. He glanced over at Rebecca, but she merely appeared satisfied the disturbance had ended. Great white wings. The heat Evan generated by his looks, by his presence, began to warm him in a different way—for which he gave thanks as desiring an attractive young man made him acutely uncomfortable. Desiring an angel could be considered a mystical experience, he supposed.

An angel . . . An Adept of the Light . . . It made a certain amount of sense and he marveled at how calmly he was taking it. His sense of wonder must have shut down for a time, fearing overload.

"There now," Evan sat back down on the couch and picked up his mug, "where were we?"

"I said I liked the way you looked then you said you liked the way I looked," Rebecca told him. "Do you want more tea?"

"Yes, please."

She took the empty mug and padded over to the table where a teapot sat under a hand-crocheted cozy. "Do you want more tea, Roland?"

"Got coffee?"

"No, just tea."

Roland glanced at the inch of greenish-yellow liquid remaining in his mug. "No thanks." Carefully avoiding claws and teeth, he slid Tom back toward Evan and sat down. The cat shot him a scathing look, uncurled, and leaped off the couch. "I think the time has come for explanations."

"Yes," Evan accepted his tea with a nod of thanks, "you're right, it has."

"You can start with what you did to Mrs. Grundy."

"That's not her name," Rebecca pointed out, refilling her own mug and returning to her place on the floor.

"It's just a nickname," Roland explained. "It's what you call a nosy neighbor." Rebecca repeated the name silently to herself, filing it away for future reference. Roland turned to Evan who gave another of his whole body shrugs.

"I merely let more of the Light show through. Fortunately, she had enough goodness in her to respond."

"She'll probably be back in the morning, making trouble. You should've made her forget she ever saw us."

"I couldn't. Neither the Light nor Dark can do other than work with what is already present." Evan took a long swallow and continued. "When I told her things would be better in the morning, I gave her a chance to build her own explanations. She'll probably decide that the entire incident was a dream."

And she'll probably spend the rest of the night dreaming about you, Roland added to himself. With the image of great white wings at the front of his mind, he said, "Are we in the middle of a battle between heaven and hell?"

"Heaven, hell; good, evil; Light, Dark. Names mean very little."

"Is that a yes?"

Evan nodded. "Essentially."

"Oh, great, oh, that's just great." Roland buried his face in his hands, ignoring the little voice in the back of his head that kept crowing, *What a song! What a song!* Mrs. Ruth had told him pretty much the same thing, but it sounded more definite coming from Evan. *This is what comes from being a nice guy. Do a friend a favor and what do you get; front row seats at the Apocalypse.* He didn't hear Rebecca ask him if he was all right. He didn't hear anything but the roaring in his head as all the strange events of the night caught up with him and hit at once. Fear and confusion, but mostly fear, raced around and around and around, chasing a tail of panic. Under it all, he felt vaguely reassured that he was finally having the kind of reaction this stuff called for.

The soft tick tick of claws on vinyl yanked him out of the maelstrom and he whirled to snarl over the couch back; "Touch that case again, cat, and you're potholders."

Tom removed his paws from the guitar case with one last tick and stretched out on the floor looking bored.

"Roland," Evan's touch was warm and comforting on his bare arm, "you needn't be involved any further. I will understand if you choose to walk away."

And he would understand, Roland knew that, but Rebecca wouldn't and without him being aware of how it had happened, the girl's opinion had become important to him. She stared up at him now, sure of his answer. He couldn't betray her trust. He just couldn't.

"Hey, it's my world. I'll do what I can to protect it." Acceptance, commitment, and peace. He felt good. *Still scared shitless, but good.*

"What do we have to do, Evan?" Rebecca stirred her cooling tea with a forefinger, then popped the finger in her mouth.

"You know that an Adept of the Dark walks in your world, more powerful than any who have come through in many centuries but he is only a gatekeeper. On Midsummer Night . . ."

"Next Friday," Rebecca added.

Now how does she know that? Roland wondered. *I wouldn't know when Midsummer Night was if it bit me on the ass.*

"Next Friday," Evan agreed, acknowledging Rebecca with a small bow, "the barriers that keep this world from interference thin. The Dark One will open a gate on that night, allowing his kind to enter as they will. He must be stopped."

"Well, if we've got a week . . ." Roland began.

A raised hand and a jangle of silver cut him off.

"A week is no time to find a mortal man in a city

this size, let alone one with the powers of Darkness at
his command and already he begins to tip the balance,
killing or driving out the Light and the Gray.''

"He killed Alexander!" Rebecca snagged her bag
and dumped it on Evan's lap.

His lip curling in disgust, Evan pulled out the rolled
towel and carefully unwrapped the dagger. "Yes." He
hissed the word out between clenched teeth. "He
killed your friend, Lady, and others; there are many
lives bound up in this evil tool."

"Don't touch it!" Rebecca cautioned.

Evan smiled, a strange, fierce expression. "I can't."
He brought his hand to within an inch of the black
metal, but not even Rebecca's two hands pressing on
top of his could cause it to go closer. "Blood and lives
guard this obscenity against my kind and it would take
blood and lives to lift that guard." Flipping his hand
over, he clasped Rebecca's for a moment. "Too great
a price to gain control of a dagger."

Rebecca nodded, face serious, as she asked, "What
should we do with it?"

"Keep it. Guard it. Do not touch it."

"I can do that."

His smile was a caress "I know."

The look they exchanged made Roland very uncomfortable—he had no wish to discover why—so he
cleared his throat and they both swiveled to face him.
"Well, how do we go about finding this guy?"

"I don't know." Evan sighed. "I am not even certain
where he will attempt to open his gate. If I knew . . .''

"You could meet him there and send him back where
he came from!" Rebecca caroled bouncing a little.

"No, Lady, it will not be that easy. The Dark Adept
and I are evenly matched for the balance must be
kept."

"Why don't you open your own gate?" Roland
asked. "Then the Dark and the Light'll still be evenly
matched."

"And they will fight a terrible war across your world
and your world will be laid waste regardless of the
winner." He shook his head, his multishaded hair

drifting about his shoulders. "No, our only chance is
to find him and stop him ourselves. My only fear is
that he will find us first . . ."

"Rebecca!"

Only Tom managed to regard the door with his usual
élan.

Tap. Tap. Tap. "Rebecca, are you okay? Open up!"
Tap. Tap. Bang. "I know you're awake, I heard talking."

"It's Daru!" Rebecca scrambled to her feet, and
headed for the door.

Roland checked his watch. "It's four-thirty in the
morning," he muttered.

Rebecca flung open the door and Daru strode into
the room, her sari an exotic contrast to her expression;
worry and exasperation about equally mixed. Roland
felt his jaw drop for what seemed the hundredth time
that evening and wondered how a woman could look
so concerned and so intimidating at the same time.

"What is going on, Rebecca?" Daru took the
younger woman by the shoulders and examined her
quickly. "I just got back from a family party and found
the damnedest message on my answering machine.
Have you killed . . . Who is he?"

Daru's expression, Roland realized, was not one of
adoring fascination, an expression he'd almost come
to believe was Evan's due. She was curious only, and,
he noticed, completely ignoring him.

Evan rose and bowed, a gesture that, considering
his appearance, should've looked theatrical and false
but didn't.

"I am Evantarin, Adept of the Light."

Daru inclined her head graciously. "And I am Daru
Sastri, Metro Social Services." Something that was
almost recognition surfaced for a moment in her eyes,
then it faded; she sighed and turned back to Rebecca.
"Rebecca, stop bouncing, close the door, and tell me
what's happening."

With a visible effort, Rebecca brought her feet back
to the ground, pushed the door closed and chained it.

"We're going to save the world from Darkness," she declared, beaming.

Daru sighed. "Honey, I've had a long day, so why don't you make me some tea and start at the beginning, okay?"

"Okay. The beginning is when Alexander got stabbed."

Rebecca headed for the kitchen and Daru glided over to the couch.

Which came first, Roland wondered, *the woman or the sari?* He'd never seen a sari worn where the woman didn't move with regal grace.

Evan waved Daru into the seat he'd just vacated and she sank down looking grateful.

"You're taking this very calmly," Roland said to her.

An ebony eyebrow rose.

"Oh." He flushed. "My name's Roland. Roland Chapman. I'm a friend of Rebecca's."

"Well, Roland," she slid her sandals off and tucked one small foot up underneath her, "I just spent over twenty-four hours with my very extended family. For the moment, I have lost my ability to be surprised by anything."

"That," Evan said thoughtfully, settling himself on the floor, "may make explanations easier."

Chapter FIVE

In the master bedroom of the Imperial Suite at the King George Hotel, the sleeper stirred. He savored for a moment the feel of the sheets brushing against his skin, the pressure of the mattress firm beneath his shoulder blades, the softness of the pillows, and the texture of the shadows upon his closed eyes. The full lips curved up into a smile of complete contentment and the eyes opened.

As clear and brilliant a blue as a summer's sky, they focused on the patterned ceiling, followed the pattern's loops and swirls to a wall, and slid down it. Light, made rosy by the curtains, spilled into the room.

The young man on the bed stretched, bringing to the action the single-minded determination of a particularly self-satisfied cat, then swung bare feet to the plushly carpeted floor and padded naked to the window. Throwing aside the masking fabric, he gazed out at the heart of the city.

"Another beautiful day," he murmured, brushing thick black hair off his face. "Sunny and hot." He pronounced the word "hot" almost like a command.

Resting on the skyline of the city, the sun blazed and, although the day had barely begun, the air wavered with heat distortion.

He placed his hand against the glass, long fingers spread, and a wheeling pigeon plummeted down seven stories to the pavement. It narrowly missed an elderly couple out for a stroll, crashing practically at their feet and spraying them both with feathers and blood.

The shrill shriek of the old woman brought back his contented smile.

In the shower, he gloried in the sensation of the water, changing the shower head from needle to massage and back again. He towel-dried briskly, rubbing the creamy ivory of his skin to a warm pink glow, then stood for a time posing before the full-length mirror, admiring the smooth ripple of muscles. His body, he knew, was a work of art, each piece in perfect proportion to the rest, just as he had designed it.

But such a body needed something to sustain it.

With the receiver tucked beneath his chin, he dressed as he ordered breakfast.

". . . and the coffee is not to be made until seconds before the pot leaves the kitchen." He pulled a light blue Oxford cloth shirt out of the closet and shrugged into it, tucking it down into his jeans and buttoning the fly. "Yes that's correct, Mr. Aphotic." Hanging up, he grinned in appreciation of his own cleverness. Aphotic meant dark, and Dark was all the designation he had, for the Darkness kept its bits and pieces too close to allow them the individuality of names. Reaching for a pair of deck shoes, he checked the loafers he'd worn the night before.

The blood had not, as it turned out, stained the leather. A bit of a surprise really, as there'd been rather a lot of it. In a city of this size it hadn't taken him long to find a young woman who would allow him to "cut" her for a ridiculous sum and once her permission had been given and the money had changed hands not all the screamed, moaned, or whispered "no's" could invalidate the contract. And as he'd worked with her agreement, the balance of Light and Dark had not been unduly disturbed. And as the balance had not been disturbed, he had attracted no attention that might make his purpose here more difficult to carry out. Freed from the constraints of ritual, for last night had been solely for his own enjoyment, he'd allowed his imagination full reign and had taken his time.

Breakfast, when it arrived a few moments later, was superb. He rolled the flavors of eggs, and sausages, and mushrooms fried with garlic and ginger around on his tongue and washed them down with juice so fresh it had still been in the orange when it left the kitchen.

"Master!"

A shadow, six inches high and occasionally humanoid, swarmed up the walnut legs of the table and paused by the coffeepot.

"Master! An Adept of the Light has passed the barriers!"

"Yes, I know." He sucked at his fingertips, getting the last of the butter and croissant crumbs. "Did you think I wouldn't notice such a shift in the balance?"

"No, Master, but . . ." It rose up and created arms in order to wave them about.

"But?" His tone made the word a threat.

"But I function to give you information, Master. I am your eyes and ears."

"Then see, hear, do something useful, and find out how this Adept came through." He poured himself coffee, added liberal helpings of cream and sugar, and drank half of it before he spoke again. The shadow wavered and fidgeted. He put down his cup with a satisfied sigh, then his expression hardened. "Tonight, find out who provided passage for this Adept, how much they know, and whether they can be used in the ritual."

"Yes, Master, but . . ."

"Again but?"

The shadow writhed and keened, a high-pitched, drawn out sound like nails on a blackboard. "No, Master. No but."

He sighed and stretched as it fled. These smaller pieces of Darkness were almost useless and he wondered if breaking it off had been worth it. His glance fell on the morning paper and the headline caught his eye. *Jays and Tigers Neck and Neck as All-Star Break Approaches.*

"A ballgame," he mused, scanning the article. "Just what I need, a sunny Sunday afternoon at the ballpark. Crowds of people, the competitive spirit . . ." Just for a moment, he wished he could postpone the opening of the gate for a few days; next weekend the Yankees would be in town. "Ah, well," he tossed the paper onto the floor, "you can't have everything."

He shoved his room key into the pocket that held his wallet and headed for the door. Throwing it open, he almost collided with a chambermaid carrying a load of towels.

"Houseke . . ." She lowered the hand raised to knock and stared at him, her eyes wide with need. She was very young and very pretty and he'd taken her brutally the first two mornings he'd stayed in the suite, twisting her responses until pain and pleasure became indistinguishable.

This morning, he merely looked at her with disgust and pushed past.

He could hear her tears and feel the heat of her shame on his back. His step became jaunty. It was going to be a great day.

"What've you got, Steve?" PC Patton got out of the squad car and slammed the door. Behind her, she could hear Jack doing the same. They'd been off duty, heading back to the station, when the call had come in and as it was on the way they'd pulled into the supermarket parking lot to see if they could help. She noticed that Police Constable Steve Stirling, a veteran who in his years on the force had acquired a reputation for being completely unshakable, looked decidedly pale. His partner, a rookie policewoman mere weeks out of the academy, had obviously thrown up and was just as obviously considering doing it again.

"It's in the dumpster," Steve said shortly, glaring at the gathering crowd.

Frowning, she swung herself up on the dumpster's side and took a deep breath before peering in; the stink alone could've caused Steve's partner to puke. Spread out on top of the usual, rotting, grocery store garbage was what looked like the entire contents of the meat department, chops, sideribs, roasts, all covered in a moving carpet of flies. And then she noticed that one of the roasts had a face.

Teeth clenched, she dropped back down to the pavement and thanked God and all the saints it had been hours since she'd eaten. As Jack stepped by her, she grabbed his arm.

"Don't." It wasn't their call. He didn't have to look.

He looked at her instead, reading the horror of what she'd seen in her eyes, nodded, and moved away.

"What a fun start to the day." Steve had come to stand beside her and together they watched another three cars arrive, one carrying the police photographer. "You could be sitting down at the station with a cup of coffee about now. Don't you wish you'd kept going?"

"Yes." She didn't have to add anything else; "yes" said it all.

"All right, let me see if I've got this straight." Daru rubbed her eyes and accepted a fresh cup of tea with a nod of thanks. "This coming Friday, Midsummer Night, an Adept of the Dark is going to open a gateway between this world and the Darkness. You," she inclined her head toward Evan, "have been brought from the Light to stop him. You two," she nodded at Roland and Rebecca, "are going to help."

"That's it in a nutshell," Roland agreed.

"Fine. Count me in."

"What?"

She swallowed her mouthful of tea, sighed, and said slowly and distinctly, "I'm going to help, too."

"You mean you believe us?" Roland stared at her in astonishment. The tale had taken the rest of the night in the telling and now, in the bright light of Sunday morning, he wasn't sure he believed it himself.

"I believe the evidence of my eyes," Daru said testily, the sweep of her hand covering both the black dagger and Evan. "Haven't you ever read Sherlock Holmes?"

"Huh?" The lack of sleep, combined with the roller coaster ride he went on every time Evan looked at him—*Just keep telling yourself it's a religious experience.*—had put Roland on less than firm mental footing.

"When you have eliminated the impossible, that which remains, however improbable, must be the answer. If Evan exists, and he does . . ." Evan flashed a smile at her over his shoulder, then went back to enjoying the different textures of light as it poured through the curtains. ". . . and if I believe what he is, and I do . . ." A moment staring into the Adept's eyes had been almost enough without the more blatant show of glory. ". . . then the rest of it must be true as well. And if our world is about to be overcome by Darkness," her mouth thinned into a hard line, "then I don't intend to sit by and let it happen."

No, Roland thought, *I bet you never have.* As a caseworker at Metro Social Services, Daru fought in the front line against Darkness every day.

"Rebecca, honey," Daru swiveled around and tried to see into the kitchen, "what are you doing?"

Rebecca popped her head back out into the living room. "Making breakfast." With full light she'd pulled on an old pair of turquoise track pants and a yellow sweatshirt with the sleeves ripped out. "There's scrambled eggs made with milk, 'cause I got some last night, and sausages done under the broiler. I unfroze the whole package instead of just three for me. I'm making toast, too."

"All that at once?" Daru sounded doubtful.

"The stove does most of the work," Rebecca explained seriously. "And the toaster."

"Do you have any jam?" Roland asked, wandering over and sticking his head in the fridge.

"The jam is behind the catsup. It's peach." She leaned farther out of the kitchen and handed him a small can and the can opener. "You can feed Tom."

He juggled the can on his palm, sighed, and glared at the cat.

Tom, who knew very well what a can of that size and a can opener meant, leaped off the couch and wove a pattern around Roland's feet; a dignified pattern, of course, expressing anticipation and only the smallest amount of hunger.

"Oh, all right." Roland moved forward and set the cat food down on the table, Tom modifying his dance to accommodate the steps. "But I want to make it perfectly clear," he called to the kitchen, "I'm doing this for you, not for him."

"Tom doesn't care, as long as you open the can."

Cramming the blade of the can opener down, Roland glared at Daru. "Why do you let her waste her money on this stuff?"

Daru raised an eyebrow. "You prefer another brand?" she asked, pitching her voice just to one side of sarcasm.

"Skip it." He wrestled the top off, his nose wrinkling at the smell, then he placed the open can on the floor. Tom sniffed it, gave it cautious approval, and began to eat. Daru flashed him what Roland interpreted as a superior smile and headed for the bathroom. Feeling outnumbered, Roland reached for his guitar and soothed his spirit by putting music to the

pattern of sunlight and leaf shadow that played across
Evan where he stood in the window.

"So much pain," the Adept murmured, watching
an ant traveling the length of the window ledge, a
smaller insect held in its jaws. He filled his lungs,
tasting the concrete and steel and asphalt, tasting the
sorrow and hatred and pain, and sighed. The Dark had
so much to work with. But the sunlight warmed him
and breezes brought the sound of children's laughter
and he had neither the ability nor the desire to deny
hope.

Roland saw Evan's shoulders sag and added a minor
scale, then he saw them lift again and picked up both
tempo and tone. He felt an audience and with a skill
honed by years on the street, where a direct glance
could scare away a paying customer, he slid a peek
out of the corner of one eye.

Daru stood beside the couch, her gaze flicking from
him to Evan and back.

Under the weight of her regard, he stopped playing
and turned to face her.

"I could see your music," she said, wonder in her
voice. "Like a mirror made of sound . . . I could
see . . ."

Roland felt his face go hot and he dropped his eyes,
fumbling with his pick.

"Breakfast." Rebecca poked a filled plate out of the
kitchen and Roland scrambled to get it, the action covering his embarrassment. He could only handle praise
when it came as cash. Praise from Rebecca, for rea-
sons he'd never quite been able to fathom, was the only
exception.

Watching Evan eat kept distracting Daru and Roland
from their own food, for he took delight in not only
the taste but the textures and the smells, making
scrambled eggs and sausages a sensual experience.

"Don't they have food where you come from?" Rebecca asked as Evan drew his fingers down a piece of
toast, examined the gleam of margarine, then licked
his finger tips.

"Of course," he bit off the end of a sausage and his

eyes widened with pleasure as he separated all the many tastes it contained, "but this is new. And every facet of newness should be discovered and enjoyed."

Rebecca nodded. "That's what I think, too."

Daru hid a smile, remembering the first time she'd taken Rebecca out for pizza and the girl had poked her fingers into the melted cheese, then spent close to five minutes experimenting with the stretch factor of mozzarella.

Her face softens when she smiles, Roland thought, having placed himself where he could see Daru as well as Evan. *Makes her look less like a hawk.* After years of protesting that it didn't mean anything, Roland had decided, looking at Daru, he knew exactly what *striking* meant when used as a physical description. Not pretty, not beautiful, but, well, striking—dark gold skin, eyes so black the pupils and irises were one, a high forehead, a proud arch of a nose, a pointed yet still determined chin, and the whole thing surrounded by a thick fall of ebony hair. Not exactly cold, but stern. He made plans to pick up his flute if he ever got home, for her song flew too high for his guitar.

"You got something to say to me?" Daru snapped, suddenly aware of his regard.

And bitchy, Roland added to his mental list, dropping his gaze. *Stern and bitchy.* Behind the pale curtain of hair, Roland could see the Adept grinning and wondered, not for the first time, just how much of his thoughts Evan could hear.

"So, uh," he got up and began stacking empty plates, "feels like its going to be a hot one again today."

"Yes," Evan sighed, the grin banished. He rose lithely and returned to his place by the window. "And when it's hot like this, with blinding glare and the air heavy and still like a sheet of heated glass, tempers fray and good people can be pushed to the edge and over."

"You mean *he's* causing this?" Roland asked over the sound of the sink filling.

"Yes," Evan said without turning.

"But it's summer," Roland protested. "I know Canada gets called the Great White North, but it does get hot here in the summer."

"Not like this," Daru put in thoughtfully. "Not this hot, for this long, in June. A week or two in August maybe . . ."

"What are you going to do about it?" Rebecca asked, getting right to the point.

"I'm doing it, Lady."

Daru's brow quirked for that was the first time she'd heard Evan title Rebecca.

"There are rain clouds to the south and west and I'm encouraging them in this direction. In two days, the city will have relief."

"Why not sooner," Roland wanted to know, handing the pile of clean plates to Rebecca to put away.

Evan spread his hands, his bracelets chiming softly. "Rain travels at its own speed. Move it too quickly, it dissipates. Move it too slowly, it gets bored and falls."

"Rain gets bored?"

"A simple word to cover a complicated . . ." He tugged on a strand of pale hair, searching for the word.

"Thing?" Rebecca offered.

"A complicated thing, yes." They shared pleased smiles and again Roland sensed another level in the exchange.

"There's something I've been wondering about." Daru paced the length of the small apartment while she spoke.

Join the club, Roland thought, settling Patience on his lap. The last time he'd been sure of anything had been just before Rebecca showed up on his street corner.

"You came here because Rebecca invited you, right?"

"Roland had a voice in the invitation," Evan pointed out, "but that's essentially correct."

"Well, how did *he* get in."

In the silence that fell while they waited for Evan's answer, the only sound was the scrape of Tom's tongue smoothing the black stripes of his tail.

"There are two possibilities," Evan said at last. "That a man or woman in this world did a deed of evil and called to the Darkness while doing it . . ."

"Black candles, and pentagrams, and human sacrifice," Roland murmured, and Patience wailed a discordant accompaniment to his words.

"Yes," Evan sighed, "the Darkness has been called that way. But this time, this time I think it moved on its own to take advantage of the weakened barriers of Midsummer Night. Although, in a way, *he* was invited, too. . . .

"This world has much darkness in it and it calls always to the Darkness outside the barriers. After a time, the barrier weakens enough for a bit of Darkness to slip through. Usually a bit so small it comes with no real body of its own and either dissipates, leaving a general feeling of bad humor in its wake, or it finds a host and does what it can to create a permanent residence. These bits of Darkness can't survive long where even a little Light stands against them."

He filled his cupped palm with sunlight, then scattered it off his fingertips in lines of delicate filigree. "Of course, the Light in your world calls in like kind. Sometimes, a deed of such Dark or Light is done that larger creatures can answer; goblins and boggins, unicorns and fauns. To pass an Adept, the Darkness waited until the call became almost unbearable, saving up the wearing at the barrier, directing all its resources to a single goal." He sighed again. "Which, thankfully, it seldom manages, self-discipline not being one of its stronger characteristics. When the time was right, it moved, forcing through a bit of itself large enough and strong enough to open the gate for the rest. I don't imagine the passage through the barrier was a pleasant one."

"You sound almost sorry for *him*," Daru said, frowning.

"I regret anyone's pain," Evan told her, no trace of apology in his voice. "Even his. But that will not stop me from destroying him."

"I don't understand what you mean, 'forced through

a bit of itself'?'' Roland had turned and twisted the statement but still could made no sense of it.

"There is only one Darkness as there is only one Light. As he is a piece of the Darkness, so I am a piece of the Light. The Darkness holds its pieces close, not trusting in them to stay, but the Light wants nothing to be a part of it that doesn't choose to be there.''

"If you love something, let it go. If it comes back to you, it's yours. If it doesn't, it never was.'' Rebecca blushed as they all turned to stare at her. "I read it on a T-shirt,'' she explained, chewing her lower lip, afraid from the reaction she'd said something wrong.

Evan tossed his hair back off his face and his eyes sparkled. "But that's it exactly.''

"It is?''

"Exactly,'' he repeated.

Rebecca nodded, content. "I thought so.''

Daru reached over and gave her hand a squeeze then turned again to Evan. "Are you strong enough to defeat him?''

"One on one, just him and me?'' Evan shrugged, the sparkle gone. "To keep the balance we are of equal power, but the Dark is often self-indulgent, bleeding power away to keep itself amused.''

Daru sighed. "That was a straight yes or no question and your answer was neither.''

"All right, then,'' he smiled, "probably. But first I have to find him.''

"Can't you just, oh, I don't know,'' Roland plucked a scale up his G-string, "cast a spell and know where he is?''

"No. Unless he actually tips the balance, I must find him the same way you would find any mortal man.''

"In less than a week?''

"Yes.''

"Do you know what he looks like?''

"I'd recognize him if I saw him.''

It was Roland's turn to sigh. "Do you know just how big this city is? With how many people?''

"Yes,'' Evan said again, "but I have help.''

Roland and Daru exchanged looks that placed them in complete agreement for the first time since being introduced.

"And as well," Evan continued, ignoring the expressions of disbelief on the faces of two members of his audience, "we should find where he plans to open the gate . . ."

"Can you put any parameters on *that?*" Daru interrupted.

"Oh, yes . . ."

She relaxed a little.

". . . the area must be fairly large, open, and the earth must not be bound by concrete and steel."

"A park," Rebecca suggested, bouncing.

"Do you know how many *parks* there are in this city?" Roland protested.

"Yes." Rebecca's tone was so perfectly serious that Roland could only conclude she did, indeed, know how many parks there were in the city.

"We need a map." Daru stood and adjusted the folds of her sari. "I have one in my car. I'll be right back."

Hoping no one noticed, Roland watched her leave. He felt like a shit, but the sway of her hips beneath the draped silk was worth it.

When she returned, she held a folded map of Toronto, what appeared to be clothing draped over one arm, and a yellow rectangle of paper about eight inches long.

"I don't suppose you fix parking tickets?" she asked Evan, tossing both the ticket and the map on Rebecca's table.

"Sorry, not my department. Give unto Caesar and all that."

Daru nodded, unsurprised. "You've read the Bible."

"I've read all your great works of literature, the Bible, the Koran, Shakespeare, Wells, Harold Robbins . . ."

"What!"

He winked, taking five years off his apparent age. "Kidding."

Daru rolled her eyes at him and headed for the bathroom to change.

"Have you read Winnie the Pooh?" Rebecca asked. "He's my favorite."

"Of course I have," Evan told her, perching carefully on the windowsill between two plants, stretching out his legs, and crossing his booted feet, "there's great wisdom in Pooh."

"For a bear of very little brain," Rebecca agreed.

This was another side of Rebecca Roland had not been aware of. "Do you read it by yourself?" he wanted to know.

"Yes." Rebecca's brow furrowed in indignation. "I can read harder books than Pooh." She paused, thought for a moment, and added, "But not much harder."

"Rebecca," Daru said, returning to the living room in white cotton shorts and a matching shirt, "has a complete set of Paddington Bear books."

"I like bears," Rebecca told the company proudly. "I have a bunch of the Berenstain Bears books, too."

Rebecca, Roland realized, probably read for pleasure more often than the majority of college graduates.

Daru spread the map out on the table and Rebecca bent over it.

"Are the parks the green bits?" she asked.

"Yes, that's right."

"Sometimes," Rebecca sighed contentedly, "things make sense. Parks are green bits," she explained to Evan as he joined them.

The table was small, the apartment was warm, and Roland, who'd never had much interest in parks anyway, soon decided he'd rather watch from a distance than be part of the crowd. From the sound of it, Rebecca did, indeed, know every park in the city, how many trees each contained, and who—or what—lived in each tree.

Tom leaped up on the sill, balanced for a moment in the open window, then disappeared. Roland assumed he wouldn't have jumped if he hadn't thought he could make it safely to the ground, so he continued strumming and didn't mention the cat's departure.

Probably has to take a leak. In fact, that's not a bad idea.

He wandered into the bathroom, did what he had to, and returned to find the other three still poring over the map.

". . . no, that's all up and down and there's too many trees . . ."

"Parks," he muttered. And, "Parks!" he said louder. There was one park he knew about . . . "Rebecca, does this tv work?"

"What?" she looked around the apartment, as if unsure who'd spoken.

Roland repeated the question.

"Oh, yes, it works. But it only works on channel five and channel nine."

"That's great, just great. I need channel nine. Can I turn it on?"

"Sure." She bent back over the map. "No, that one's too long and skinny."

Like everything else in the apartment, the small portable television on the shelf over the radiator was spotless. Roland unwound the cord from the hooks on the back—Rebecca, apparently, was not a big tv fan—found the nearest outlet, and plugged it in. If he remembered the starting time correctly, he shouldn't have missed much more than the opening pitch.

As the picture faded in, black and white and a little fuzzy, he saw he'd judged it just about right; top of the first with one out and a runner on second. With the volume turned low, he settled down to watch something he understood.

In the bottom of the third, he felt the couch shift and heard the soft chime of Evan's bracelets as the Adept settled down next to him.

"Who's winning?"

"Detroit—one, nothing."

"The Jays' prima donna still benched?"

"Yeah," Roland sighed, "he . . . Wait a minute!" He spun to face the Adept, found him almost unbearably close, and successfully fought the urge to discover whether his hair was as silky as it looked. "What do you know about baseball?"

Evan waited until the Bluejay at bat popped out before answering. "Television signals pass easily through the barrier."

"You mean you watch tv in heaven or elfland or whatever you call the place you come from?"

"I call it home. And yes."

"What on," Roland asked facetiously, unable to help himself, "crystal balls?"

"Of course not, balls roll all over the place. Any good sized piece of crystal with a reasonably flat surface will do."

"You're not serious." He took a closer look at Evan's face. "You are serious. Well, I'll be damned."

Evan grinned and stretched. "Not likely," he said.

Roland found himself mesmerized by the pulse that beat at the base of Evan's throat. He heard the crack of a bat and the crowd at the stadium yelling but couldn't seem to tear his gaze away. He noticed Evan had the same clean smell as Rebecca's apartment. He sighed and closed his eyes, seeing again the vision of great white wings.

"Daru and the Lady have gone to the store. I hope you didn't want anything. You seemed pretty involved in the game."

Opening his eyes, Roland glanced around the apartment. He and Evan were alone. "No, nothing." He watched the sunlight glint on the golden tips of Evan's lashes. They were sitting very close. Desperately, he searched for something to say as the silence was beginning to say too much. "Why do you call her that . . . Lady?"

"It's a term of respect."

"Not of endearment?" Roland asked suspiciously.

"Aren't they often the same thing?"

"You know, it's next to impossible to get a straight answer from you."

"The Light has never provided easy answers."

Roland snorted. "That's exactly what I mean."

What's wrong with this picture, he thought as with an effort he turned his attention back to the broadcast. *The women folk go shopping while the men folk watch the game. Except that one of the women folk is a few pickles short of a barrel, the other keeps wondering what rock I've crawled out from under, and one of the men folk is an angel. Of sorts.*

"Daru, why don't you like Roland?"

Daru picked up a third can of lemonade concentrate, studied it for a moment, and dropped it in the basket. "What do you mean, Rebecca?"

"Well," Rebecca squeezed the rye bread gently while she spoke, "you show him your government face all the time."

"I don't dislike Roland. Have you got mustard at the apartment?"

"Yes."

"I just don't know him very well."

"Then you should get to know him better. Roland is nice."

Daru sighed; three years as Rebecca's case worker and almost that long as her friend enabled her to leap ahead to what Rebecca actually meant. "I'm not going to sleep with him," she said quietly. "Get a head of lettuce please."

Rebecca obediently picked a head out of the pile, weighing it in her palm before passing it over. "Why not?"

"Because I don't want to."

"Why not?"

"Because I don't know him."

"But you would get to know him if you slept with him."

The woman at the cash register looked up, interested. Daru felt herself flush, glad her complexion was too dark for it to be easily seen. The most obvious, and annoying, manifestation of Rebecca's disability was her lack of a volume control. Everything she said, she said in her normal speaking voice. Her normal, fairly loud, speaking voice.

"He wouldn't sleep with me."

"Rebecca, hush." Daru's opinion of Roland rose upon hearing he'd refused Rebecca's offer—the odds were better than good that Rebecca had been the one who'd offered—and simultaneously fell for she felt she knew why. Rebecca might appear to be a precocious ten year old, but she was an adult woman for all that and Roland had no right to think of her as a child. Of course, she was amazingly childlike and Roland deserved credit for not taking advantage of that. Except she wasn't a child and . . . Tangled up as usual in Rebecca's sexuality, Daru sighed and paid for their groceries.

But after they'd left the store, while she was still thinking about it, she asked, "Are you remembering to take a pill every day?" God knew she'd had enough trouble getting the pills approved; considering mentally disadvantaged adults as sexually active gave most of the department spasms.

"Don't worry, Daru," Rebecca shifted the grocery bag and smiled reassuringly, "there won't be any babies." It wasn't exactly a lie. She didn't exactly say she took the pills. Daru just wouldn't understand that babies came when babies came and little pills wouldn't make any difference. Rebecca wished she could explain it, then everyone could stop taking the little pills.

"He's there. He's at the ball park."

"What?" Roland whirled to stare at Evan. "Look, just because the outfield misses an easy catch doesn't mean *he* had anything to do with it. The Jays have been known to snatch defeat from the jaws of victory before."

"And have balls changed direction as they fell before?"

"Sure. The stadium's right on the lake. It's one of the windiest in the league."

"Look at the flags, Roland." Evan pointed at the screen and Roland had a sudden vision of the ghost of Christmas yet to come at Scrooge's grave. "There's no wind."

"Yeah, but . . ."

"And that earlier decision . . ."

"He could've been out; after all, the second base ump was right there."

"But he looked safe, didn't he?"

"Yeah." Roland had to admit it.

"And what of that error that the umpire just didn't see?"

"It happens." But even to his own ears he didn't sound so sure.

"It's him." Evan rose, lips set in a thin line. "He's there. I don't know what he thinks he's doing, but he's there. I have to try to find him. We may never get this kind of a chance again."

"I hope he arrives a little more conventionally than he left," Roland muttered, suddenly alone in the apartment. He reached out and with a trembling hand touched the empty indentation smoothing out of the couch. "Gone. Just like that." He laughed nervously and went back to watching the game. It was the only thing he could think of to do.

"Well, hello, Becca." The large blonde-lady-from-down-the-hall beamed as Rebecca and Daru came into the small lobby of the apartment building. "Have we been grocery shopping, then?" she asked brightly, wiping at her face with a large square of pink cloth. Not waiting for an answer, she turned to Daru and added in the same artificial tones, "It's just so sweet of you to come here on your day off and help our Becca out."

Daru smiled tightly.

"You're probably wondering why I'm waiting down here. Well, my sister's boy is coming to pick me up and take me out to their lovely house in Don Mills. They have central air conditioning."

"He must be very strong," Rebecca said, intrigued.

"Who must, Becca dear?"

"Your sister's boy who's coming to pick you up."

"Isn't she just precious?" the large-blonde-lady-from-down-the-hall asked Daru in a stage whisper. A

horn honked at the curb and she lumbered to her feet.
"You be a good girl now, Becca. And you," she waved
a pudgy finger at Daru, "you let me know if I can do
anything to help."

Rebecca watched as she made her way out to the
street and sighed. She'd been looking forward to seeing someone pick up the large-blonde-lady-from-down-
the-hall, but the sister's boy had come in a car instead.

"I guess Evan made her a dream that worked," she
said as they climbed the stairs.

"I guess," Daru agreed. "Rebecca, do you want
me to talk to her again?"

"You can talk again, but she won't listen again."

Daru had to admit that she wouldn't.

"I don't mind," Rebecca continued, " 'cause
mostly I feel sorry for her."

"Sorry for her? Why?"

" 'Cause she always has to be her and that mustn't
be very nice most of the time."

Daru was still mulling that over as they entered the
apartment which felt almost cool after the baking heat
of outside.

"Where did Evan go?" Rebecca asked, setting the
bag of groceries on the table and pulling out the package of ham.

"To the ball game," Roland said shortly, not taking
his eyes off the television.

"Why on earth . . ." Daru began.

"Because *he's* at the ball game."

"Oh." She sat down beside Roland and peered at
the screen.

The crowd roared as a pitch swerved and the umpires inspected both the ball and the Tiger's pitcher.
The crowd roared louder when both passed the inspection.

In the bottom of the sixth, a Jays' runner slammed
into the Tigers' second baseman and in the screaming
match that followed both managers were tossed from
the game.

As Rebecca handed out ham sandwiches—"People
still have to eat."—a ground ball leaped out of the

shortstop's glove, rolled between his legs, and away. The roar of the crowd had become a constant and ugly background noise.

During the seventh inning stretch, BJ Bird stepped backward and fell off the dugout roof. The announcer said he thought the mascot had been trying to avoid a bottle thrown by a Detroit fan when it happened.

"I didn't see a bottle, did you?" Daru asked.

"No," Roland told her. "I didn't."

Several fights broke out between fans wearing head-phones, the radio announcer having said the exact same thing.

In the eighth inning, two obvious errors went un-called and a star player, a favorite with the fans, put up an argument over his third strike and got thrown out of the game. The roar became a snarl.

The Tigers hit the only home run of the game in the ninth but the Bluejays couldn't seem to find the ball.

The final score: three to two, Tigers.

From the general admission seats came screams of "Cheat! CHEAT!" and the stands erupted.

"This is so fucking un-Canadian," Roland mut-tered. "A riot? I don't believe it."

They watched in silence as the camera zoomed in on the seething mass of people, some screaming in anger, some screaming in panic. The play by play an-nouncer did his best to report what he saw;

"The exits appear blocked with bodies . . . I can see parents trying to lift their children up out of dan-ger . . . The police are trying to regain control . . . My god, that man has a bat . . ."

The color commentator kept repeating, "Oh shit, oh shit, oh shit . . ." until someone turned his micro-phone off.

As the camera swept the stadium, it found one tiny island of calm. Up behind home plate, a double row of empty seats between him and the riot, a dark haired man watched and waited and, as he felt the camera focus on him, he looked up and smiled.

"That's *him!*" Roland and Rebecca yelled together.

Daru felt her heart thud as the bright blue eyes on the screen met hers.

Then suddenly, a blaze of white light burned out the image and the television went dark.

Chapter SIX

". . . And to recap our top news story of the day, a riot at Exhibition Stadium results in four dead and seventeen injured. No charges have been filed yet in the incident. Police are withholding the names of the dead until next of kin can be notified. I'm Heather Chan and this has been the news at six."

The constable who had the desk turned the radio down as the news ended, and shook his head. It all sounded so tidy once it hit the news; four dead and seventeen injured, no muss, no fuss, no mention of the noise, or the stink, or the hopeless feeling you got facing a riot involving almost forty thousand. Of course, that was from a cop's point of view and no one ever seemed much interested in that.

He pulled a stack of arrest reports over to his terminal and began inputting the information they contained. The thing that really pissed him off about what had gone down at the stadium was the paperwork. With all divisions undermanned—the flu bug sweeping the city seemed to have a preference for the police—the last thing they needed was a doubling of the workload. He squinted at a colleague's scrawl, decided the name had to be O'Conner, and hoped Fourteen Division appreciated what the other stations in the city were doing for them.

"Hey, Harper." An auxiliary dropped another pile of paper on the desk.

"Hey, yourself," he grunted. "There'd better be a stack of those for you, Wojtowicz, or you're toast."

She patted the pile beside her own terminal and for

a few minutes the only sound was the faint click click of the keyboards. "So, have they figured out what caused the riot?"

He glanced over, envying the effortless way her fingers moved over the keys compared to his own hunt and correct method. "Didn't you hear the news? The Jays lost."

Wojtowicz snorted. "That's not news. And no cause for a riot."

"Not all by itself maybe." Harper ticked the points off on his fingers. "One, the Jays lost to the Tigers. That upset a lot of people. Two, the umpires called a bad game. It happens. It upset a lot more people. Three, which may also be the reason for two, it's hot out there; you could fry an egg on a batting helmet if you wanted to. In hot weather people get irritated faster and are more likely to do something about it." He grinned at her sceptical expression. "They teach us that psych stuff at the academy. A hot, angry crowd like that and I'd have been more surprised if there hadn't been a riot."

"But what about all the tv cameras burning out?"

"What cameras? I didn't hear about that."

"There was a flash of bright light, and all the tv cameras burned out. I was watching the game at home before I came in."

"Aliens," Harper said dramatically.

Wojtowicz rolled her eyes. "Right. Little green Bluejays fans."

"Okay, terrorists."

"Up from Buffalo for the game? Get real."

He spread his hands in surrender. "Okay, I give up. I don't know why the tv cameras burned out. Nor do I particularly care."

"What about the way the riot stopped, as suddenly as it began?"

"Who can tell what a mob will do?"

"No," she shook her head, remembering her reaction while watching the game. "Something about the whole thing felt wrong."

"It was a riot," Harper pointed out. "It's not supposed to feel right."

"You know what I mean."

He thought about it for a moment, but finally shrugged. "Hot weather makes people do strange things."

"But it's only June!" she protested.

"Yeah, I know." He looked out the glass doors and watched the heat shimmer up off the road. "God help us in July and August."

Daru turned off the television. The news had told them nothing they didn't already know and Evan still hadn't returned. "Well . . ." she said, with a helpless shrug at the other two.

"Deep subject," Roland murmured, reaching for his guitar, "turn it sideways and you've got a tunnel."

"Oh, that's a lot of help!" Daru snapped at him.

"Turn what sideways?" Rebecca wondered.

They ignored her.

"What do you want me to say?" Roland sneered. "Let's put the wagon train in a circle? Form up an intrepid band of rescuers and go after him? We don't know where he is. We don't know *if* he is. He might have lost already and we're fucked. Have you thought of that?" He slashed his hand down on the strings, then sighed and leaned his forehead against the smooth wood.

Daru opened her mouth to tell him just what she thought of his defeatist attitude, but Rebecca tapped her lightly on the shoulder and shook her head.

"Don't be mad at him, Daru. He's worried about Evan and being worried makes him cranky."

Roland looked up, his expression unreadable, met Daru's eyes, and shrugged. "I'm sorry. She's right."

The phone rang. Daru and Roland jumped, but Rebecca, almost as though she'd expected it, dropped to her knees and dug it out from under the couch. It rang again.

"It's Evan," she said, holding the phone out.

"How do you know?" Roland asked as Daru took it and lifted the receiver to her ear.

Rebecca held up the end of the cord, the plastic jack between thumb and forefinger. "It's not plugged in."

"Yes, yes, I understand. I'll be right there. Fifty-two Division? Why all the way up . . . Overcrowding? Oh. Yes, I know where it is. No more than fifteen minutes. You, too." She hung up, took a deep breath, and said, "It was Evan. I have to go and bail him out."

"Bail him out?"

"Well, vouch for him." She paused and her lips twitched just a little. "He doesn't have any ID."

Roland chuckled. Daru chuckled. Then the two of them roared with laughter while Rebecca watched, completely confused.

Still laughing, Daru stood, scooped up her purse, and headed for the door. "We'll be back as soon as possible," she said, and left.

Roland wiped his streaming eyes. "No ID," he repeated, setting himself off again. "No ID."

Rebecca shook her head. Sometimes so-called normal people made no sense.

She crossed the cobbles in front of Fifty-two Division with short, jerky steps, her mind paying no attention to her feet. How dared they give her a parking ticket when she was only in the spot for a minute or two. Okay, maybe ten, but where else was she supposed to park? Getting a spot downtown was like pulling teeth, no, harder than pulling teeth, and she'd give the cops an opinion or two along with her twenty bucks. She felt the impact of a shoulder, began to fall, then a strong hand pulled her straight and steadied her.

"Thanks," she snarled at her rescuer. As she pushed past, she glanced up at his face. Her frown curved up into a smile, and she got lost in the smile he flashed in return. Not caring how it looked, she stood and stared after him until he and his companion got into a beat up old Japanese hatchback and drove away. He wasn't even her type, too young, too flash, way too pretty—she made it a point never to get interested in men significantly prettier than she was—and completely irresistible.

"Now that," she sighed to the evening air, "is a man worth making a fool of yourself over." With a final melting glance in the direction he'd disappeared, she pulled open the door and stepped inside the station, her earlier pique forgotten.

"Play the one about the unicorn again." Rebecca bounced where she sat. "The one your friend wrote."

"I played it already, kiddo. Two songs ago."

"I know," she told him, rolling her eyes, "I said play it *again*."

Roland smiled. "Oh, *again*. Pardon me."

Rebecca thought about it, brows drawn down, teeth working on the edge of her left thumbnail. "Okay," she said, after a minute. "You can play what you want to, but you've got to play the unicorn song first."

"You win," Roland surrendered, still smiling. He didn't mind playing for Rebecca—even though she usually wanted the same songs sung over and over—because she listened so intently, becoming completely involved in the music. Audiences like that were few and far between.

He plunges through the forest night,
his eyes are wide with fear.
Behind him, he can hear the sounds
that say the hunt is near.

Out of his whole repertoire, Rebecca's favorites were the simple tunes with the fantastical lyrics that one of his oldest friends had been sending to him in every letter she'd written over the last five or six years. He'd tried to fool her a couple of times with songs that were alike in theme and structure, but Rebecca always knew. Once, he'd played her one of his own pieces of music. She'd listened as intently, head cocked to one side, and when he'd finished said, "It's very good, Roland, but it isn't quite." And then had not been able to tell him *what* it wasn't quite. He never played her one of his pieces again. Mostly because, deep down, he agreed with her.

As he finished, they heard voices in the hall and the door opened.

"Evan!" Rebecca flung herself to her feet and across the room, rocking to a halt inches from the Adept. "Are you okay?"

"I'm fine, Lady." He smiled; a little wearily, Roland thought. "Thank you for your concern."

"You got arrested!"

"Yes." He stroked a curl back off her face. "I did."

Rebecca turned to Daru and her eyes widened. "You got chicken!"

"Yes." Daru handed her the red and white striped bag. "I did."

Rebecca buried her face in the bag, took a long appreciative sniff, then turned and showed it to Roland. "Roland! They got chicken."

"I can see that, kiddo." He stood, holding Patience against him, scanning Evan for any signs of . . . of . . . anything. In his experience, cops weren't kind to young men with no ID they pulled in out of a . . . situation. "Are you all right?"

Even spread his arms. "As you see, I'm fine."

Roland continued to look. *Taking advantage of the excuse to look your fill and hide the feeling under concern,* said a small voice in the back of his head which he ignored. Rebecca put a plate heaped with chicken and french fries and coleslaw in one hand, lifted his guitar out of the other, and replaced it with a fork.

"Eat," she said, so he did.

Later, when the bones had been picked clean and he'd recovered his equilibrium—a process he hoped he wasn't going to have to go through every time he saw Evan though he rather suspected he would—he asked, "What happened?"

Evan fed Tom a piece of skin. The cat had arrived just as they were sitting down to eat. "I stopped the riot," he said simply. "I couldn't stand the hurting, the fear. He got away. I think he knew it would happen like that. I think he's somewhere laughing at me, right now.'' His fine features looked pinched and drawn. ''Stopping the riot took all the power I had.''

Daru almost didn't recognize her own voice as she said, ''By saving those people, by letting *him* go, you may have doomed the rest of the world to Darkness.''

''I know.''

And there was nothing more to say, because he did know, better than they ever could, and the pain in his voice, in those two words, was enough to bring tears to a heart of stone.

PC Harper pushed his keyboard to one side, laced his fingers together, and stretched. His shift was almost over and he could practically taste that icy cold beer waiting for him at home. He could coast through the next hour and a half. What was going to happen at nine-thirty on a Sunday night in Toronto the Good?

He heard the door open but before he could turn to look, he had a pretty good idea of what he'd see. The air conditioning, already straining to defeat the heat, simply couldn't cope with this new assault as well; old dirt, old sweat, unwashed clothes, and over it all the pervasive stink of stale urine.

''Hey, bubba, you gotta minute?''

Breathing shallowly through his mouth, Harper stood and walked slowly over to the counter. This was the worst part of being so shorthanded, he had no choice but to deal with this old lady, no chance to suddenly have to go to the washroom, leaving her to the other guy on the desk. Damn. ''And what can I do for you?'' he asked, keeping his tone neutral with an effort.

''You know the girl what got killed last night? I think I seen who did it. You interested?''

''Wha . . .''

Mrs. Ruth sighed and shook her head. ''The girl what got killed last night,'' she repeated slowly. ''I think I seen who did it.'' He still appeared a little shell-shocked, so she added, ''I was on my way to the dumpster and I seen this guy leaving the parking lot. I didn't think nothing of it at the time, but he smelled a little funny. Then I heard about what happened through the grapevine, so I come in to tell the cops.''

"Smelled funny?'' He wondered how she could possibly tell.

"Yeah. Not like expensive perfume or hair junk. Like blood.'' Her voice took on a grimmer tone. "And I know what blood smells like.''

"But if you went to the dumpster, you must have found the body.'' *It always happened,* Harper sighed to himself. *Any kind of sensational crime brings out the nut cases.*

Mrs. Ruth's eyes narrowed. "I didn't say I went to the dumpster,'' she snapped. "I said I was on my way. I got distracted and never made it. Now, are you going to call someone out here who can take my statement and a description of this guy or am I going to have to get angry?''

Her voice so reminded him of a teacher he'd lived in terror of all through third grade that his finger hit the intercom button before he even knew he'd moved it.

Mrs. Ruth smiled.

". . . I mean, why should I let him push me around?''

"Why, indeed.''

"He thinks he's hot shit just because he drives a BMW and has some hot shit computer job, but I'm just as good as he is.''

"Better.''

"Damn right!''

The Dark Adept leaned forward, placing his forearms carefully between the beer rings on the table. "After all, where would his type be if not for you. One of the men who actually makes what they consume.''

"Yeah. That, too!'' He tossed back the beer in his glass and held it out for a refill, long past the point of wondering why the pitcher never seemed to empty. "And you know what else? That son of a bitch has the nerve to tell me I can't put my garbage at the edge of the driveway. We share the fuckin' driveway, you know, and he thinks he can tell me not to put my fuckin' garbage there.''

"Perhaps it's time to do something about him.''

"Yeah.'' He scowled. "P'raps it is.'' Abruptly he pushed back his chair and stood, swaying slightly. "Do something about him right now.''

"Do you still keep your shotgun in the back of the hall cupboard?''

"Yeah.'' His eyes narrowed. "Yeah. That'll show the son of a bitch.'' He staggered off through the crowd, bouncing off chairs and tables and people, letting neither curses nor spilled beer distract him from his course home. And his hall cupboard. And the lesson he was going to teach that fancy-ass that lived next door.

"That,'' the Adept sighed, "was almost too easy.'' He caught the attention of one of the waitresses and beckoned her over with a toss of his head.

"Oh, he's a cool one,'' she murmured to her companion, tucking her tray under one arm and twitching her short skirt into place.

The other girl peered in his direction. "He looks dangerous.''

"You think anyone with a gleam in his eye looks dangerous.''

She shook her head, teased hair bobbing with the motion. "Yeah, but he looks really dangerous. Like, like a sharp knife.''

"Poetic.'' Moistening bright red lips, the summoned girl sashayed off, with one last comment, "Don't worry, honey, I can handle him.''

"That's settled it, then.'' Daru slipped her pen back into her purse and tore the top sheet of paper off the pad in her lap. "I'll go in tomorrow, do everything that absolutely has to be done and book the rest of the week off. Roland and Evan will start showing Evan's drawing around the hotels.'' She glanced at the sketches Evan had done of the Dark Adept based on the glimpse he'd gotten of him at the ballpark. The sketches were good; detailed down to the collar buttons and the faintly contemptuous expression. "Are we sure he's going to keep looking like this?" she asked.

"Oh, yes," Evan told her. "Until he goes through the barrier again, he's as tied to that body as I am to this one."

Daru nodded, satisfied, and Roland shoved an image of being tied to Evan's body out of his mind.

"And tomorrow after I get off work," Rebecca announced, "Evan and me . . ."

"I," Daru corrected automatically.

"Yeah. Evan and I will go and ask the littles to help look." She sighed. "I wish I could take the rest of the week off."

"As much as we need you, Lady, you are needed there more."

"Yeah, but . . ."

"Did you not say there are three of your co-workers off sick already?"

Rebecca sighed again. "Yes, three. It wouldn't be fair to Lena for me to go away, too. Then she'd have to make all the muffins herself."

"Don't look so sad." Evan pulled his happy-face button free, leaned forward, and pinned it to Rebecca's shirt. "You see many people in your job; hear a lot of conversations. If anything strange is going on, people will talk about it and you can pass it on. Someone listening to people carrying on their ordinary lives may give us the clue we need. It's the ordinary lives he'll disrupt the most."

"Okay." Rebecca nodded reluctantly, raised her hand and trapped his. She ran a finger down the line of bracelets, causing them to ring together, smiled at the sound, and did it again. "But why can't we start tonight? It isn't too late."

"It is much too late," Daru declared, standing. "None of us got much sleep last night, and you and I," she said pointedly to Rebecca, "have to be up early in the morning." She turned to Roland. "We are leaving. And you," she turned back to Rebecca, "are going to bed."

"Maybe I should stay?" Roland offered.

"Maybe you should go home and get some clean clothes," Daru replied.

"But . . ." He looked from Evan to Rebecca and then up at Daru. Their expressions were merely curious. Hers was almost challenging. "Yeah, I guess you're right."

"Daru is almost always right," Rebecca told him.

"Really." He stretched over the back of the couch, looking for his guitar case. "Doesn't that get tiring." The case had slipped down and was lying flat on the floor, just out of reach.

Daru smiled. "No. It doesn't."

"Mrs. Ruth is *always* right," Rebecca added to the room at large.

Daru rolled her eyes. "Mrs. Ruth is a bag lady, Rebecca. That in itself is not very right."

"Have you met Mrs. Ruth?" Roland asked, coming around the couch to stand by his case.

"I haven't had the pleasure."

"You're missing a treat." He bent over and flipped open the unsecured lid. "You've . . . Get out of there, cat!"

Tom glanced up, blinking a little in the light, and yawned. His back followed perfectly along the curve of the case and all four paws lay flat, claws securely anchored in the felt lining.

"Go on! Scram!"

"I guess he thought it was a cat bed," Rebecca offered as Tom stood, stretched, and poured himself out over the side.

"I don't care what he thought," Roland snarled, kneeling and brushing off the covering of cat hair. He grunted as Tom butted against his ribs with almost enough force to knock him over, and pushed the cat away. Tom looked pleased with himself, came back, and did it again.

Daru stifled a laugh. "I think he's trying to piss you off. Cats always know."

"Know what?" He eased Patience gently down, snapped the lid shut, and straightened. "Come on, let's go."

"You'll meet me here tomorrow morning?" Evan asked.

Roland's expression softened as he turned to the Adept. "Yeah. Eight-thirty, like we agreed." He waggled a finger at Rebecca. "Take care of him until then, kiddo."

Rebecca nodded matter-of-factly. "Oh, I will." She smiled at Evan and he mirrored her expression.

Roland could no longer deny what was right in front of his eyes.

"Hey, if you think . . ."

Daru's hand closed like a steel band just above his elbow and she had him hustled out the door and it shut behind them before he had any idea of what she was doing. When she released him, he rubbed his arm and glared at her.

"Do you know what's going to happen in there tonight?" he sputtered.

"I know." Her voice was ice. "Do you?"

"Yes, I do. They're going to . . . uh . . ."

Daru sighed and her voice grew a little kinder. "Think about it for a moment, Roland. Think about what Evan is. He certainly isn't going to take advantage of a poor little retarded girl." Unexpectedly, she smiled. "And I don't think Rebecca will be taking advantage of him. Come on." She started toward the stairs. "I'll drive you home."

Thinking about it as commanded, Roland scrambled to catch up. "Doesn't it bother you?" he prodded as they crossed the small lobby.

"Why should it? Evan, by his nature, is incapable of doing evil and Rebecca, for all her disability, is a physically mature woman with all the—" she considered her next word as she pushed open the door— "urges that entails."

"You mean when she asked me to sleep with her . . ."

"She meant it euphemistically? Yes, probably." Daru glanced both ways and started across College

Street, Roland trailing in her wake. "Look, you can't
keep the mentally disadvantaged so protected from the
world that they never get a chance to learn from it.
Rebecca has a job and an apartment, why shouldn't
she have lovers, too?"

"Because she could get hurt!"

"Emotionally? So can we all. And actually, her
simplicity protects her from creating a lot of the emo-
tional torments we lay on ourselves. Physically? There
isn't a woman in the world safe from that. It stinks,
but there it is. You think she lacks the judgment to
avoid the men who'd take advantage of her? Well,
you're wrong. Rebecca has a childlike ability to see
right to the heart and the fakes, the phonies, and the
psychos can't touch her. Now that's not some kind of
special power that applies to all the mentally disadvantaged, but it certainly applies to Rebecca." She
stopped by her battered green hatchback and fished in
her purse for the keys.

Roland lifted his head and watched something that
was definitely not a squirrel scamper along the hydro
wires.

"She sees little people in bushes," he muttered.

Daru followed his gaze and snorted. "So do you."
In answer to Roland's unspoken question, she shrugged
and said, "So do I. After looking into Evan's eyes, I'd
be more surprised if I didn't see them." She tugged
open her door, slid in, and leaned across to pop the
lock on the passenger side.

"Doesn't *that* bother you?" Roland asked, stowing
his guitar in the back seat.

"Why should it?" Daru put the car in gear and
pulled carefully out of the parking space. "They'll live
their lives and I'll live mine. Poverty, hunger, and dis-
crimination bother me a lot more. Where to?"

"Neal, just east of Pape, north of the Danforth."

"I know it."

They drove in silence for a while; Roland's mind
turning over the way he saw Rebecca, Daru's on the
traffic.

"Until she was twelve," Daru said suddenly, braking for a light, "Rebecca was a normal little girl. Then one Sunday, on a drive out into the country, a truck broadsided the family car. The impact threw Rebecca clear and when the emergency vehicles arrived the truck and the car were burning and she was the only survivor. They found her lying in a ditch by the side of the road, covered in mud and blood. According to the medical report, she began to menstruate that day, probably during or just after the accident."

Roland squirmed, made more uncomfortable by the reference to menstruation than by the deaths of three people. *It's not my fault,* he excused himself, *that's woman stuff.*

"Her most serious injury was a skull fracture; a large piece of bone pressing down on her brain. She'd lost so much blood that the doctors were afraid she wasn't going to make it, but she sailed through the surgery to a quick and complete recovery. Well, physically complete. It didn't take long for the brain damage to become apparent. In less than a year, her reading skills deteriorated down to a very basic level, she lost all her math, and most of her ability to deal with abstracts."

"With what?"

"Abstracts. All the things that people have created to clutter up their lives. A hundred years ago, maybe even fifty in parts of the world, she would have been fine. She'd have gotten married, raised children, cared for living things, spending her whole life within established parameters dealing with things she is quite capable of dealing with. But life today," her hands left the steering wheel for a second and spread helplessly, "it just doesn't give her that option. Doctors and social workers soon found that since she couldn't deal with abstracts, she couldn't take shortcuts. Everything, thoughts and actions, had to be done one well-defined step at a time. Still, it wasn't bad enough to institutionalize her, so she stayed in a series of foster homes."

"What about relatives?"

"She hasn't any." Daru slammed the car into third, the motion violent and barely under control. "When she was fifteen, her foster father came to Children's

Aid and confessed to a long string of sexual attacks on children supposedly in his care.''

Roland had a sudden vision of the man drawn and quartered. Prompted, he had no doubt, by the grinding anger in Daru's voice.

''He'd tried the same thing on Rebecca. He said he didn't remember what happened, that the next thing he knew he was on his way to confess. I read the report. He kept repeating, 'I didn't realize,' and bursting into tears. All Rebecca ever said about it, both in the report and later when I asked her, was, 'I showed him what he'd done.' '' She paused as she maneuvered the car around a bus and onto Neal Street. ''No, I don't think you have to worry about Rebecca. Besides, I've never seen her as stable as she was today.''

''Evan?''

''Well, it's hardly the situation.'' Her smile flashed white in the darkness, a gleaming counterpoint to the heavy sarcasm in her voice. ''It would make sense. He is the Light, after all, and one would think he's *supposed* to bring out the best in people. Say when.''

Roland pointed at his uncle's house and Daru pulled over. He got out, fished his guitar from the back, closed the door, then leaned back in the open window. ''Thanks for the lift. And for the information. You've . . .'' he sighed. Evan and Rebecca. Right. ''You've given me something to think about.''

''Here's something else.'' She met his eyes and he almost flinched, so uncompromising was her expression. ''You were upset because of Rebecca, granted, but I don't think her disability had anything to do with it. I think you're more upset because she gets to sleep with Evan, and you don't.''

He watched the car's taillights until they disappeared around the corner and, with Daru no longer there to argue the point, he said, ''That's ridiculous.'' Then he turned and went into the house, ignoring whatever it was that snickered at him from the peonies.

Evan rested his cheek against Rebecca's hair, his eyes half-closed, his breathing shallow. She snuggled hard against his chest and he smiled sleepily, stroking one hand lightly down her damp back. An hour in her arms had done much to replace the power he'd expended quelling the riot. By morning . . .

The balance shifted, suddenly, painfully, and he barely managed to stop himself from crying out.

Here I am, said the Darkness. *Come and get me if you dare.*

He knew it was a challenge intended to take him when he was weak and unprepared, still drained from the afternoon's effort. Knew the Dark would not have issued it if it thought he could win. Knew, and knew that the Darkness knew, that he couldn't refuse.

Gently, he lifted Rebecca to one side of the bed and slid out from under her outstretched arm. She stirred, and half woke, calling his name. He leaned forward and lightly kissed her brow.

"Sleep, Lady," he said, tasting the salt tang of her on his lips. Tonight he would keep her safe, and tomorrow, and for all time if he could. She had enchanted him with her clarity from the moment he first saw her and what Darkness would do to such sweet simplicity . . .

Rebecca sighed and settled back against the pillows. Seen through Evan's eyes, she glowed with a warm and golden light.

Tom stepped into the alcove and leaped up on the bed, heading for his regular, now vacated, place.

"Watch her, little one," Evan murmured. "Stay with her while I am gone."

Tom spread one paw in the air and began to wash between his toes. He didn't need Evan to tell him what to do.

Evan straightened, fully clothed in the instant between one heartbeat and the next, touched the flaring curve of Rebecca's hip one last time to keep the memory fresh, and then moved toward the Darkness.

. . . an alley, shadowed by more than the night. He heard voices, laughter, and walked cautiously forward.

"No. . . . Please. . . ."

He stumbled as a wave of Darkness roared down on him, and then he broke into a run.

At the end of the alley, under the weak red light of a flickering fire exit sign:

A boy, mid teens, up against a wall, both hands to his face and blood seeping through his fingers.

At his feet, another. Facedown in a spreading puddle.

In front of him, five laughing shadows with knives.

Beyond, a well-dressed man who spread his arms and smiled a welcome. A smile only Evan could see.

"Not so pretty now, are you, shithead?" One of the shadows strutted forward and prodded at the boy's shoulder with the butt of his knife. The red light reflected off his shaved head and turned the tattoos covering it to purple. "We're gonna have us some fun with you."

"Here I am," purred the Darkness. "Your chance to take me out."

Behind his hands the boy whimpered, and his pale pants suddenly darkened at the crotch.

"Hey! He pissed himself!" One of the shadows found this hysterically funny.

"Bad boy," sneered another. "And bad boys have to be punished."

"Shall we cut his prick off?" asked the first, dropping his knife point to the top of the stain.

"Cut his prick off!" screamed the shadows in enthusiastic agreement.

"Or maybe there's something you should take care of first," the Darkness suggested. He glanced at his watch. "Do hurry. I haven't all night."

Evan moved forward, into the shadow's circle, conscious of a cold fury that lives would be so blithely spent to trap him. He couldn't not save the boy.

"Well, what have we here?" The leader of the gang, sensing new prey, turned and sneered. "Some sort of fucking white knight riding to the rescue?"

The others laughed and the circle closed about Evan. The pleasure they took in causing pain lapped at him, surrounded him, isolated him, and would weaken him in time.

"Please," he said softly, his hands open, his arms spread, "let the boy go. Put down your knives. Release the Darkness." All beings capable of choosing had to be given the choice.

"Turn from darkness?" The leader advanced, knife cradled loosely in his right hand. "We got us a fucking preacher here, gentlemen."

"Looks like a fag," observed a gang member with swastikas tattooed on both cheeks.

"Let's cut *his* prick off!" The third voice rose and almost cracked with excitement.

That afternoon, Evan had given himself to a stadium full of rioters, reminded them of the Light and helped them push away the Darkness. The five he now faced only narrowed their eyes against the glare and gripped their weapons tighter. They had no Light left in them for him to reach.

He saw the blade out of the corner of one eye and ducked. The steel slid through his hair and he slammed an elbow into the wielder's stomach. A boot heel, sticky with blood, just missed his knee and he kicked out in return, sending the gang leader to the ground.

"Bastard!" the leader shrieked, scrambling back to his feet. "Take him OUT!"

Leaning against the alley wall, Darkness laughed.

It was the wounded boy, who could've run to safety but instead grabbed a dangling scalp lock and yanked a knife away from Evan's ribs, that gave Evan the strength to do what he had to.

A great blaze of light flared up from his clenched hands.

The fight ended very quickly after that.

"So He drove out the man," the Dark Adept said, straightening, "and He placed at the east of the garden of Eden cherubims, and a flaming sword which turned every way, to keep the way of the tree of life."

Evan sighed and drew the bar of light back into himself. "If you want a quote," he said wearily, scrubbing his hand across his face. "Think not that I am come to send peace on earth: I came not to send peace but a sword.''

"For behold, the darkness shall cover the earth, and gross darkness the people.''

"That's only half the verse,'' Evan pointed out.

The Dark Adept shrugged. "I forget the rest.'' He moved gracefully out into the alley, confident that the Light had so depleted its power it was not, at present, a threat. That it retained enough power to deal as it had with the gang of toughs had surprised him a little, for he knew that calming the multitudes at the stadium had left it virtually helpless. He could have taken it then, wiped the Light from this world for a time, but it wouldn't have known what hit it and where would be the fun in that? Fortunately, the Light, so predictable, was easy to trap. And, also fortunately, his shock troops had worn the enemy down further. Although he wouldn't have minded if they'd finished the job, it was perhaps better this way. He raised his hand and snapped it forward.

Evan grinned and threw up his arm, his exhausted stance vanishing with the motion. His silver bracelets caught the whip of Dark power and broke it into a thousand harmless splinters. He didn't know why so much of his strength had returned so quickly—perhaps this world had more good in it than he thought—but he rejoiced in the surge of power. The Darkness was in for a nasty shock. Quickly he threw a dozen shining disks and his grin grew wolfish as one got through a hastily erected defense, and the Dark Adept cried out in pain. His eyes began to glow and he advanced palms up . . .

. . . on nothing.

He stood alone in the alley with the wounded boy and the corpse of the boy's friend.

He extended his senses as far as he dared, but the Dark Adept had left no trail to mark its retreat.

Sobs tearing at an innocent's throat drew him back to himself.

Gently, he reached down and touched the boy's shoulder, giving comfort and easing pain.

"Richard's dead," he heard whispered from between bloody fingers.

"Yes."

Hazel eyes peered up at him, lashes matted together into points. "Can you bring him back?"

"No."

"But you made those others," his voice broke, "disappear."

"I did," Evan admitted. "But I cannot defeat death."

The barricade of hands dropped, one falling to rest lightly on Richard's stiffening back. The boy was no more than fifteen, if that. Blood continued to seep slowly from the gash across his cheek. "What are you?" he asked.

"I am a warrior against the Darkness, Matthew." The boy's head jerked up at the sound of his name. "As you have become this night. Your scar will be a warrior's mark. Wear it proudly."

And Matthew knelt alone.

"Wear it proudly, indeed," Mrs. Ruth snorted, stomping out of the shadows. "What bloody help is that? Men!"

Matthew started and spun around. When he saw the short, round shape of the bag lady trudging forward, dragging an overloaded bundle buggy behind her, the terror on his face slid into confusion. "Who . . ."

"Just someone picking up the pieces, bubba. Let me see that face." She pinched his chin and he tried to flinch away, although not from pain; the breath washing down over him was redolent with onions and garlic. "Prompt medical attention to this and it may not scar at all. Warrior's mark. Humph."

"Wha . . ." Matthew tried to look away and found he couldn't. All of a sudden he just didn't have the energy to turn his head. The old woman's eyes were black and deep and he had the strangest sensation of falling.

"We will go out and call the police now. You will tell them how those wicked boys cornered you and your friend and how when I came up the alley they ran away. Maybe they thought I was the Mounties, I don't know.''

Matthew let her help him up and, with him leaning heavily on her shoulder, they made their way toward the street. He saw, he heard: the punks, the knives, Richard falling, the sudden noise of the bag lady's approach, the sneering faces vanishing into the darkness. ''Why . . .'' He looked down at his hands. They were covered with blood. ''Why don't I feel anything?''

''Shock.'' Mrs. Ruth tightened her arm about his waist. ''Don't fall down on me, bubba. I'm too old to pick you up again.''

They got to the phone and Matthew somehow managed to dial the emergency number. In a shaking voice he told the story Mrs. Ruth had given him while the bag lady nodded in approval.

Let the policemen look for a gang of no-goods matching those descriptions, she thought, catching Matthew as he slid down the glass of the phone booth. The two of them sagged to the sidewalk together and waited there, listening to the sirens coming closer. *And if they never find them, which they won't, so what. It'll keep them from having to deal with other things. From trying to deal with other things.*

She remembered the laughter of the Darkness and knew he was spreading a shroud over the city. *For a while.*

Chapter SEVEN

The alarm clock had barely begun to chime when Rebecca stretched out an arm and switched it off. Knowing full well that lingering meant being late for work, and being late for work was very bad, she sighed and swung her legs out of bed. Then she paused, reached back, and stroked a finger gently down the soft skin over Evan's spine.

He stirred but didn't wake.

Rebecca checked the clock and sighed again. Four minutes after five, no time to cuddle. Daru said she had to be in the shower by five after five and as she watched, the four shivered and changed.

The shower washed away the last bits of sleep and she sang quietly to herself as she scrubbed her hair, toweled dry, and reached into the medicine cabinet for the little pink package of pills. Monday morning's pill dropped into the toilet.

She placed one hand just below her navel and with the other reached out and shoved the plastic handle down. "No babies," she murmured quietly to the sound of the water swirling away. And beneath her hand she felt her body agree.

When she returned to the alcove, Evan was watching her through half-closed eyes.

"Wind and rain, Lady," he murmured. " 'Tis but the middle of the night and yet you have risen."

Rebecca giggled. He'd talked that way during love-making. She liked it. It sounded like a fairy tale. She didn't always understand it, but she liked it.

"I'm going to work," she explained, pulling on clothes. "The first batch of muffins has to be ready by seven o'clock."

"My life shall be bleak without you."

Even Rebecca's literal mind recognized this as blatant flattery. "Silly." She grinned, drew a fingernail down the exposed sole of his foot, and laughed as he whipped it away. Slipping her own feet into thongs, she gathered up her fresh uniforms and went into the other room. Her red bag was under the kitchen table, the black dagger still inside it. Carefully, she reached in, grabbed the rolled towel, and lifted it out. She could feel the edges of the weapon even through the layers of terry cloth.

Now what? Her eyes lit on the shelf over the television. It would be safe there because nobody could touch it accidentally; they'd have to make an effort. Pleased with herself for thinking of it, she pushed her plush dragon to one side and put the towel on the shelf.

Then she packed her uniforms, took her keys off the hook by the door, and went to say good-bye to Evan.

He roused enough to twine his fingers in her damp hair and pull her face down to his. "Be careful, Lady," he whispered, "for Darkness waits."

"I'll be careful," she agreed against his mouth, took another kiss for the road, and left. *He tastes different in the morning,* she thought, *more like apricots and less like apples.*

Outside, the air was clear and still. The early morning light had a fragile feeling to it. Rebecca paused beneath the chestnut tree, looked up, and remembered.

"Oh, Alexander." She sagged against the trunk and her eyes filled with tears. She'd just realized, really realized, she'd never see her friend again.

Five thirty, called the cathedral bells, still blocks away. Five thirty.

Rebecca straightened. "I know," she sniffed. "I'm coming."

At ten minutes to six, slightly out of breath, she ran down the stairs and into the cafeteria kitchen. Waving at the elderly woman already at work wrapping danishes, she crossed into the locker room, dressed, and went to find Lena.

As expected, the supervisor was in her office and Rebecca began the morning ritual.

"Good morning, Lena."

"Morning, puss." Lena looked up from her coffee and smiled.

"Would you fix my hair, please?"

"Don't I always? C'mere."

Rebecca perched on the indicated corner of the desk, handing Lena a brush and an elastic.

Balancing her cigarette on the edge of the chipped saucer she used for an ashtray, the older woman shook her head at the state of Rebecca's curls. "You forgot to brush this morning."

"I'm sorry."

"Never mind. Did you have a good weekend?"

Rebecca's memory traveled from Alexander to Evan.

"Not exactly," she admitted. "But it got better at the end."

"Want to tell me about it? Tilt your head, puss."

Rebecca tilted obediently. "Well," she said at last, "the little man who lived in the tree outside the building where I live got killed, then Roland and me got attacked by a lawn, then Ivan the ghost went for help, then Evantarin came through from the Light and he stayed with me."

"Evantarin stayed with you? Who is Evantarin?" Lena snapped the elastic around Rebecca's newly tamed hair with unnecessary force. She worried about the girl spending her weekends with no supervision and wondered why Social Services didn't have her safely in a Home somewhere.

"He said to call him Evan and he's sort of an angel, I guess. He glows and he came to fight Darkness." She reached up and touched her netted ponytail, hoping, as she always did, that her hair could breathe while it was bound so tightly. "Am I done?"

"You're done," Lena told her, relieved Rebecca's visitor had turned out to be just another figment of an uncontrolled imagination. "And you'd better get started. Those muffins won't bake themselves."

" 'Cause if they did I'd be out of a job," Rebecca replied seriously. She liked it when she knew the proper thing to say. Gathering up her brush, she headed out into the kitchen.

"What are you grinning about?" asked the last woman of the shift to arrive, sticking her head in the office as Rebecca skipped away.

Lena took a long pull on her cigarette. "Rebecca has an angel visiting her." The smoke trickled back out through her nose. "His name is Evantarin and he's come to fight Darkness."

"Yeah?" The other woman's gaze dropped to the newspaper she held and the headline, *Man Shoots Neighbor; Claims "The Yuppie Son-of-a-Bitch Deserved to Die."* "Well, I wish him luck, he's gonna need it."

* * *

"And what are you doing up so early in the morning?"

Roland turned from the bookcase and shrugged. "I couldn't sleep, Uncle Tony, so I thought I'd look something up. Do you mind?"

"Mind? Hell, no." He peered at the book in his nephew's hands. "An encyclopedia eh? I don't suppose you're looking up something pertaining to gainful employment?"

"Not exactly." Roland closed the book and slid it back on the shelf. "I got called a bard this weekend, I just wanted to see what it meant. This wasn't very helpful."

"What do you expect?" Tony asked, doing up the last few buttons on his work shirt. "We got that set at the grocery store, $1.99 with every five dollar purchase. Siddown and have a cup of coffee with me and I'll tell you all I know about bards before I leave for the shop."

Roland followed his uncle into the kitchen and watched him fill two mugs from the automatic coffee machine on the counter. "How do *you* know about bards?" he asked, fishing the cream out of the fridge.

"Books," Tony told him, handing him a mug and waving him into a seat. "I read the right kind of books. That's the problem with you kids today, you don't read the right books. You need more history and less of this Hollywood adultery crap. Now, for starters, a bard was more than just a musician." He studied the cream swirling into his coffee and added two heaping spoonfuls of sugar. "Where was I? Oh, yeah . . . A bard used music the way a wizard would use magical spells, using his music to influence reality . . ."

Spellbound, Roland listened, the events of the weekend having banished disbelief.

". . . course not every musician was a bard. It took a special talent and years of study. Seven years studying, seven years practicing, and seven years playing is how I think it went." Tony snorted. "Twenty-one years. And I thought a five-year electrical apprenticeship went on forever. So anyway," he stood and put his empty mug in the sink, "you're what . . . twenty-eight? You started with this nonsense at about fourteen; hell, you've barely done your second seven years."

Don't get cocky . . . Mrs. Ruth's words came back to him and finally made sense.

"And even if I believed all that stuff—which I'm not saying I do or I don't—if you're a bard, things have gone downhill since the old days. Johnny Cash, now that was a bard. You, you'd be better off if you got a job."

Roland started, his thoughts had wandered miles away. "Uh, I think I've got one."

"Good." Tony paused at the door. "Try to see this one through to the end for a change."

As the door closed, Roland studied the guitar calluses on his fingertips and wondered whose voice kept muttering sepulchrally in his head that the end was near.

"It's not like Michelle to be late."

"Everyone's late sooner or later," her companion pointed out philosophically.

"Yeah, but Michelle's gone gaga over one of the guests, taking a little extra time to clean his room if you know what I mean. You'd think she'd be here early with bells on."

"Come off it. Sweet, little, innocent Michelle?"

"Well, sweet, little, innocent Michelle could hop into every bed she makes for all I care." The key jammed in the lock and it took vigorous jiggling to free it. "Just as long as she's on time for work. I don't want to get stuck doing her half of the shift as well as my own. That's weird, it's unlocked already." The door swung open and she groped around the corner for the light. "Smells like a toilet in here. And there's something all over the floor."

"Oh, no! Look at this mess."

Brushes, cleansers, shampoo, and soap fanned out from an overturned cleaning cart.

And then they looked up.

Dangling above the cart, her tongue black and protruding, was Michelle, a curtain sash tight around her neck and great scratches down her throat where she'd tried to tear it away.

Hands behind his head, the Dark Adept listened to the distant sounds of screaming.

"I might as well stay in bed," he mused. "Breakfast is likely to be delayed."

"Master?"

His gaze flickered off the ceiling and down to the shadow squatting like a stain against the blue sheets. "Get off the bed," he commanded coldly. "If I have to tell you again . . ."

"Not again, Master." The shadow moved from the bed to the small table beside it. "Master, the Adept of the Light . . . I saw, I heard."

He frowned, remembering the pain the Light had caused him. He had expected to win and the pain had been greater for that. "What did you see?" he asked, his voice cold. "What did you hear?"

The shadow quivered at its master's tone, but it knew better than to hesitate. "There are three, Master. A man and two women. They help and they know they help the Light. They hunt you, Master."

"Fools." He stretched and then worked the fingers of his left hand into the muscles of his right shoulder. A white pucker marked the perfect flesh and the wound, although it had healed in the hours since their confrontation, still throbbed. Four nights and five days until he could open the gate and this world had suddenly ceased to be amusing. Not for the first time, he wished his original passage through the barrier had been made closer to Midsummer Night, but the barrier had to be passed when the opportunity arose and Midsummer Night could not be moved. His entire body convulsed with the memory of the crossing.

"How did you get so strong, my shining brother?" he wondered aloud when his breathing had steadied and the sweat that beaded his skin had dried. "After all you'd been through, you should have fallen into my hands.'' The Light, like the Darkness, could draw strength from many things, and the Light had found friends. ''Give me their essences!'' he demanded suddenly.

''Yes, Master.'' The shadow flattened to paper thinness against the polished oak. ''But I hold only two, the man and one woman. The other was . . . was . . . was too . . .''

''You failed.'' The Dark Adept waved away the shadow's excuses.

''But, Master, she was . . .'' The shadow's protest became a howl and it snapped through several shapes until it lay pulsating weakly and wearing no shape at all.

''I said, you failed.''

''Yes, Master.'' It barely had a voice remaining.

''Give me the two you took.'' He showed his teeth as the shadow slid over to his outstretched hand. ''And we will see, my pretty adversary, what we can do about removing you from your strength without leading you straight to me.''

Daru threaded her way through the rabbit warren of overflowing cubicles that made up the Department of Social Services, a computer printout in one hand and a bagel balanced precariously on a cup of coffee in the other. She sidestepped a sullen teenager without looking up, muttered a greeting of sorts to a colleague, and scowled at the list of names and numbers she held. Things couldn't possibly have gotten this bad over the weekend. Could they?

She turned into her own tiny square of office space, scooped a stack of file folders off her chair, and searched, without much hope of success, for a place to put them. Sighing, she piled them with others on the floor, grabbed at the falling bagel she'd forgotten she still held, and splashed coffee across an overdue report.

''Ms. Sastri?''

''What?''

The young woman backed up a step at the expres-

sion on Daru's face. "Uh, Mr. Graham just went home
sick with that flu bug—he threw up in the elevator,
said he felt fine until the fifth floor then, blammo—
and Ms. Freedman and Mr. Wu both called and won't
be in." She offered the armload of files she carried.
"The director says you're to deal with these." Backing up another step would take her out of the cubicle,
so she settled for leaning away and smiling nervously.
"Don't shoot me, Ms. Sastri, I'm only the piano
player."

Muttering under her breath, Daru took the papers
and set them with exaggerated care on the desk. "Is
that all?" she growled.

"Uh, no. I'm supposed to remind you, you're due
in court in twenty minutes. But you probably knew
that . . ." she added, exiting a lot more quickly than
she'd entered.

Daru sank into her chair and buried her face in her
hands. In less than thirty seconds, her case load had
tripled.

"I'll just finish up what has to be done and take the
rest of the week off." She mocked herself and her
blithe promise of the night before. She should've
known it wasn't going to be that easy.

"Uh, Ms. Sastri, police on line one. Apparently
they picked up a derelict with your name and this number on a card in his pocket."

It was never that easy.

"I thought you said you'd be early?"

"Yeah, well I got delayed." Roland pushed past the
Adept and into Rebecca's apartment, Tom following
close on his heels. He leaned Patience gently against
the wall, the motion obviously carefully controlled as
he practically quivered with suppressed energy. "First,
the subway took forever to arrive." Unable to remain
still, he began to pace, arms waving for emphasis.
"Six—not one, not two, but six—trains went by going
the other way. The platform got packed. Some turkey
dropped a lit cigarette on my case. I barely avoided
going up in smoke, and then I got yelled at for flicking

the damned thing to the floor. Okay." He spread his hands and took a deep breath. "I can deal with that. So the train finally comes and we're crammed in like sardines, then, between stations, in the middle of nowhere, we stop and the lights go out. A kid starts to scream and the fat, smelly lady behind me grabs onto my ass. I try to get out of her reach, step on a foot not my own, and a riot nearly breaks out. Are you smiling?"

Evan brushed his hair back off his face and schooled his expression. "I wouldn't do that." It hadn't exactly been a smile.

Roland scowled, stomped along another two lengths of the room, and aimed a kick at the cat. He missed by a considerable margin, but Tom hissed and dove under the couch. Irrationally, Roland felt better.

"The cat had no part in your troubles," Evan pointed out gently.

"You don't know that," Roland snarled. "He was waiting for me at the corner."

"I sent him to watch for you."

"Oh."

"I think you owe him an apology."

"Forget it." Roland stopped pacing and glared. "I am not apologizing to a cat."

Evan merely looked at him.

After a moment, Roland's gaze fell.

"Oh, all right," he muttered and turned his head vaguely in Tom's direction. "I'm sorry I kicked at you."

Safe under the couch, Tom growled.

Only Evan's presence kept Roland from growling back. He straightened out the fingers that had turned to fists and made a conscious effort to calm down. So he'd had an irritating morning. That didn't give him the right to make everyone else's day miserable. He could feel the weight of Evan's regard and he let it sink down over him, smoothing out jagged edges and filling in gouged nerves.

"I guess I'll laugh about this later," he sighed.

Evan grinned.

"I said *later.*" The grin remained and Roland found himself returning it. He couldn't help it; a morning's worth of petty annoyances just couldn't stand before the strength of Evantarin, Adept of the Light, which, when he came to think about it, was a damned good thing considering what they'd be facing later on.

Evan's gaze grew speculative as the silence stretched between them and Roland felt himself begin to flush, suddenly very aware that Evan wore only his jeans. The skin of the Adept's chest and stomach stretched smooth and golden over lean lines of muscle, and Roland's hand slowly rose toward it.

Oh, no! Not that, too. Not this morning. Calling up the last of his earlier irritation, Roland forced his hand back down, wet his lips, and asked curtly, "Have you had breakfast?"

In the moment Evan took before answering, Roland realized that should the Adept force the issue he'd be unable to resist and his entire sexual orientation would crumble. He wasn't sure how he felt when Evan merely turned to the table and pointed proudly at the toaster.

"I made toast."

He sounded so much like Rebecca that Roland allowed himself to relax. "Well, put some clothes on and we'll grab coffee before we start."

"Sounds good." Evan nodded and went into the bed alcove.

Roland followed Evan's progress by the soft music of his silver bracelets. He wondered if he took them off to sleep. Which led him to wonder if he took them off to . . . *Stop that!* he railed at himself. *You are developing the worst case of gutter mind.*

Evan dressed was a lot easier to deal with and the two of them gathered up the sketches and left the apartment, with Tom slipping out just as they were about to close the door.

"So where do we start?" Roland asked as the three of them moved down the hall.

"At the top," Evan told him. "The Darkness is every bit as predictable as it accuses the Light of being. And besides, would you stay in anything less than the best if you didn't have to?''

"You aren't," Roland pointed out, nearly tripping over Tom who darted suddenly ahead and down the stairs.

"Haven't you heard that friendship buys a better bed than money?''

Roland snorted. "That sounds like it came out of a fortune cookie.''

"Ever wonder where fortune cookie fortunes come from?''

"Give me a break.''

"No, really, they're our second biggest export.''

"I know I'm going to regret this . . ." They stepped into the sunshine and Roland squinted up at his companion. "What's your first?''

"Light beer.''

Roland rolled his eyes.

"Get it, Light beer. Light . . ." Evan sighed. "I'll work on it.''

"You're sure you haven't see him?''

The woman on the desk at the King George Hotel shook her head. "No, I . . .''

"Think carefully, Sheila," Evan broke in, his voice pitched to elicit confidences. "This is more important than you can know.''

Roland spent an instant wondering how Evan had known the woman's name, then he saw the brass name tag pinned to her uniform blazer. *Score one for the real world,* he thought.

She studied the sketch again, chewing the pale gloss from her bottom lip. "No, I'm sure I'd remember if I'd seen him.''

"Damn," Roland cursed under his breath. "Strike seven." They hadn't quite started at the top—the King George most definitely—for there were a number of lesser hotels between it and Rebecca's apartment. It had occurred to Roland when they were starting out that they might have a little trouble getting hotel employees to cooperate, given that they had no official reason for their request, but Evan's presence seemed to inspire everyone from the manager to the cleaning staff to help. And in every hotel so far someone—male, female, young, old; it didn't seem to matter—had slipped the Adept a private phone number and the whispered confidence that perhaps later they might remember more.

"But you see," Sheila continued, handing the piece of paper back to Evan and smiling shyly, "I've been on vacation for the last two weeks. Let me just get one of the others."

"Thank you."

Her eyes went dewy at Evan's gratitude and Roland had to bite down on his tongue to keep from saying something cutting as she went into the office. He sincerely hoped he didn't look quite so soppy when Evan smiled at him. That he rather suspected he did, did nothing to improve his mood.

Unnoticed, a bellhop moved from the end of the marble counter and headed toward the elevators. Mr. Aphotic would want to know there were people looking for him. He'd probably be grateful enough to hand over another packet. *And another packet*, the bellhop's pale eyes gleamed, *would get me through the next few days on top of the world.*

"Jack," PC Patton nudged her partner. "The two at the desk."

"That's them," he agreed. "Fits the description to a T."

They started across the lobby.

"Uh, Evan."

Evan looked up. He'd been following the pattern of the marble, fingertips stroking the cool stone.

"I think we've got a problem." Roland had been approached by too many cops during too many years on the street not to know when the minions of the law were bearing down with him in mind. The man and the woman advancing toward them didn't look angry but neither did they look pleased.

"Can we have a word with you, gentlemen?" It wasn't quite a question. It wasn't quite a command.

Evan inclined his head graciously. "Certainly, officers."

Somehow feeling as if she'd just been granted a boon, PC Patton led the way to a quiet corner. They'd been off shift for barely eight hours, were beginning a double thanks to that damned flu bug, and she had no wish to be patronized by some long-haired juvenile delinquent no matter how pretty he was. That she recognized how pretty he was, and that a direct look from his stormy gray eyes caused her heart to dance, pissed her off further. "They told us at the Ramada you two were showing around a picture. Let's see it."

Roland considered the reaction he'd likely invoke by asking for a warrant, decided against it, and watched silently as Evan handed over the sketch.

PC Brooks opened the file folder he carried and the two constables compared the identikit picture to this new one.

"Accurate to about ninety percent," he murmured.

"Where did you get this?" PC Patton demanded, waving the sketch.

"I drew it," Evan told her mildly.

"Don't get smart with me, punk," she snapped. "This man's a suspect in a murder and if you're withholding information I'll have your ass behind bars so fast your hair will curl."

Roland didn't know whether Evan was capable of lying but he didn't think this was exactly a good time to find out. "We got it from the same place you got yours," he said quickly. To his relief, Evan kept silent.

Both of PC Brooks' eyebrows rose. "The old lady . . ." he began but broke off as his partner glared at him.

The old lady? Roland repeated to himself. *The old . . .* "Mrs. Ruth." The expressions on both faces told him he'd guessed correctly. He could almost feel the tension ease, so he assumed they had no idea that it was a guess. They still weren't happy, but they no longer fingered handcuffs.

"I don't know why she came to you two," PC Patton growled. "Whether you think you're some kind of vigilantes or what." She crumbled the drawing of the Dark Adept into a tight ball in one fist. "But stay out of this. Do you hear me?"

"We hear you," Evan said softly.

She jerked her head toward the exit. "Now get!"

They got.

After the air conditioning in the lobby, the heat outside hit them like a solid wall, pulling sweat out on their skins in seconds. The trapped exhaust from thousands of cars filled the air with a grayish-yellow haze bitter to breathe. Although two blocks away on Yonge Street brightly colored summer crowds surged back and forth, here the sidewalks were blessedly empty.

"I don't believe we got out of that," Roland marveled as they walked down the three shallow steps and away from the hotel.

Evan shrugged and shoved his hands behind one studded leather belt. "We were a complication, with paperwork they'd rather avoid, so I pushed on that. It wouldn't benefit the Light if we spent the next few hours at a police station making statements none of them would believe."

Roland shook his head; if only it were always so easy. "Let me guess. You don't ask the cops for help because none of them have the ability to See?"

"That's right. And the ones who do, get blinded or ground up and spit out by the system pretty fast, the system being interested in Justice not Truth."

Heavy philosophy for a man who just learned to make toast, Roland thought, leaning on a newspaper box, carefully keeping bare skin off the hot metal. "Now what?"

"We wait. The police will leave, the Darkness can easily shield itself from them, and then we . . ." He trailed off, his eyes focusing on the newspaper.

"We go in and talk to the other clerks?"

"No. There's no need."

Roland turned and squinted at the paper, trying to find what had brought that note into Evan's voice. *Police Hunt for Murder Suspect Intensifies* read the largest headline. *But we knew that.* He wondered how Mrs. Ruth had been able to give the police a description of the Dark Adept and then he saw the smaller type, almost hidden by the glare of sunlight on the box. *Chambermaid Suicides at King George* and it drove the question from his mind.

"He's here," Evan said, his expression now stern and cold. "Come on. There has to be another door, one the police can't see from the desk."

"It's a big hotel, Evan. How will you know what floor he's on? What room?"

"Now that I know he's here," his lips pulled back to show his teeth, "I can find his room."

They found a side door, marginally smaller than the ornate brass and glass monstrosity leading into the lobby, and slipped through it, managing to reach the fire stairs undetected.

"He'll have shielded himself in the lobby," Evan explained as they climbed, "but I doubt he bothered on his own floor. He'll have left a residue."

As they peered out through every door, Roland had visions of sticky tarlike trails of Darkness ground into the plush cream colored carpets but when Evan pulled him out onto the sixth floor and said, "This is it," he didn't see a thing; the carpet, and the salmon pink walls were unmarked. Then Evan reached back and brushed a hand across his eyes and he almost lost his lunch.

The Adept moved without hesitation down the corridor, Roland following behind, his gaze not dropping from the small of Evan's back. The glimpses he got with his peripheral vision were bad enough. When Evan stopped, Roland looked up. The brass number on the door read, "666."

"Well, at least the Dark has a sense of history," he murmured under his breath, wondering if the number was an accident, a joke, or a warning. If he were watching this in a movie, he'd be screaming, *No! Don't*

open that door! about now. A sense of, well, evil, for
lack of a better word, seeped through the wood and
paint. He swallowed and wet his lips, nervous but not
afraid; the whole thing seemed too unreal to be frightening.

Evan laid his palm just above the lock and the door
swung silently open.

Darkness lay everywhere in the suite. It hung in ebony spider webs from the ceiling and pooled in vis-
cous puddles on the floor. Great moldy patches grew
from the walls and in some of them Roland thought
he saw faces. He could hear the hum of the air con-
ditioner, but the room still stank of stagnant water and
things less savory.

"Gone," Evan growled, turning around slowly in
the center of the suite.

Roland threw up an arm to cover his eyes as Evan
flared and the Light burned all traces of Darkness from
the room. As much as he wanted the whole thing to
be over, relief over the postponement of Armageddon
made his knees weak. And then he heard the elevator
open and a familiar voice echo down the hall.

"For chrisakes, Jack, we don't need backup to question a suspect. Besides, if he tries anything, I'll *gladly*
shoot him."

Now he was frightened. Cops, he understood.

He grabbed Evan by the back of the T-shirt and
yanked him close, filling him in on their situation with
a few choice words. Evan ignored him and Roland
thought of a few other choice words he wanted to deliver even though he didn't have the time.

Evan appeared disoriented and the voices were getting closer. The hall, Roland remembered, stretched
straight and wide from the room to the elevator. No
possibility of slipping out without being noticed. Desperately, he scanned the suite. The bedroom or the
bathroom? No, they'd be trapped. Behind furniture?
Nothing big enough that wasn't right up against a wall.

Maybe they should just try to brazen it out.

"The door's open."

In the following silence, the sound of holsters opening was unnaturally loud and completely unmistakable.

Maybe not.

Roland shoved an unresisting Evan into the only hiding place they had time to reach; the coat closet near the door. During the next few seconds of noise and confusion, he closed his eyes and prayed.

It might not have helped, but it certainly didn't hurt. When things calmed down, the police stood in the center of the sitting room with their backs to the closet.

"I think he's flown," PC Brooks said softly, his head cocked to catch the smallest sound.

Roland tried to get his heart to beat a little less loudly. Any minute now, any second, he knew those blue clad backs would turn and it would all be over; they'd be up as accessories to murder and the Darkness would move on unopposed. A small voice in his head cried "Shame!" that he cared more for the former, but Roland ignored it. He dug his elbow into Evan's ribs and again got no response.

"I think you're right," PC Patton agreed. "But let's make real sure. Come on."

The bedroom. I don't believe it, they're going into the bedroom! Roland got a tight grip on Evan's arm and laid his other hand against the inside of the closet door. The tiny opening he'd left limited his line of sight and although he saw the police starting toward the bedroom, he had no way of knowing if they'd actually entered. He forced himself to wait, watching his watch count off fifteen seconds—the longest fifteen seconds of his life—and then he moved, dragging Evan out of the closet, out of the suite, and out of the hallway, not stopping until the two of them stood, reasonably safe, back in the stairwell.

No shots. No shouts. No sounds of pursuit.

Relief hit so hard his knees almost buckled and he sagged against the bannister, eyes closed, waiting for his entire body to stop trembling with adrenaline reaction.

"Roland? Are you all right?"

"Am I . . ." His eyes snapped open and he

slammed Evan up against the wall, his fingers digging into the Adept's shoulders. "Where the fuck were you? I needed you and you buzzed out!"

"I was searching for our enemy," Evan explained calmly, acknowledging but not reacting to Roland's anger. "I thought I had a trail. I was wrong. How did you need me?"

"While you were gone, the cops showed up! I thought you said the Darkness could shield himself from them?"

Evan managed to shrug, despite Roland's hold on him. "He must have let the shields drop when he left." Then his expression softened. "How did you need me?" he repeated quietly.

Roland's voice grew shrill and it bounced around the stairwell like a swarm of angry bees. "I needed you to get us out!"

"But *you* got us out." Evan reached up and covered Roland's hands with his own. "Thank you." He smiled.

Roland tried to snatch his hands away, but his arms refused to cooperate. He could feel the warmth of Evan's skin through the thin cotton T-shirt and that warmth began to spread, drying his mouth and snatching his breath away before it did him any good. It moved lower, igniting an answering warmth in him.

"Evan, I . . ." He didn't know what he wanted to say and could only stare helplessly at a pulse in the golden throat, afraid to meet Evan's eyes.

"There is never shame in loving, or in wanting to love," Evan said softly, lifting his hands and freeing Roland's. "Nor is there harm in wanting without having if you are not so inclined." One eyebrow arched. "Although your body may try to convince you otherwise."

Roland felt his ears turn red, his body's reaction all too evident against the crotch of his jeans. *The flesh is willing, but the spirit is freaked.*

"Being wanted does not hurt my feelings or insult me." Evan smiled again but much more gently, without the blazing heat of before. "Rather the opposite, actually."

Wetting his lips, Roland managed a smile of sorts in return, his arms falling slowly to his sides. "All I want to do is beat your head against a wall." His voice was a little shaky, but not so much it couldn't be ignored. "You left me to save our asses."

Evan brushed a shock of hair back out of his eyes. "And you justified my faith in you," he pointed out, respecting Roland's need to pretend, at least externally, that nothing had just happened.

"Well," Roland lifted his chin and squared his shoulders, "let's get out of here before the cops decide to search the stairwell." Evan nodded and Roland started down the first of the six flights. He wondered if Evan knew how close he'd come that time to tossing aside twenty-eight years of social and sexual conditioning. What had Evan said; *there is no harm in wanting without having*. He hoped the Adept was right; he might be able to come to terms with the wanting but the having would be more than he could handle. On the other hand, less than twenty-four hours ago, he'd denied the wanting, too. Did that mean that twenty-four hours from now . . .

A middle-aged man in a maintenance uniform came through the fourth floor fire door and plodded upward past Roland, past Evan. Just within earshot, obviously intending to be heard, he muttered, "Damn queers in the stairwell."

If he had anything more to add, it drowned in Roland's laughter.

Chapter EIGHT

"But where's he gone?" Rebecca asked, handing out tall glasses filled with an equal amount of pale green liquid and ice cubes.

Roland took a cautious sip and grimaced; iced herbal tea. Wonderful. He'd meant to pick up a couple of cans of pop on the way back to the apartment and now he was paying for his memory lapse.

"Has he gone to another hotel?" Rebecca settled to the floor, her back up against the couch, her eyes on Evan who sat perched on the window ledge.

"It's unlikely," Evan told her, taking a long drink with, Roland noticed, every evidence of enjoyment. "He's probably gone to a private house."

Her eyes widened. "But who would want to have him?"

Evan sighed. "You'd be surprised at how many people would love to have him, Lady. He can make himself very agreeable."

"Let me use your guest room and I'll cut you in for shares when my side rules the world?" Roland guessed.

Evan nodded. "Something like that." He turned and looked out the window, murmuring softly to the night, "And the devil took him up onto an exceeding high mountain, and sheweth him all the kingdoms of the world, and the glory of them; and said, All these things I will give thee, if thou wilt fall down and worship me." He sighed and faced into the room again, his eyes shadowed. "He won't, of course, give up anything, but mortals never seem to realize it. And what can I offer to fight that?"

"Your sparkling personality?" Roland suggested. Both Evan's brows rose and he stared at Roland, who only shrugged. "I hate to see an Adept of the Light feeling sorry for himself," he explained. He wondered for an instant if he'd gone too far, if he'd misjudged Evan's mood. He didn't think so, he'd seen that expression in his mirror often enough to recognize it when he saw it again.

Evan frowned, opened his mouth to speak, seemed to reconsider, and suddenly smiled.

Roland relaxed muscles he hadn't consciously tensed.

Rebecca tilted her head and chewed on a bit of hair,

not entirely certain she understood what had just passed between the two men. "I believe in you, Evan," she offered, reaching out to touch him gently on the knee.

He covered her hand with his. "That gives me both strength and joy, Lady."

Roland looked at their two hands lying against the faded denim of Evan's jeans, fingers intertwined, and reached for his guitar. He had to give a voice to the music that he heard.

The phone rang.

"Damnitalltofuckingshit!"

Rebecca jumped and sat blinking at Roland in astonishment. *She* disliked the jangling bell that broke the peace into pieces. She hadn't realized others felt the same.

The phone rang again.

"It's probably Daru," she pointed out, dragging the phone from under the couch. "She always calls on Monday nights. I always plug the phone in the wall on Monday afternoons when I get home from work. Hello?" She dropped the receiver away from her mouth. "It's Daru."

Roland buried his head in his hands, as the music danced tantalizingly out of reach. "Of course it is," he muttered. "Who else?"

"She can't come tonight."

"What?" He lifted his head. "Give me the phone." Almost snatching it from Rebecca's hand he barked, "What do you mean you can't come tonight? We're trying to save the world here, not fucking get together for bridge!"

"Fine." Daru's voice worked like sharpened steel on the words. "You do that. You go save the world. I'm trying to save the people on it!"

Roland barely got the receiver away from his ear in time as Daru slammed down her end so hard it could be clearly heard throughout the room. Even Tom looked up from his meal. "She, uh, can't come tonight," he said, hanging up.

"But I already told you that."

"Yeah." He pushed the phone back under the couch. "I know."

Rebecca swiveled around to face Evan again. "What will we do without Daru?" she asked anxiously. All their plans had been made for four people.

"Roland will have to come with us."

"To see the littles?"

"Yes."

"No." Roland raised his hands as Evan's gray eyes and Rebecca's brown ones fixed on him. *They've the same kind of single-minded intensity,* he realized. *Once you've got their attention it's a little overwhelming.* Until Evan arrived, he'd never understood how Rebecca's simplicity could be strength. Now he wondered how he could have missed it. "I'm not spending the evening talking to things in bushes and down sewers. I'll stick to the original plan and see what I can hear on the street."

"I don't like you being alone," Evan said, making one of his disconcerting shifts into Evantarin, Adept of the Light.

"Daru's alone," Roland reminded him.

"So why put two of you in danger."

"Is Daru in danger?" Rebecca demanded.

"Alone, we are all easier prey for the Darkness."

"Fortune cookie platitudes again," Roland scoffed.

Evan's eyes narrowed. "But truth nevertheless."

"Look, if I'm alone, too, Daru's chances are fifty percent better because he might just come after me."

They were both on their feet now, bodies leaning forward, chins up, and teeth showing.

"And if he does?"

"You can fight him for my body."

"That's not funny, Roland!"

"It wasn't meant to be."

"You're not supposed to be fighting each other." Rebecca pushed between them. "Stop it. Now." She glared from one to the other, her expression daring them to continue.

Evan spoke first. "I'm sorry," he said softly. "I don't want you hurt."

Roland drew a long shuddering breath. "I don't want me hurt either. But I've been with you all day. I need some time to myself." His voice begged Evan to understand.

Understanding, unexpectedly, came from Rebecca. "Caring for someone makes more bits and pieces than you can deal with sometimes. Doesn't it?"

Caring? Was that it? Is there more here than just sexual attraction? He might be able to handle caring. He managed a grin, a nod, and a shaky, "Yes."

Evan sighed but all he said was, "Be careful."

The heat of the day seeped back out of concrete and asphalt, keeping the temperature high even though night had fallen. A hundred heads bobbed up and down as the current on the sidewalk swept them from one patch of bright light to the next and a dozen different stations blared from car radios as drivers cruised up and down the strip. Sweat and perfume mingled with car exhaust into the distinctive smell of a summer night in the city.

The streets feel different. As Roland joined the surging crowds heading south on Yonge, he could feel the difference against his skin. Others felt it, too, for the laughter had a brittle edge and the crowds surged back and forth with a kind of jerky desperation.

You don't want to know, he told them silently. *You really don't want to know what it is.* Trouble was, *he* knew. Knew that somewhere in the city Darkness moved. And should it move on him tonight, he'd be facing it alone. He searched the faces that swept past, in and out of his vision in a kaleidoscope of eyes and mouths and noses, cheeks and chins, smiles and frowns, brown, black, white, yellow in a thousand combinations.

Fuck it! He dropped his gaze to the ground, his stomach tying itself in knots. *I wouldn't know him if I saw him.*

Rebecca was with Evan. Daru was nice and safe in her office. He was all alone.

"I must be out of my fucking mind," he muttered.

A pair of teenage girls stared and swung wide around him.

He considered stopping and busking for a while at Gerrard but the smell from the pizza place combined with his case of nerves had him swallowing convulsively, so he kept moving south. At Edward, an old man sat playing the accordion, badly, and at Dundas, at the north end of the Eaton Centre, an entire four-piece band, complete with amplifiers, raised the ambient noise at the corner by about a hundred decibels. The lyrics they screamed tied sex to pain and Roland tried not to listen as he pushed his way through the gathered crowd. He passed junkies and rummies, runaways and hookers, heading for the relative security of his usual spot at Queen.

Across the street, he saw two kids, no more than fifteen, buy a small package from an older man in a black leather jacket. They did it openly, knowing no one would bother interfering. Roland gritted his teeth and walked on. *And I'm one of the good guys.* He tightened his grip until the plastic handle of the case cut into his palm. *And we wonder who asked the Darkness in. Every fucking one of us.* Anger, even anger at himself, made him feel stronger, so he held onto it.

A man stood on Roland's corner. Long dirty hair hung lank and greasy down his back, bare feet stuck out from under stained and filthy jeans, and a dark red cross, recently painted, gleamed damply on his soiled T-shirt. "The end," he cried, his voice surprisingly deep and resonant, "is near!"

"I don't need this," Roland groaned. "I really don't need this. Not tonight." Eyes forward, refusing to see the crazy, he stepped over a puddle of vomit—the smell lost in a hundred others—and headed for the other spot he frequented.

The large open area at the Bay Street end of the Simpson's Building held a dispirited looking flower seller, a hot dog vendor, and a steady stream of tourists heading for both old and new City Hall. Roland set his guitar case carefully on the pavement, lifted out Patience, and left the case lying open. He checked the tuning, watched a young woman walk by, her breasts moving almost languidly under her loose tank top, and, suddenly melancholy, began softly playing "If."

While he sang, voice and fingers on automatic, passing conversations flowed over and through him.

". . . doesn't start until nine-forty, I checked the paper."

"Of course, he says it was just a business lunch . . ."

"Look Marge, I'll make a deal with you. You let me keep the beard and you can get your ears pierced."

". . . coming on top of that chambermaid's suicide this morning, too."

The two men were walking slowly and Roland strained his ears to catch the rest.

"Well this wasn't a suicide. Just some junkie who scored big."

"A bellboy shoots most of a gram of heroin into his arm and it's an accident? *I* think there's something going on at the King George."

"Yeah? But who can tell with junkies?"

Who indeed? Roland mused, letting the song trail off. Had they seen the bellboy that afternoon? Talked to him perhaps? Could they have saved him? He pushed those thoughts away and tried to bury his feelings in sarcasm. *At least he's marking his trail.* It didn't work. Sarcasm was too frail a crutch to support the load he carried now. *And we're always one body behind.*

"And just what do you think you're doing?"

Roland turned and came guitar to belly with one of the fattest cops he'd ever seen. The guy looked like he'd stepped out of a bad Burt Reynolds comedy right down to the little piggy eyes gleaming out from within folds of fat.

"I asked you a question, boy."

He even sounded like he came out of a bad Burt Reynolds comedy, but Roland felt no urge to laugh. Give these types a nightstick and the right to use it, and they did.

"Is there a problem, officer?" He kept his voice level, calm, empty of any possibility of insult. If Darkness had sent this man, it had barely taken a touch.

"If there wasn't a problem, would I be wasting my time talking to you? You're blocking the sidewalk. Move on." And under the first layer of words, ran the second. *Go on, you no-good hippy, argue. You aren't worth shit and we both know it.*

Years ago, Roland might have protested. Pedestrian traffic moved easily around him and no one had complained. Years ago, Roland had ended up spending the night in jail with three busted ribs. He squatted, laid Patience away, and snapped the guitar case closed.

The cop stood, watching him, until the curve of Bay Street hid his bulk.

With the roar of the subway vibrating the entire western slope of the Don Valley, Evan and Rebecca crawled through a hole clipped in the fence and scrambled up under the massive cement support of the Bloor Viaduct.

"Look at the plants!" Rebecca yelled over the shriek of the rails.

The plant life covered the ground with luxuriant greens in spite of the almost constant noise and vibration from the Viaduct above and the exhaust fumes wafting up from Bayview Avenue below. Even the recent scorching temperatures seemed to have had no effect on it.

"The troll takes care of it. It's what he does." The subway passed and her last word rang out into relative silence. She giggled and added in a lower voice, "He takes care of the bridge, too."

Evan glanced up the length of the huge pillar to where steel girders angled away into the night then he dropped his gaze back to the ground. The troll was their last hope for information. None of the gray folk they'd met and warned had been able to offer anything in return. Many had simply shrugged the warnings off. Most of the gray folk in this city were young, with scant concern for anything outside their immediate sphere. The older, more traditional creatures, were few and growing fewer.

A tree, standing where no tree should be, caught

and held his gaze. He cleared his mind and the troll graciously inclined his head.

The troll's manner gave the impression of height—although he wasn't really very tall—and bulk—although he wasn't very large.

Rebecca smiled and stepped forward. "Lan," she laid her hand on his arm and the moss he wore bent under her touch, "this is Evantarin. He's my friend."

The troll thought about that for a moment, while another subway train screamed by up above. His whiteless eyes studied the Adept, then he nodded again.

"There is a Darkness in the land," Evan began, but the troll held up a gnarled hand. "If you know," Evan asked, "why haven't you gone to safety? Trolls are enough in the Light that destroying you would add to its power."

The troll smiled. "I am safe," he said, his voice rolling out as slow and sure as a river moving to the sea. "This small Darkness will not try to destroy me. It knows I am too strong. It will not waste strength it needs to deal with you. And if the barriers break and the large Darkness comes, I will not leave my garden."

"We're trying to stop the Darkness, Lan," Rebecca told him earnestly, pleased he wanted to talk. Sometimes when she visited, they just sat quietly for hours. "Evan says trolls are wise. Do you know anything that will help?"

"I know how to help things grow. I know bridges." He bent and straightened a tiny seedling twisted by the wind. "I have not thought of other things in many years."

"Perhaps it's time," Evan said softly.

The troll raised his head and looked down the length of the viaduct, across the two huge arches and the smaller supporting ones at each end, then he dropped his gaze back to Evan.

Under the troll's steady regard, Evan's chin went up and he tossed his hair back off his face.

The troll held up a cautioning hand. "You need not

show me your glory, Adept. I have walked in the Light. Lady . . .'' Evan started, hearing his name for Rebecca from the troll. ''There is a small bird tucked up in the ivy. It has fallen from its nest and I am too heavy to climb up and put it back.''

''Would you like me to, Lan?'' Rebecca gave a little bounce.

''If you would.''

''I'll be right back, Evan.'' She scrambled farther up the slope and disappeared around the base of a bridge support, obviously familiar with the ivy the troll spoke of.

They waited while another train passed, cocooned by the noise, then the troll said, ''If you win, take her with you.''

''What?''

''In another time, where she could grow roots, her innocence would not matter, but this time uproots her constantly. It is cruel to her and I wish her to be at peace. Do this and I will be in your debt.''

Completely taken aback, Evan turned and walked a few steps away. Men and women had gone through the barriers in the past, although none in recent memory. He held Rebecca up against the world he came from and she slipped into place, barely rippling the image. *Perhaps she draws me so because she reminds me of home.* He shuddered as he thought of how he would feel, trapped in *this* world, and he marveled that her clarity had stayed unblemished for so long.

''It must be her choice,'' he said softly. ''But if we win, I will ask her to come with me.''

''If you lose, Adept, it will no longer be a problem.''

The World's Biggest Bookstore stayed open late and drew a steady stream of customers, although nothing like the crowds that still jostled together a block away on Yonge. Roland pulled Patience up to his chest and just let his fingers run over the strings for a moment, soothing his jangled nerves with her familiarity. His wariness of police could tip easily over into an irra-

tional fear if he let it and he had no intention of allowing it.

Unfortunately, suspecting that Darkness sat just out
of sight playing on his insecurities made it worse.

"I said get in the car!"

*Roland opened his mouth to explain that his jacket
had snagged and he couldn't free it with his hands
cuffed behind him when the nightstick came down on
his shoulders. He tried to twist away and fell back
against the cop, knocking him to the ground. Back,
ribs, legs, head; he lost track of the blows . . .*

*Resisting arrest, they'd said in court. Attacking a
police officer. And the cop's partner, who'd done nothing except watch, did nothing again. Because of his
youth, he was given a suspended sentence. He'd just
turned fifteen.*

"You got a reason to be blocking the sidewalk?"

Guitar strings cut into Roland's fingers as his hands
clenched and he turned. A trickle of sweat, that had
nothing to do with the heat, rolled down his side.
There were two of them, standing close enough that
he could smell soap and aftershave.

The larger, red-haired cop pulled out his occurrence
book. He knew fear when he saw it and in his business, fear meant guilt.

Darn sighed and pushed the file across the desk.
She'd finished off what paperwork she could, but a
stack, at least as large, still waited on court dates and
personal visits. Her week was already full, but that
wouldn't stop new problems from occurring, new people from needing help, new battles from having to be
fought.

Switching off her desk lamp, she was suddenly aware
that only the emergency lights remained on.

"Ten-forty?" she snapped at her watch, as though
it were somehow at fault. Her voice echoed in the
silence and when it died away, she realized the only
sound she could hear was the beating of her own heart.

"Sounds like I'm the last one off the floor again."
She stood, scooped up her purse and headed out of

her cubicle for the elevators, threading her way carefully through cluttered narrow corridors which seemed even more cluttered and narrow in the dim light. The quiet was so complete that she wondered if she might not be the very last person in the entire building.

She pushed the elevator button and waited. And waited. Occasionally they turned the elevators off at night, leaving her with a long walk down seven flights of badly lit stairs. She hated those stairs; the lines of sight extended only half a flight up and half a flight down and the tiniest noise echoed and reechoed off the cement walls, creating imaginary dangers and masking any real ones. The chime of the arriving elevator made her jump and, stepping inside, she chided herself for being startled by a sound she heard a hundred times a day.

The underground garage was brightly, almost garishly, lit, angles standing out in sharp relief. Daru squinted and, ignoring the signs that instructed pedestrians to keep to the walkways, strode diagonally across the empty lot to the section where she had parked her car. She rounded a corner, stopped and swore. The lights were out.

She leaned back around the corner. Through the open door of the elevator, a patch of cooler yellow spilled out into the white glare of the fluorescents. *I should go up to the lobby and tell security.* But as she watched, the doors closed, and she could hear the machinery hum as the elevator began to climb. Behind her, the darkness waited.

No more than thirty feet away, her beat up hatchback sat, a shadow in the dark. By the time the elevator returned, she could be in the car and on her way home. She took a step, and then another, surprised at how quickly she moved into a complete absence of light. Surely the brightness from the rest of the garage should spill over.

She found the car with her shins.

"Damnit!"

The word dropped into the darkness and disappeared.

With one hand on the car, and the other fumbling in her purse for her keys, Daru moved around to the driver's door and searched for the handle. *I've opened the stupid thing a thousand times . . . ah, there.* Keeping her thumb against the edge of the lock, she brought the keys forward and stabbed them into the hole. They jammed halfway and her violent tug to free them flung them to the ground.

Biting back profanity, Daru dropped to her knees and began to pat the concrete.

Then she froze, arms extended, fingers spread, suddenly aware she was no longer alone. She felt the hair on the back of her neck lift, and she held her breath, senses straining. And heard a soft, almost silken sound. And then again, closer.

And she remembered that Darkness walked the city.

Her search became a frantic scramble, masking all further sounds. She didn't need to hear it. She knew it was still out there. The tip of one finger touched metal. Her knuckles left skin on the concrete as she snatched up the keys and scrambled to her feet.

Then she couldn't find the handle. . . .

Then she couldn't find the lock. . . .

Then the damned key wouldn't fit. . . .

Then something touched her back.

She shrieked and spun around, arm raised.

"Here now, Miss, be careful. I just thought you could use a little light on that." The security guard lifted his flashlight and shone it against the car's door.

Daru took a deep breath and forced herself to stop trembling. The old man smiled kindly, neither surprised nor upset by her reaction.

"It's a pretty spooky place down here when the lights are out," he added, glancing around.

She followed his gaze, noting that the darkness had become more gray than black. She could see her car, not clearly, but she could see it. Wetting dry lips, she murmured, "Thanks," unlocked the door and climbed in. As she drove away, she thought she saw, just for a second, a shadow in her headlights where no shadow should be.

* * *

With no reason to hold him—no outstanding war-
rants, no previous record, not so much as an unpaid
parking ticket—the police had no choice but to let Roland go. He'd spent a bad twenty minutes, stammering
over his name, forgetting his address. Every time he'd
opened his mouth, they became more convinced he
had to be guilty of something. They'd asked him to put
the guitar down, so he didn't even have the comforting
weight of Patience in his hands.

Finally they waved him off, sending him on his way
with a stern, "We'll be watching you."

It struck him, about a block later, that one, and
possibly both of the cops were younger than he was.
He had a feeling it wouldn't have helped if he'd realized that earlier. Shaken, his balance eroded, he
headed for Yonge Street and the anonymity of the
crowds. At the moment, Darkness seemed preferable
to another run-in with the Metropolitan Toronto Police.

The four-piece band still blasted out its version of
rock at the north end of the Centre, but its audience
had thinned. As he watched, another group of teen-
agers wandered away, joining the steady stream of
people moving south. No one was coming north.

Puzzled, he followed the crowd.

The open area, just down from the big central doors,
was packed with bodies, some swaying, some nodding
in time, all standing quietly listening to a single voice
and an acoustic guitar.

Roland pushed his way forward, using his case as a
battering ram where necessary, until he stood just one
row back from the singer. He couldn't see the big attraction. A dark haired man, about his own age, stood
strumming a shining new, black Ovation, his voice
pleasant enough but not really great. Certainly not up
to the quality of the guitar. And then, his curiosity
satisfied, he listened, really listened, to the song.

He couldn't understand the words, if it had words,
but he picked up the feeling easily enough. Despair.
Disillusionment. Hopelessness. He found himself

swaying in time, agreeing with the sentiment. What was the point of it all anyway. No one else cared, why should he?

Evan cares, chided a small voice in his head.

It's Evan's job to care, he told it, wishing it would shut up so he could hear the music.

What about Daru? it asked.

Her job, too, he pointed out gleefully, getting the better of that small voice for the first time in his life.

And Rebecca?

He didn't have an answer for that. Rebecca cared because Rebecca cared, no other reason. Suddenly the music didn't make as much sense and he jerked his head to clear it.

The singer looked up and smiled right at him.

Roland backed up fast, ignoring cries of outrage as he banged into people, disregarding the muttered curses he left marking his path. He didn't stop until his back pressed up against an ad pillar and a mass of bodies were between him and the Darkness. His heart pounded so hard that he couldn't hear the music, but he knew it went on.

And he knew he had to do something about it.

I can't. The police will come again and this time they won't just talk.

He was panting as if he'd just run a race.

I can't. I can't fight Darkness alone. Evan is supposed to be here!

All around him, men and women of all ages swayed and nodded, their faces growing bleaker.

I can't.

But he fumbled for the clasps of the guitar case and pulled Patience free, holding her before him like a shield.

He had to, for the Darkness was taking something he loved, warping it and making it ugly. He couldn't let that continue.

There wasn't anyone else.

But what would be strong enough to lift the disillusionment that lay like black syrup over the crowd? What was strong enough to span the generations listening spellbound to Darkness? He chose and discarded and chose and discarded again. Then he realized if he had only one chance, he had only one song. His fingers strummed the opening chord and he prayed that John Lennon, wherever he was, would lend a hand.

By the fourth line, the heads closest to him began turning.

By the sixth, they'd shaken off the Darkness and the effect was spreading.

Roland let the song sing itself, giving himself to the lyrics and the music and blocking everything else from his mind. The song had to be all there was, leaving no room for Darkness to get in.

As he finished "Imagine" and moved without pausing into "Let It Be," he saw tears glimmering on more than one cheek and suspected his own were wet. He felt the power of his singing, of his playing, move out from his voice and fingers and find a place to grow. *This* is worth believing in, said the power. Hope. Life. Joy.

He slid into "Can't Buy Me Love" and saw toes beginning to tap. And then he saw the smiles and knew he was winning.

He stopped singing when his voice had died to a croak and saw without any real sense of surprise that he'd been at it for a little over two hours. The crowd, laughing and talking, began to break up. The occasional frown or mutter remained, but the overpowering sense of despair had vanished.

Roland stretched cramped fingers and grinned. *Beatles, one. Darkness, zero.*

"I think," said a quiet voice at his shoulder, "we should talk."

Roland's grin widened. After this, he could deal with the cops. He turned, and froze.

Darkness smiled.

Chapter NINE

"You play very well," the Dark Adept nodded at Patience still cradled in Roland's arms. "You'd be superb with a better instrument."

Roland's hands tightened against the polished wood. "I'm happy with what I have," he said, indignation breaking through his fear.

"Of course, you are." Standing his own guitar case on end, the Dark Adept leaned companionably against the top of it. "If you weren't happy, you wouldn't be so good. But surely you must have wondered what it would be like to play on a really top of the line guitar. One with a decent resonance and strings that don't go sharp when you least expect it."

Of their own volition, Roland's fingers found the A-string. It did tend to go sharp, regardless of how many times he changed the string or how carefully he tuned it. And Patience, for all she'd been the best he could afford at the time, had always had a slightly shallow sound. *I must have been crazy to go up against him with just . . . Hold on!* He forced his gaze away from the Darkness and out over the last of the dispersing crowd. *I won.* His sense of accomplishment came flooding back and with it his self-confidence.

"I'm happy with what I have," he repeated, his tone refusing all further discussion. He laid Patience carefully in her case, caressing her gently as he settled her against the felt. When he straightened, the plastic handle secure and familiar in his hand, the Dark Adept had moved around in front of him, blocking his path.

"Walk with me."

"Do what?"

"Walk. You have nothing to fear from me now. You defeated me. You can afford to be magnanimous."

Talk about taking a walk on the wild side. Roland

stared fixedly at a point beyond the cotton clad shoulder and tried to get his thoughts in order. He was not going to go for a stroll with this deceptively friendly young man and that was final. But Evan needed information—where the Darkness hid, where the gate would be—and this might be the best, probably the only, chance to get it. Sure, there'd be risks, but wouldn't it be worth it? He could still feel the residue of the power he'd put into the music warming him. Besides, up close, the Darkness didn't seem that frightening. He *had* defeated him and he could do it again.

Two large, blue clad figures coming into his line of sight from the south made up his mind.

"Walk where?" he asked, moving away to the north.

The Dark Adept fell into step beside him. "Oh, just around."

They walked in silence until they turned left onto Dundas and then the Adept said, "I'd like to make a deal with you."

Roland's head snapped around in astonishment. "A deal? What kind of a deal?"

"In return for what you most desire, you will cease to help the Light."

The tone was so matter-of-fact, Roland could only say, "You're tempting me?"

The Adept smiled a little sheepishly. "Well, it is what I, uh, do."

In spite of everything, Roland couldn't help but laugh. They turned left again, into the small park behind the Centre, moving across the grass toward the looming spires of Trinity United Church. "So tempt, but I'm warning you, I don't want anything you can give me."

"But you have been wanting different things of late."

The curve of Evan's cheek, the long line of thigh, the heat in his hands . . .

"No," Roland shook his head violently. "No. No, I haven't."

The Dark Adept looked surprised. "You deny your desire for the Light?"

His mouth opened to say, "Yes," because he couldn't admit to Darkness something he wasn't ready to admit to himself. Then he stopped, suddenly aware of the danger in giving Darkness a lie. The lie, he realized, would deny the Light, the words that made it up were unimportant.

"No," he said again, slowly and carefully. "I don't deny my desire."

"But you said . . ."

"I denied that I've been wanting *different* things of late." That wasn't exactly true, but Roland thought he could get away with it. "I've wanted love before. What difference does plumbing make?" *What indeed?* he asked himself, turning the idea over and feeling like he'd just been hit with a brick. *Holy shit, Evan was right. There* is *no evil in loving. Wait until I see him again, I'll* . . . He stopped the thought, unsure of just what he would do but sure, at least, that he'd stopped running. The light by the church door illuminated the face of Darkness and Roland realized he'd won again.

"That wasn't my offer," the Adept snapped as they headed back toward the Centre. "That isn't what you most desire."

"Well?" Roland prodded, willing to be, as Darkness had suggested, magnanimous in winning.

The Adept took a deep breath and placed his hand against one of the glass doors leading into the mall. It swung open.

"Hey, it's after midnight. That shouldn't be unlocked."

"It wasn't." The Adept grinned back over his shoulder, his blue eyes almost black in the dim light. "Coming."

Roland shrugged—*In for a sheep, in for a lamb* . . . —and followed.

The inside of the Eaton Centre looked like a different place at night, like a set waiting for actors. Their soft soled shoes made no sound against the tiles as they crossed the wide concourse and paused just inside the glass doors leading out onto Yonge. On the other side of the glass, the area they'd played in was now empty of everything but trash.

The Darkness waved a long-fingered hand. "I offer you what you had out there tonight . . ."

"That's already mine," Roland scoffed, touching the last warmth of the power. "That came from within me, not from something outside. You can't give it, and you can't take it away."

"You didn't let me finish," the Dark Adept sighed. "I give you what you had tonight, with your own songs."

"With my own . . ."

"Yes. Your words, your music will have the power to move people. Not just you singing and playing the words and music of others."

"Mine . . ."

"Now," Darkness smiled, "is that not what you desire above all else?"

"Yes." Roland barely got the word out. To have the piece that was somehow missing from his songs. To finally have a voice of his own. To have music he'd created mean something to others; to move them to tears, or laughter, or anger; to last and have the same effect long after he was gone. He'd often thought he'd sell his soul for that. Now he was being given the chance.

"Well, do we have a deal?"

Evan didn't really need him. Besides, tonight he'd done his bit to defeat the Darkness. He'd beaten it not once but twice. Wasn't that enough?

"Roland?"

His songs. His music.

"Do we have a deal?"

A red and white fried chicken wrapper blew up against the doors.

Roland, they've got chicken.

I can see that, kiddo.

Would Rebecca want to listen to his songs if he gave in? Somehow he didn't think so. But weighed against the rest of the world, did it matter what one simple-minded girl thought?

He could feel himself trembling and he couldn't raise his head. His voice was scarcely audible. "No."

It mattered.

"No?"

He knew he should feel exalted that he'd proven strong enough yet again, but he only felt an aching sense of loss.

"You're making a mistake, Roland." The Dark Adept shrugged. "But it's your mistake to make."

"You're taking this very calmly," Roland said with some surprise, not entirely sure he liked this nonchalant attitude toward his sacrifice.

The Adept placed his hand against the door and the lock snapped back. "You win some, you lose some. Oops," he paused, "looks like your friends in blue are still out there. I don't think they'd be very happy to see you coming out of a locked and closed building."

Roland looked from the two cops to the Dark Adept and knew he was saying quite possibly the most stupid thing he'd ever said, but his fear of the police was immediate and his fear of the Darkness was, well, confused. "What should we do?"

"We go out the back, of course."

They made their way back across the concourse to a door that would bring them out on the other side of the church.

"We've circled right around Trinity," Roland said as they paused under the same exterior church light.

"Yes," said the Dark Adept, "I know."

Roland leaned back against the stone and took a deep breath of humid air. "I can't figure you out. You're not at all what I expected. You're so, well, up close, you're not very frightening."

"Oh?" said the Dark Adept. And suddenly he was very frightening.

Roland's legs gave out and his knees slammed down on the concrete. His mind, trying to deal with the immensity of the evil it faced, could deal with nothing

else. He tried to look away and couldn't. He tried to
scream and couldn't. He fought his mouth around one
word and it came out as a whimper. "Evan . . ."

Darkness smiled. "Too late."

"Hey Marge!"

PC Patton paused, one hand on the station house
door, and waited for the auxiliary who, having gotten
her attention, ran up waving a piece of paper.

"I found that guy you were looking for!"

"That was fast." She let the door close and held
out her hand.

The auxiliary relinquished the paper, grinning
widely. "It wasn't hard. I mean, he's a little distinctive. I'm not surprised you remembered seeing him."

Scanning the printout, PC Patton nodded thoughtfully. "No, neither am I." The picture didn't do him
justice; it couldn't capture the moving highlights in his
hair or the incandescence of his smile. She'd known
when she saw him at the hotel that she'd seen him
before. "So, we scooped him up at the riot . . . Evan
Tarin eh? Well," she shoved the paper in her pocket,
"thanks, Hania, you never cease to amaze me with
what you can pull out of that computer."

Hania shrugged and smiled. "It's what I do. *That*
was an easy one."

A few minutes later, sliding into her seat in the patrol car, PC Patton tossed the printout on her partner's
lap.

"Told you so," she said as he picked it up.

PC Brooks merely grunted as he read the information.

Her expression smug, PC Patton drummed her fingers on the dashboard. "I knew there couldn't be *two*
men that good looking in the city."

"Well, thank you very much, Mary Margaret." He
handed back the paper and started the car. "What do
we do now?"

"He was released to a Daru Sastri from Metro Social Services."

"Yeah. So?"

"So we finish this shift, and maybe tomorrow we check her out. This Mister Tarin has some connection to our murderer and I want a few words with him and his friend."

"Should've had them this afternoon."

PC Patton frowned. "Yeah, I know." She still didn't understand why she'd let those two walk out the way she had; no names, no nothing. It wasn't the sort of thing she normally did. She shot a glance at Jack from the corner of her eye. It wasn't the sort of thing *they* normally did. "I guess the heat got to us."

"You really believe that?"

She laughed humorlessly. "Since that night in the Valley, I don't know what I believe."

"Personally, I believe what I always did."

"You always believed in unicorns?"

"Yep."

"Elves and pixies, too, no doubt."

"Uh-huh."

"Ghoulies and ghosties and things that go bump in the night?"

He didn't answer for a moment and all kidding had left his voice when he said, "That goes without saying."

And then they sat quietly, watching the night go by.

"But where is he, Evan?"

"I don't know, Lady. I can't find him."

"Is he dead?"

"No. I'd know if he were dead . . ."

The world felt wrong. Roland forced his eyes open and instantly closed them again as even that little bit of light drove spikes into his brain. He had the worst hangover he could ever remember having; his mind had been put through a blender, an iron bar cinched his stomach toward his spine, and his entire body wanted to puke. Again. The smell made it pretty evident that he already had. If his head would just quit flopping around, maybe he could . . .

He remembered the Darkness, the terror, the pain, and he began to keen, arms and legs thrashing feebly.

"Told you it lived."

A tightening of the vise around Roland's middle squeezed him out of his hysterics, leaving nothing in his world but a fight for breath. When he no longer seemed to be in immediate danger of passing out, he opened his eyes again.

The ground bobbed by about four feet from his head, just beyond the reach of his flopping fingertips. A blurred brown blob came into and out of his line of sight and he wondered muzzily what it was. By focusing everything he had, which at the moment wasn't much, he managed to gain enough control of his arms to push against whatever held him. It didn't budge although it felt warm and vaguely resilient under his hands.

It tightened again and his arms dropped, his vision went yellow, then orange, then . . .

"Killing it now!" boomed a second voice followed by a sound like a clap of thunder, then, blessedly, the pressure eased and Roland sucked in great lungfuls of foul smelling air.

When his vision cleared, it cleared completely and he suddenly recognized the blurred brown blob as a bare and dirty foot.

About a size thirty, triple E, he thought dreamily, swinging back and forth. Then the implications hit him. "Jesus!" Panic gave him the strength to twist his head and look up.

The giant that carried him tucked beneath one massive arm had to be fifteen feet high. His buddy, walking alongside, was a little shorter. Each wore a number of foul and rotting hides, roughly shaped into a sleeveless shift.

He punched and kicked and when that had no effect, he tried to squirm free. He disturbed large numbers of flies which lifted from the hides, circled and settled again. But the giants ignored him. His strength gave out and his head fell, reality condensing to the patch of ground that swayed below him. Watching the dirt path turn to rock, he muttered, ''I don't think I'm in Kansas anymore.'' It wasn't original, but it was the best he could do under the circumstances. He didn't seem to have any fear left—it had seeped out with his strength and now he just felt numb—but he supposed that would change as soon as more information gave him a better idea of what to be afraid of.

The giants waded through a pile of rotting garbage and the stench wafting up from it sent Roland's stomach into spasms. He began to retch again. This proved too much for his oxygen-starved body and he slid back into unconsciousness.

He came to, minutes later, when he landed to sprawl across a soft, yielding mound laced with rigid chunks that dug into his bruised ribs. It was the best resting place he'd ever had. Not even the smell bothered him as he lay there and gloried in his ability to breathe freely. He couldn't see a thing and his ears buzzed loudly, but he felt better than he had in—his mind skirted around the memory of the Darkness—hours. Suddenly, there was light and, without moving, Roland could see one of the giants standing about ten feet away, his shadow dancing over a stack of oddly angled objects that sparkled in the firelight. In his hands, looking like a toy when measured against his size, he held Roland's guitar case.

Roland started and tried to push himself up. His hand sank through its support with a wet, tearing sound and into a cavity filled with what felt like rice pudding. But the grains of rice were moving. Scrambling back until his knees touched rock, he stared in horror at what he'd been lying on. Most of the bodies had decayed past recognition, the buzzing had come from a billion flies, and the chest cavity he'd broken into writhed. Given the flies, it didn't take a genius to figure out why, even in the bad light.

Only his reaction to the bodies kept Roland from reacting to the maggots. Although a good part of him wanted to run about screaming ''Get them off me! Get them off me!'', he only gave his arm a shake and knelt, eyes wide with shock.

Like most of his generation in his part of the world, the only body Roland had ever seen had been laid out like a wax doll, looking as if it had never been alive. These bodies were both more and less real and the only reference Roland had for dealing with them came from movies he'd much rather have forgotten. No chance of mistaking this for a movie though, or even a nightmare. Neither movies nor nightmares had this kind of immediacy. His knee began to ache as something dug into it and he shifted to one side, glancing down. Three quarters of a finger had been crushed under his weight, the joint glistening and exposed. He began to tremble uncontrollably and felt a scream welling up from his gut.

"I wouldn't scream if I were you." The jaw of one of the corpses was moving and its voice was the voice of Darkness. "Remind those two that you're here and they may decide to have an early lunch."

Roland whimpered, but that was the only sound he made. He peered back over his shoulder. One giant still tended the fire, the other dug through the rubbish against the far wall of the cave.

"There is a way out," the Darkness continued. "All you have to do is call on me. Ask my help and I'll take you home." The lips of the borrowed mouth were incapable of it, but Roland could hear the smile in the Dark Adept's voice as he added, "Don't wait too long."

"Wait too long," Roland repeated weakly as the corpse fell still. His mind tottered on the edge of insanity and he stared into the black depths with something close to anticipation.

That's it, quit, sneered the little voice in his head. *Take the easy road, just like Uncle Tony always says.*

Escape beckoned. Roland stepped back. *The hell I will.* He forced his body to stillness. *These guys are dead. They can't hurt me. And if they tried, one good shove would break them apart.* Brave words even if he didn't entirely believe them. His overactive imagination kept animating the grisly remains. *He wants me too terrified to think, so my only option is to call on him. Well, he can just* . . . He pushed his thoughts away from the Darkness—that way would only lead back to the edge—and turned them to the immediate task of getting away from the giants. The Dark Adept had, in a way, done him a favor for his terror at the Darkness so overwhelmed him it didn't leave much room for more mundane fears and, by concentrating on survival, Roland found he could cope.

"Drink now. Eat it later."

That sounded encouraging.

"Eat it now. Before it dies."

That didn't.

Roland turned cautiously. The larger giant sprawled on the floor by the fire, his back propped against a heap of debris, a wooden keg cradled on his lap. The smaller sat chewing on the end of a femur.

"Eat it now," he repeated sulkily as the bone splintered with a loud crack. Roland winced. "Not as good dead."

"Won't die," insisted the other, taking a long pull from his keg. "Nothing broken."

"Always die," muttered the first.

It would, Roland realized, be very easy to fall into the trap of considering the giants foul-smelling buffoons. They might not be very intelligent, but the pile of bodies behind him testified to their effectiveness. As he'd been unconscious when they picked him up, he was, he suspected, probably the first meal they'd ever dumped in their larder that hadn't been beaten almost to death. And if no one had ever tried to escape before, his odds of success improved immeasurably. All he had to do was move silently through the shadows by the wall, slip unseen out of the cave, and run like hell.

Trouble was, the smaller giant was sitting between him and Patience and he wasn't leaving without her.

He watched the larger giant pour a seemingly endless stream of liquid into his mouth, while the smaller sucked the marrow from the bone he chewed like it was some kind of yellow-gray peppermint stick. Surely they would have to piss, or something. Sometime.

Hopefully they'd leave the cave to do it. To occupy his mind, he picked maggots off the hand and arm he had inadvertently plunged into the corpse. In a way, that was the most horrible thing that had happened so far for in it he had been an active participant, not just an observer. The temptation to shriek, "Get me out of here!" and to pay any price for that deliverance grew with every moment he waited, with every larva, with every fly, with every glimpse or half glimpse of the rotting bodies around him until his nerves were stretched tighter than his guitar strings.

Finally, the smaller giant stood and kicked his companion, who only snorted and closed his hands more firmly about his keg.

"Going out," he declared. "Don't eat!"

That sounded fine to Roland. He froze as his captor stomped by, then scrambled across the bone-strewn cave until the giant's bulk cleared the cave entrance. *Get Patience and get out. Get Patience and get out,* was the litany Roland moved to. *Get Patience.* His hands clutched at the guitar case. *And get . . . holy shit.* Although Roland didn't play the harp, he had friends who did and he'd spent enough time with them to recognize that the instrument so carelessly tossed on the pile of rusting armor—all rosewood, tarnished silver, and twisted gold—had at one time belonged to a master. His fingers itched to run over the remaining strings or to stroke the smooth curve, but he held back. He knew if he touched it, he'd take it, and that was theft. Even from this pair of steroid cases, theft was wrong. And a man walking in Darkness had better be damned careful about abusing the Light.

He leaned away, paused, and suddenly decided; leaving the harp on this pile of garbage, leaving it to be shattered or, worse yet, fall slowly to pieces from neglect would be a greater abuse of the Light than stealing it. As he lifted it, careful not to sound the few strings still intact, he hoped the Light would see it that way. Tucking it up under his arm, he again reached for his guitar case.

With the plastic handle back in his hand where it

belonged and Patience's familiar weight hanging at his side, Roland turned and discovered that the larger giant was not, as he'd thought, asleep.

Surprisingly pale eyes peered out at him from under bushy brows and an incredibly vapid smile stretched the thin lipped mouth.

Great. He's pissed. Maybe he'll think I'm a hallucination.

''Meat?''

And then again, maybe he's got the munchies. Shit! Roland ducked a wild grab and raced for the entrance of the cave, abandoning stealth for speed. *Maybe I should stop and try a lullaby.* The giant roared and lurched to his feet. *Maybe not.* He exploded out into early morning sunlight, swerved around the very startled smaller giant who made a half-aware attempt to scoop him up, and took off down the rock strewn slope. If he could get to the forest, a mere hundred yards or less away, he would easily outdistance his larger and clumsier pursuers among the trees.

He hoped.

''Are you sure I should go to work, Evan?'' Rebecca stood in the doorway anxiously watching the Adept pace the length of her small apartment. ''I could stay home and help you look.''

''And I would love to have your help, Lady.'' Evan added two steps to his pacing and caught up her hand. ''But you know that every disruption further weakens the barriers between your world and the Dark. And if you don't go to work . . .'' He rested his cheek against her palm.

''If I don't go to work, it would disrupt a lot of people.'' Rebecca nodded solemnly. ''But Roland is one of my specialest friends. I wish I could help find him.''

''We each have our part to play, Lady.'' The storm had died in his gray eyes and he appeared unnaturally still.

''I understand.'' She sighed. ''But I would rather be with you.''

"And I would rather you were with me, Lady." And he would, for he felt stronger when she was with him, more confident, better able to reach the Light although he didn't understand why. But he suspected Roland had been taken to trap him and he didn't want Rebecca around when the trap was sprung. He couldn't risk that. He couldn't risk her. At her job, she'd be safe. And the rest of it, as far as it went, was true.

Branches slapped at his hair, caught and tore at his T-shirt, and raised painful welts on the unprotected skin of his arms. Roland ducked his head to keep a particularly aggressive evergreen out of his eyes and swore as his toe caught under a protruding root and he nearly pitched onto his face. He could move faster and more easily if he dumped the harp, leaving one hand free to force a path through the brush, but the same streak of stubbornness that kept him out on the street in all kinds of weather kept the instrument under his arm. He barked his shins on a log, swore again, and stopped running.

At first, he could hear only the sound of his own breathing. After a time, he stopped puffing like an entire aerobics class and the other sounds of the forest began to filter through.

Bird song.

Leaves rustling in the wind.

Two branches rubbing together with a soft shirk, shirk.

More importantly, he didn't hear the crashing of underbrush or the bellowing of giants. It had been touch and go for a while, but not even the smaller giant could get up any kind of speed among the trees and Roland, with an agility born of desperation, had soon pulled ahead. From the sound of things, he was now safe.

He set the harp gently against the log and leaned Patience out of harm's way behind the bole of a huge tree. Then he indulged in a well-deserved fit of hysterics.

When it was over, he felt much calmer. Tired, and still afraid, but no longer stretched almost to the breaking point. He sat down on the log, wiped his damp cheeks with the back of one hand, and sighed.

"Now what?" he asked the harp.

One of the broken strings stirred in the breeze and chimed softly against the whole string next to it.

Roland smiled, for the first time in quite a while. "You're welcome," he said, then reached back a long arm and drew Patience from her refuge.

The case had picked up a few more dents and abrasions but the guitar seemed fine when he took her out to examine.

"This is my lady," he told the harp, unsnapping the guitar strap and setting Patience back gently against the foam and felt. "I imagine you were someone's lady once." Cradling the harp in his lap he managed to attach the strip of embroidered canvas to the curling end pieces. "And a lady deserves a better resting place. There." He slung the strap over his shoulder and stood.

"A little low, perhaps, but it does leave me a hand free for defense." *Or de-giants,* he added silently, his inner voice sounding very who-are-you-trying-to-kid.

He shifted Patience slightly, settling her securely, more for the feel of her in his hands than any other reason, and firmly closed the lid. By his hip, a soft tone sounded. From inside the case came a muffled but firm response.

He opened the lid.

Patience looked no different. He ran a finger over her strings. She sounded no different. Except that she never used to sound without him playing her. Finally, as minutes passed and both harp and guitar remained silent, he shrugged and closed the case again. Considering everything else that had been happening to him, this rated about a three out of ten and no more than the amount of worry it had already evoked.

"Okay," he straightened. "My loins are girded. How do we get out of here?"

He seemed to remember having read something, sometime, about moss growing on the north side of trees. The moss around him grew where it liked and in a couple of places that meant all over the tree. The forest stopped him from getting a fix on the sun and no helpful boy scout eager to earn a woodsman's badge appeared to direct him.

"And I don't know where I'm going anyway."

Finally, he decided to keep heading the way his wild flight had been taking him—vaguely downhill—holding tight to the thought that eventually he had to meet someone who could show him the way home. Turning to the Darkness *couldn't* be the only answer.

And that damned little voice asked, *But what if it is?*

"Excuse me, don't I know you from somewhere?"

Evan turned and glanced at the young woman. She was just as she seemed and not a construct of the Dark, so he smiled and said, "No, I don't think so."

She reached out and gently touched his arm above the bracelets. "Are you sure?" Her fingertip drew tiny circles on his skin.

"Yes."

Moving slowly, she ran her hand up his arm until it kneaded his shoulder. She swayed closer until her breasts pressed up against his chest. "It doesn't matter," she sighed, "we're together now."

For a moment, Evan stood stunned by the burning desire in her eyes, then with a shake of his head he gently pulled himself free. *Light is attracted to Light,* he thought walking on with a smile as the young woman continued on her way with only a vague memory of the entire incident, *but it's never worked quite that way before.*

By the time he'd walked the two blocks between Rebecca's apartment and Yonge Street, it had worked "that way" with another three women, one old enough to be a great-grandmother, two men, a thirteen-year-old boy, and an embarrassingly amorous dog. He stopped at the corner to think about it, aware that at least two pairs of eyes were gazing at him in open need.

He can do nothing to me directly, lest I find him, so

he thinks to slow my search for both him and Roland by throwing these people in my way. As he'd put no one at risk, Evan had to admire the deft touch the Darkness had shown. It would be impossible to do any searching if he had to stop every two feet and disentangle himself from another *admirer;* the cost in both time and power would be enormous if these first two blocks were any indication. And then he thought it through to another level and went cold with rage.

He is manipulating the Light in these people; not the Darkness, but the Light!

As Evan's power flared with his anger, the three people closest to him, their desire for the Light already forced open by the Dark Adept, fell to their knees, their expressions rapt and beatific. Evan felt himself responding to their need, felt his power manifesting, and knew that each could see a private vision of the Light. The urge to continue, to pull at least these three over fully into the Light, was strong and perhaps the greatest temptation his kind faced in this world.

For Light could destroy the balance as easily as the Darkness.

And any destruction of the balance weakened the barriers and aided the Dark.

He forced his power down and moved to repair the damage. The Light had been too strong for him to erase the memory of it completely, but he did what he could to lessen the impact. Then he retreated to the safety of Rebecca's apartment and brooded over what to do next.

Roland's stomach growled and his mouth flooded with saliva, as he fought to free the harp.

"Oh, you picked a perfect time to get intimate with a bush," he muttered, trying to untangle the mess of leaves and twigs and harp strings. His fingers seemed unusually clumsy, probably because his entire mind was on the enticing smell of roasting meat. If he turned, he could see the outline of a building in a clearing just visible between the trees, a building he'd be at right now if the harp hadn't jerked him off his feet when it tied itself to the bush.

He frowned as he carefully unwound one of the broken strings from about a sturdy branch. Granted he'd been charging forward pretty fast, his feet propelled by his hunger, but he thought he'd secured the string to the harp better than that; it shouldn't have come loose. His stomach growled again. It had been over twelve hours since he'd last eaten and he was starved.

"There." He got the harp free at last and swung the strap over his shoulder. "Now if you don't mind, I'm going to see about getting some food." With Patience back in his hand, he headed for the clearing. "Maybe I can sing for my supper. Breakfast. Whatever."

The harp chimed softly. Patience answered.

Roland sighed. "All right, I'll be careful. After all," he reached back and patted the carved wood, "I don't suppose you enjoyed that any more than the bush did. But you," he added, giving Patience a gentle shake, "you're in a case. What have you got to complain about?"

Muffled by felt and vinyl came the unmistakable sound of a G-string, violently plucked.

"Women." Roland rolled his eyes. It didn't really bother him that his guitar now made noise independently of his touch. He'd always thought of her as having a personality of her own and this just seemed an extension of that. *Besides,* he thought, pushing his way slowly through the underbrush, *when you've almost been eaten by giants at dawn, nothing that happens during the rest of the day can surprise you much.*

He paused at the edge of the clearing and stared in astonishment. *Except this.*

The walls of the small gabled cottage were squares of gingerbread, stacked one on the other and mortared with a hard white icing. The round shingles on the roof were cookies—chocolate chip by the look of it—and the door and the window shutters appeared made of peanut brittle. In the yard beyond, Roland could see several round pens he assumed were for livestock as these were made of wood. A small brick oven smoked by the side of the cottage and from it came the delicious odors that Roland had been following.

He drew in an appreciative noseful and raised his foot to step forward into the clearing. Then he put it down again, an elusive memory nagging at him. This all seemed so familiar. . . .

The door to the cottage opened and he froze as a little, old, white-haired lady bustled out. She carried a large wooden paddle and Roland realized she was on her way to remove whatever roasted in the oven. He'd never seen a paddle of that type used outside a pizza parlor before, but then he'd never seen an outdoor oven or a house made of gingerbread before either, so he shrugged it off. He wouldn't bother her now, she could burn herself. He'd wait until she'd moved a safe distance from the heat and then he'd see about getting some breakfast.

Her hand wrapped in her snowy white apron, she pulled open the oven door and the smell from inside intensified.

Roland swallowed rapidly as his mouth flooded. *I'm so hungry I could eat a . . .*

. . . child.

A boy about seven years old lay curled in a fetal position on the end of the paddle. His hair had been reduced to frizzy stubble by the heat. His skin, except where the fat had broken through and still sizzled and popped, was a well-done golden brown.

Roland's stomach heaved, the world twisted, and his last hysterical thought before he turned and fled was, *In the story, she never undressed them first.*

Had it been capable of it, Evan's astral form would have sighed as it moved in ever widening circles out from the Eaton Centre. Although without a body he could take no action, Evan had spotted the residue of power easily enough—the Dark Adept had made no attempt to hide it—and he now knew what had happened to Roland although he still didn't know exactly where the musician was. He could find him, in time,

but time was what he didn't have, not if he hoped to
stop the Darkness by Midsummer Night.

With Roland's life balanced against all the others in
this world, Evan could make only one decision; the
Darkness had to be stopped. If he failed, then Roland
was no worse off than the rest of his people. If he
succeeded, and Roland still lived, he would find him
then. He only hoped by then Roland would still want
to live.

Back in Rebecca's apartment, Tom jumped up on
the Adept's lap and butted his head into the crease
between jeans and T-shirt. The lack of response
seemed to annoy him and he sat back, tail lashing.
Anchored by claws sunk deep into denim, he leaned
forward, sniffed delicately, and snorted. Ears back, he
dropped to the floor and stalked toward the window,
pausing on the ledge to express his opinion with an
eloquent howl. Then he snorted again and leaped down
out of sight.

Except when the cramps dropped him to his knees
to spew bitter tasting bile on the forest floor, Roland
continued to run, getting as far as he could from that
horror in the clearing. He didn't see what he stumbled
over or slammed into or plunged through, his mind
reeling with images of giants and corpses and children
baked a toasty brown.

When at last he fell, without the energy to rise again,
the images danced round and round and round, leaving him with a single thought.

I want to go home.

I don't care what it costs. I want to go home.

I can't take it anymore.

Nothing happened. Apparently, the Darkness wanted
him to surrender out loud.

He sobbed, a tortured, choking sound that ripped at
the lining of his throat, then he managed a breath deep
enough for words.

"I want," he cried . . .

"Well, what have we here?"

The voice was a warm, deep, and friendly drawl and

so far removed from everything that had been happening to him that Roland grabbed onto it with everything he had left.

"Are ya'll hurt, young man?"

"I . . ." He managed to get up on an elbow and turn until he was looking up into the concerned features of a large brown bear. A large brown bear wearing a pair of overalls and with a spotted kerchief knotted around his neck.

"I . . ." Roland repeated weakly. And fainted.

Chapter TEN

"Now just as soon as ya'll finish eating, Papa'll guide you to the edge of the forest."

"Me, too! Me, too!" Baby Bear banged his spoon against his wooden porridge bowl and nearly spilled his milk.

Roland grabbed the mug and moved it to a safer spot, receiving a smile of thanks from Mama Bear that he tried to accept in the spirit in which it was offered, ignoring the mouthful of sharp teeth now revealed. Not that he appeared to be in any danger from these bears; from the moment Papa Bear had carried him into the cottage, they'd shown him nothing but kindness.

"Uh, no thanks." He waved away another helping of porridge. The bowls, even Baby Bear's, held an obscene amount of food and Roland, afraid of offending the cook, had eaten all he'd been given.

Mama Bear shook her head. "Ya'll don't eat enough to keep a squirrel alive," she scolded, clicking her claws against the scarred tabletop. "Why, you'll fall ovah from hungah before you've been on the trail ten minutes."

"Now leave the Bard alone, Mama," Papa Bear growled, picking up his bowl and licking it clean. "He

knows when he's had enough. And if you're not goin'
to finish that honeycomb . . ."

"Please, go ahead." Roland pushed the piece of
comb across the table and watched as Papa Bear ate
approximately a pound of honey in two bites. *It's
amazing what you can get used to,* he marveled. When
he'd come to, tucked snugly into Baby Bear's bed with
Mama Bear draping a cool cloth across his brow, he'd
whimpered and shrunk away from what looked like a
new installment in the day's nightmares. Mama had
merely continued to wipe his face and murmur comforting words in her gravelly voice. Finally, convinced
he was safe, he'd started to cry and she'd held him,
stroking his back, careful of her strength and his relative frailty. Worn out by terror, he'd eventually drifted
off to sleep.

Baby Bear's cold nose investigating his right ear had
jerked him awake a short time later. His startled yell
had started Baby Bear squalling, brought Mama Bear
running, and resulted in such a normal domestic scene
that there was no room for fear.

"Nothin' like a little snack between breakfast and
lunch." Papa Bear pushed back from the table with a
satisfied belch. "You've got a long way to travel, Master Bard, so we'd bettah get goin'."

"I don't know how to thank you," Roland began,
as the whole family moved to the door with him. He
slung the harp over his shoulder and picked up the
guitar case. "You saved my life." His throat closed
up and he felt perilously close to tears. "I've no way
to repay that."

"Nonsense." Mama Bear patted him on the back
and almost knocked him to his knees. "Bards are special and we'd do the same for any of them." She
handed Papa Bear his hat, beaming benevolently.
"Still and all, it's a good thing Papa heard youah instruments calling or he'd have just thought you were
some poah animal blundering by and, well, it's unlikely you'd have survived till noon."

"Yes." Roland's free hand dropped back to stroke
the smooth wood of the harp. "I know." He had no

memory of anything save horror during his wild run through the bush—Patience and the harp could have been playing "The Battle Hymn of the Republic" for all he knew—but he had a very clear memory of what had caused his panicked flight and knew he'd carry it to his dying day.

Papa Bear unwound Baby Bear from about his leg, handed him, wailing, to his mother, and pushed Roland out the door.

"Ah hate to see the little guy cry," he confided as they crossed the clearing surrounding the cottage. "But it's just too dangerous foah him in the forest. And you," he straightened to his full height and looked down at Roland, "you're lucky you've got me with you. Yup," he dropped back down to his usual hulking slouch as they stepped under the first of the trees and he bent a small sapling out of his path. "There's things in this forest with teeth that bite and claws that catch."

"Jabberwocks," Roland murmured.

"Why, that's it exactly. Mama tell ya'll about them?"

"No." Roland tightened his grip on Patience's case and carefully kept his gaze away from the deep shadows that pooled under certain trees. "I think I'm beginning to get the hang of this place."

Mrs. Ruth banged the newspaper against the edge of the garbage can, dislodging a half-eaten cherry danish and an apple core.

"People," she snorted, glaring at the damp, sticky splotch, "should have more consideration." Usually, she picked up her paper first thing in the morning and avoided the day's trash, but this was an early afternoon edition and if the glimpse she'd already managed was any indication, she needed to see it. "Hrmph. Dumping their leftovers on my paper!" She transferred her glare to a young woman hurrying past. "I ask you, why don't people take the time to eat properly? Bowel problems. Mark my words, they'll all end up with bowel problems."

The young woman averted her eyes and hurried a little faster. She just didn't have the time to deal with crazy old bag ladies.

Mrs. Ruth spread the paper across the top of her overflowing bundle buggy and squinted at the headline. *Modern Miracle; Angel Appears at Yonge and Carlton.* The story below it reported that a number of independent witnesses had spotted a glowing man with wings standing on the corner during the morning rush hour and that reactions from the various churches were still forthcoming. Mrs. Ruth snorted. ''I'll give you a reaction. Someone got a little too big for his britches.'' Shoving the paper down behind a perfectly good hockey stick found in a pile of otherwise disappointing garbage, she began to drag the squealing and protesting buggy down the street.

''If you want anything done right,'' she informed two businessmen as she pushed between them, ''you've got to do it yourself.''

''Go on! Scram!'' Papa Bear bent, picked up a chunk of stone, and heaved it at the pair of red shoes. They skipped back out of the way and danced off through the underbrush.

Roland swallowed heavily and managed to keep his gag reflex under control. There'd been feet in the shoes, wrinkled and mummified but quite definitely feet, the ankle bones gleaming dully where the dried flesh had pulled away.

''Damn nuisance, those things,'' Papa Bear growled, stomping forward. ''Not dangerous, though.''

''Great.'' Roland tried not to sound sarcastic. *Lions and tigers and bears*, he thought, *would be a nice change*. Then he glanced at Papa Bear and added, *Okay, cancel the bears*.

''Ms. Sastri?''

Daru grunted an affirmative without looking up. The bureaucracy had just spit out a new pile of forms needing immediate attention and she was already three days behind on her fieldwork; she had no time to spend on idle chatter.

"Ms. Sastri, if you could just spare me a few moments of your time."

The voice was warmly persuasive; a voice that accepted service as its right. It made the hair on the back of Daru's neck rise, this voice that sounded vaguely familiar even though she knew without a doubt it belonged to none of the men in the office.

The sooner I deal with him, the sooner I can get rid of him. She sighed, initialed the top two papers on the pile, pushed the whole stack to one side and swiveled her chair around in the same motion. "I can give you one mo . . ." she began and trailed off as she realized who stood just inside her cubicle.

His dark hair was cut fashionably short, a thick lock falling gracefully forward over his brow. His eyes were very blue, surrounded by a fringe of indecently long lashes. Teeth showed brilliant white against a café au lait tan. He wore a pale gray, raw silk suit, not an Oxford cloth shirt, but Daru recognized him immediately. She wondered if Evan knew how accurate his sketch had been. He'd even captured the contempt that lurked below the surface charm.

"Yes?" Her voice, she was pleased to note, quavered only a little and she quickly gained control of that. An enemy seen and available to be grappled with was less frightening than one skulking in shadows. "How can I help you, Mr. . . ?"

He spread long fingered hands. "My name is unimportant. And I rather think that I can help you. May I sit."

"Can I stop you?" Daru smiled tightly and waved in the direction of her second chair which was almost buried under case histories. She didn't see how he did it, but the bulging files were suddenly stacked neatly on the floor and he was crossing one leg over the other, twitching the trouser crease back into place.

"I have come to make you an offer," he said.

"If you're going to take me up on a mountaintop,"

Daru snapped, wondering if anyone would hear her if she screamed, "make it fast. I have work to do."

"A mountaintop. Yes." He drawled the words as though they left a bad taste in his mouth. "As you have no time for pleasantries, I will dispense with them myself. I offer you the power to deal with all of this." The sweep of his arm encompassed the entire department. "No paperwork. No government red tape. No being forced to stand by as situations go from bad to worse. I can give you the power to deal with problems, to solve them as they happen."

No more children destroyed in front of her eyes. No more men and women swept away as she watched helplessly, resources stretched too thin to save them. "And as my part of the deal?"

"You will cease to fight me."

"Well, that makes your whole deal kind of worthless, doesn't it, because that's what all this," the sweep of her arm mirrored his, "is. Fighting you." Her eyes narrowed. "You see, I know you and you're not some pretty young man in an expensive suit. You're the landlord who rents a shithole basement apartment with no heat and a toilet that doesn't work to an immigrant family for nine hundred and fifty dollars a month because you know they're desperate for a place to live. You're the punk who beats his pregnant girlfriend almost to death because she forgot to buy beer. You're the father who rapes his ten-year-old daughter, then blames what he did on her. And you're every judge, and every jury, and every lawyer who lets those bastards get away with it." Her eyes blazed and her fingers curled into fists. "And I will never stop fighting you."

For a moment, Daru held him pinned with her gaze, then he stood and smoothed a nonexistent wrinkle from his jacket. "You know, Ms. Sastri," his voice picked up an edge, "you are beginning to annoy me."

"Well, good," Daru snarled, "because you've *always* annoyed me. Now get the fuck out of my office!"

The Dark Adept shook his head. "Such language," he chided, but he left.

Daru straightened her hands, laid them flat on the desk to stop their shaking, and tried to remember how to breathe.

"Say, Jack, doesn't he look familiar?" Standing just outside the elevators, PC Patton pointed with her chin at the man walking out of Social Services.

PC Brooks frowned. "Isn't he . . ."

And then a pair of bright blue eyes swept the thought, and all thoughts connected to it, away.

"You look lost, officers," he said, stopping before them. "Can I help?"

Lost was the word for it all right; once past the public sections, Toronto City Hall became a hopeless rabbit warren. "We're looking for a Daru Sastri."

"Oh, I'm terribly sorry." And he looked most terribly sorry. "She's out of the office now and there's no way of knowing when she'll be back."

"Do you know where she's gone?"

"Out in the city somewhere, that's all I know." He smiled. "Would you like to speak to someone else?"

"No." PC Patton sighed. *Out in the city somewhere. Great.* "It had to be her."

The Dark Adept watched them get back into the elevator and enjoyed their disappointment. He hoped whatever they'd wanted Ms. Sastri for had been important.

The forest ended suddenly. One moment they were pushing past—or in Papa Bear's case, plowing through—the underbrush and the next moment they were looking out at a prairie that stretched to the horizon.

"Well, son, this is as fah as Ah go." Papa Bear absently scratched himself behind one ear, claws digging deep into the thick pelt and coming up with something many-legged and squirming which he absently flicked away. "Too much sky out theah foah me, but if ya'll follow the sun, things should come out all right."

"Follow the sun," Roland repeated, peering up into

the vaulting dome of blue that was the sky. His eyes, grown used to the shadowed light of the forest, watered and he blinked rapidly to clear them. The sun, almost directly overhead, burned hotter and higher than the sun at home.

"Good luck to ya, Master Bard." Papa Bear clapped him carefully on the back.

By clutching at the nearest tree, Roland managed to keep his feet. "I can't thank you enough for all you've done . . ."

"Heck, 'tweren't nothin'." The huge bear looked embarrassed. "Ya'll just put us in a song someday."

"I will," Roland nodded. "You can count on that." He stood for a time, watching Papa Bear stomp back to the cottage—and to Mama Bear, Baby Bear, and a yellow-haired kid who hadn't shown up yet—then he stepped out onto the grassland.

Walking was easy and he thankfully lengthened his stride. The grass grew to about ankle height, one blade pretty much like the next, stretching as far as he could see in any direction but back. The weight of the forest slipped off his shoulders like a discarded cloak and he left it lying where it fell, letting the sun wrap the memories in a cushioning layer of light. Heat seeped into the tattered places in his mind, warming and soothing, and as he walked he thought about nothing at all.

When a roll of the land dropped the forest out of sight, Roland sat and ate the lunch Mama Bear had packed for him. Then, still in a haze of heat and light, he stood and walked on, his shadow streaming out behind him.

Pain across the bridge of his nose brought him back to awareness. He reached up, touched his face gently, and swore. The skin, he knew, would be a bright, tight red. He squinted down at his forearms, just beginning to burn.

"I might have known," he muttered. "Nothing around here comes without a price." Now firmly back in the world, he sighed and did the only thing he could; he kept walking. A very short distance later he realized the price was higher than he'd thought. He'd seen no sign of water and he was suddenly very thirsty.

"Follow the sun and things should come out all right," he mocked, licking dry lips. "All right for who?" With every step, he could feel the sun sucking moisture out of him. The honey and biscuits lay like a lump in his stomach and the sweet aftertaste only intensified his need for a drink.

He stood equidistant from the two cathedrals, enjoying the way his presence washed out whatever influence for good they might have. They were symbols of the Light, but he was a piece of living Darkness and against him they didn't stand a chance. Leaning against a storefront, he waited for the enemy's third companion. Although his servant had been unable to take an impression, it turned out not to matter for the impressions of the other two were filled with her image.

"Rebecca," he murmured the name and considered what he knew. Were she merely an innocent he would take great delight in her destruction, but she was a simpleton as well and that saved her. What pleasure could there be when the victim remained unaware? No, he would disrupt the careful structure of her world, upset the balance she needed to deal with life, and send her weeping and wailing back into the arms of the Light as a further burden and distraction.

A slow smile spread across his face as he thought of the Light Adept so cruelly caught on the horns of a most exquisite dilemma. If he went out, the people he claimed to care so much about got hurt, used, twisted by their desire for the Light, their desire for him. Yet if he stayed in, his search was curtailed, not stopped but certainly not as effective.

"I am a genius," he murmured, and straightened as he saw his prey approaching.

Because it was what she did, Rebecca looked in all the pawnshop windows, but she hardly saw the jewelry although it sparkled gaily in the afternoon sun trying to attract her attention. The Darkness had sent Roland away and she didn't have the heart for pretties. She reached the last of the windows and frowned. Something was missing. A watch with two huge emeralds caught her eye. Two minutes past three it told her.

Past three.

What had happened to the bells?

Rebecca's heart began to beat hard, the way it did when things went wrong.

What had happened to the bells?

Three minutes past three, said the watch.

Four minutes past.

Five minutes past.

What had happened to the bells?

Unable to stand it any longer, she whirled about and stared from one tower to the next, panic rising.

"Ring," she pleaded. "Ring."

And the Dark Adept felt the bells move within his hold. He tightened his grip. They trembled and moved again.

"That's impossible," he snarled.

Slowly, bit by bit, the bells pulled free. He fought them, but he couldn't stop them and when at last they rang they rang him as well, pealing inside his head, clanging and clamoring until he cried out and clapped his hands futilely over his ears. He felt his weapon against the enemy fall, knew the enemy felt it, too, and all but shrieking in frustration, he fled.

Rebecca sighed in relief as the pattern of her world continued unchanged. The watch in the pawnshop window must have been wrong.

As the sun began to go down, the air grew chill, the heat of the day quickly dissipating. Roland shivered, his thin T-shirt now much the worse for wear, and, swaying slightly, he stood glaring into the setting sun. He didn't know how long he'd been heading toward the gray bulge in the distance, but it didn't seem to be getting any closer. Suddenly his legs gave way and he sat, heavily, on the grass.

This is ridiculous, he thought, swallowing blood. The fall had driven his teeth through his tongue and he was crazily thankful for even that much moisture. *It's only seven. I left the bears' cottage at about eleven. Only eight hours. I can't be this thirsty.* But he was, thirsty and tired and sunburned and cold.

The sun dropped below the horizon and the temperature plunged another few degrees. Hunched in on himself, Roland wondered what pleasures the night would bring. *Werewolves. Vampires. Ghouls. A herd of stampeding dragons.* Just because he hadn't seen any wildlife didn't mean it didn't exist. *And in this place it would likely come out after dark. Of course, I'd have to survive the exposure long enough for it to get to me.*

He looked up at the sky and shivered again, but not from the cold this time. All around him, the sky came down to meet the earth in an unrelieved curtain of black. Sitting there, alone in the darkness, he felt he was the only living thing left in existence, that existence itself ended just beyond his fingertips. Only the comforting weight of the guitar case against his leg, and of the harp tucked up under his arm, kept him from wailing. Had the sun left enough moisture for tears, he would've cried.

Eventually, his head fell forward and, exhausted by despair, he slept.

The harp woke him, sending a note singing into the night. Roland jerked his head up and wondered for a moment where he was. Then he remembered, and moaned. The whole wretched experience hadn't been a dream.

The moon had risen while he slept and rode high and full in the starless sky. Each blade of grass on that seemingly endless prairie stood out, silver edged against a tiny, perfect shadow. If he strained, he thought he could make out the darker shadow of whatever it was he'd been using for a landmark.

In the distance, he heard the rumble of thunder. It drew closer, growing in volume and intensity.

"Wait a minute," he lurched to his feet, eyes wide and breathing quickened, "that's not thunder, that's . . ."

A double line of horsemen pounded out of the dark-

ness, the moonlight setting the silver inlaid in their
armor and their tack on fire. Roland stood paralyzed
while they raced closer and closer until, at the very
last second, when the beasts and the riders filled all
sight and sound and smell, the lines split and swerved
off to either side to continue their gallop in a mad
circle about him.

As far as the city-bred Roland could tell, the animals were normal horses and therefore only normally
terrifying with their wild eyes and flashing hooves and
great slabs of teeth, but the riders were clad in fantastical armor and he had no idea what rode beneath it.
Two arms, two legs, and a head were all that could be
taken for granted.

He was almost ready for it when the first spear thud-
ded into the earth at his feet. Then the second grazed
his shoulder, drawing a thin line of blood, and he
flinched aside, a whimper rising from deep in his
throat. When the third took a small piece from his
thigh, the pain became a part of the terror and he lost
his grip on where one ended and the other began. They
were all around him; he couldn't run, he couldn't hide
so he shuddered and closed his eyes, clamping his teeth
shut on the scream that fought to get free. *I'll die quietly at least,* he swore bleakly. *And Darkness can stuff
it up his ass.*

The harp began to play; an eerie and peculiar tune,
for few strings remained intact.

The thundering hooves quieted and then ceased to
thunder entirely.

Roland dared to open his eyes and as he did, the
harp fell silent. He felt rather than heard something
approaching behind him and, not entirely certain it
was a good idea, he turned slowly to face it.

The horse stopped less than a body length away and
the rider hung the reins over the elaborately chased
saddlebow. Silver and black gloves were removed to
expose literally lily-white hands. Slender fingers
moved to lift the bird's head helm. Roland had no clue
what kind of a bird it represented, he only knew pi-
geons and it wasn't one of them. Masses of ebony hair

cascaded down over shoulders and breasts and jade
green eyes stared at him curiously from under slanted
brows.

Roland swallowed. Excluding Evan, she was the
most beautiful creature he'd ever seen, from the tip of
her delicately pointed ears to the sweeping curve of
her cheek to the moist gleam of narrowed lips.

"The harp you carry," her voice, although hard and
suspicious, was as beautiful as her face, "how didst
thou come by it?"

"I, uh, rescued it." He couldn't seem to straighten
his thoughts.

"From where?"

Roland shifted the weight of the harp on his hip,
dimly aware of the wound on his thigh protesting the
movement and of fresh blood soaking into his jeans.
"From, uh, a giants' cave." And then, because an
honorific seemed needed, he added, "Ma'am."

"The harp belonged to my brother."

He wondered which hunk of rotting meat the brother
had been but he said, "I'm sorry."

"Thou art human."

It didn't seem to be a question so he kept silent,
content for the moment merely to watch her.

"And yet the harp accepts thee." She frowned,
changing her beauty but not lessening it. "Art thou a
Bard perchance?"

"Uh, yes." He remembered what Uncle Tony had
told him about Bards. "That is, I am but I've, uh, still
got seven years to go."

She shrugged the remaining seven years aside and
repeated, "A Bard."

"Your Highness . . ."

Roland jerked as one of the other riders spoke. Staring into the depths of the lady's eyes, he'd forgotten
anyone else was there.

". . . what shall we do with him?"

"We shall take him with us." She smiled and Roland felt his heart do back flips. "The hill has been
long without music."

* * *

Bouncing painfully on the back of a saddle, Roland tried to keep one eye on Patience and the other on the harp and both of them on the rider in the bird's head helm, giving himself a headache to go with the ache in his other end. As far as he could see, what with the darkness and the movement and his fear of sliding off and being trampled by those galloping along behind, the instruments were doing better than he was. The rider before him wore a cat's head helm but not even his most desperate attempts to hang on to the armored torso could tell Roland whether he was clinging to a man or woman.

The hill turned out to be the bulge in the landscape Roland had been trudging toward for most of the afternoon; he was certain of it the moment it loomed out of the darkness. He saw the princess wave a hand and a large section of the hill misted away. Pale gray light spilled out of the opening. Horses and riders surged forward and Roland, still struggling to stay seated, was swept underground.

Some moments later, holding Patience protectively, his mind buzzing with images of color and light, he limped after the princess as she led the way through a set of great carved doors. He had a jumbled impression of an immense vaulted room filled with people and a murmur of surprise that tracked them as they walked the length of it. Roland kept his eyes on the princess, his head filled with paeans to her beauty that drowned out the pain and fear.

Across one end of the room was a dais and as Roland and the princess approached it, men and women moved aside to reveal a man seated on a great black throne.

Good lord, but they look alike, was Roland's first thought. His second was, *Am I out of my mind?* for the man on the throne had dark red hair and pale gray eyes.

"Thou hast returned early to my sight, Lady Daughter." He didn't sound pleased. "What hast thou brought to me?"

"Two things, Lord Father." She held up the harp.

"My brother's harp is found and he who carries it is himself a Bard." She paused briefly then added without expression. "A human Bard. The harp accepts him."

Roland felt every eye in the place on him. Pinned by the king's level stare, he realized why he thought the two looked so much alike despite their radically different coloring; their expressions and their mannerisms were identical.

"I can assume," the king said dryly, "that thou didst not best my son in battle and wrest the harp from his stiffening hands?"

"Uh, no, sir." How did he get the harp? His memory seemed to go back only as far as his first sight of the princess. With an effort, he reached further and pulled out the answer. "I, uh, rescued it from a giants' cave."

"Pity. But the giant would have silenced him, so the result is the same."

Roland got the impression that the late prince had not been very well liked.

The king continued. "Thou hast returned to me one of the treasures of my kingdom. Ask and it shall be thine."

He must know the way home. Home. Roland fought to hold onto the word but the princess was here and infinitely more real and her presence kept pushing everything else away. "I . . ." His throat closed up and his tongue stuck to the roof of his mouth as he suddenly realized how very thirsty he was. "I, I'd like a glass of water, if I could."

The king frowned.

Roland felt the people surrounding him draw back and he heard the clank of metal plates as the princess and her riders turned to stare.

"A glass of water," the king repeated.

The silence lengthened and stretched. Roland desperately wanted to scratch his nose but was afraid to move.

Slowly, the king smiled and the court began to breathe again. "Water for the Bard," he commanded.

"And when thou hast been refreshed and reclothed, Sir Bard," the smile broadened, "we will feast!"

Roland found himself surrounded by a swirling crowd of brightly clothed men and women, all laughing and talking and fussing over him. He lost sight of the princess and his leg began to hurt. The snatches of conversation he heard made little sense, so he stopped trying to listen; not difficult as no one actually spoke to him. A silver goblet was placed in his hand and he thankfully drank. Now he only felt tired, confused . . .

And short, he added silently as he came face to chest with yet another swelling bosom. Even the women stood well over Roland's almost six feet.

He was pushed and pulled and chivied along until he ended up in a small, steamy room with two young women and a deep tub of hot water.

". . . clothes."

"What?" That last statement had obviously been addressed to him. "I'm sorry, I didn't hear."

The young woman giggled and pushed a short chestnut curl up behind the point of her ear. "I said, thou hast to remove thy clothes. Unless thou wishes to bathe in them?"

"Uh, no." He leaned the guitar case carefully against a stone bench and stared stupidly at the silver goblet in his hand.

The second woman, whose black hair hugged her head in a sleek cap, sighed and stepped forward. "I have no wish to be at this all night. If thou wilt but stand still, Sir Bard, we shall manage. Moth, if thou wilt stop giggling and help . . ."

Roland meant to protest when two sets of surprisingly strong hands began dragging down his jeans, but he just didn't have the energy. Before he had time to be embarrassed, he was in the tub and the hot water started to soak away his aches and pains. The water turned pink as dried blood washed away and he shrieked as it hit the now open cut on his leg.

"Just wait." Moth pushed him down and held him.

"There's that in the bath to help thy wounds if thou wilt give it a chance."

He didn't have much choice so he sat, teeth gritted, until the pain faded. Slowly, he began to feel better than he had in—he thought back—one day. It had all happened in just one day!

It's amazing how soon you can get used to things. He'd thought it first watching Papa Bear eat. He thought it now as two beautiful young women bathed him. And then he realized his body wasn't nearly as blasé about the situation as his overloaded mind.

"Best not waste that, Sir Bard," Moth giggled, digging soapy fingers into knotted shoulder muscles, "or her Highness will in fury rage."

Roland blushed, squirmed, and discovered there was no way to hide. His brain reluctantly shifted out of neutral. "Her Highness?" he managed.

"Thou hast impressed her mightily." Moth lathered his hair and scrubbed vigorously. When she finished pouring a pitcher of warm water over his head, she added, "First thou wilt feast and then thou wilt frolic."

Roland knew what frolic meant where he came from, so he tackled the first bit of information. "I impressed her?"

"Most surely. With your request of his Majesty her father."

"My request?"

"Thou wast expected," the other woman said dryly, holding out a large towel for him to step into, "to beg for thy life."

That took care of the small physical problem.

He allowed himself to be dressed in borrowed finery and led to the feasting hall, all the while hoping that if begging was necessary he'd be given another chance. That thought vanished at the first sight of the princess who nodded approvingly and drew him to her side. He sat where she indicated, mesmerized by the startling contrast between her pale skin and the black satin of her gown.

"Alabaster and ebony," he murmured, and flushed as she smiled.

The feast passed in a kaleidoscope of sights: Although the short haired servers dressed in a bright array of colors, those being served wore only combinations of black and red and silver. Roland had never realized that red and black and silver could come in so many shades, could sparkle and shine and burn with such intensity.

And sound: Laughter rose frequently over the noise of eating and drinking, but it had a brittle edge as though the ones who laughed knew secrets their listeners did not.

And taste: Roland ate everything that appeared before him, reveling in foods that had the texture of silk and the flavor of sunshine, the sharp tang of a winter's day, the thick richness of midnight.

And smell: The scent wafting out from the heavy mass of Her Highness' hair wrapped around him, capturing and intoxicating him, leaving no room for other scents and very little room for thought.

He couldn't hold onto fear or even wariness. Everyone he saw was young and beautiful and, after the king and the princess, they deferred to him. If he was to be killed in the morning, he'd worry about it then and probably go smiling to the firing squad. Or the local equivalent.

When the last of the food had been cleared away, the huge room fell silent.

"And now, Master Bard," the king announced, "mayhap thou wouldst honor our company with a song."

A server approached carrying the harp, cleaned, restrung and as beautiful as Roland knew she would be. He ran a gentle finger down the sweet curve of her, and smiled.

"I beg your pardon, sir," he said, "but I'll stick with the lady I know."

The feel of the silence changed, but the king merely waved a graceful hand and replied, "Thy choice, Sir Bard."

Moving slowly, for he suspected he'd had just a little too much of the deep red wine, Roland opened the case and pulled Patience free. "It's called a guitar," he answered the king's raised eyebrow. Running up a scale, he felt in control of events and when he started to play he gave himself over to the music.

They kept him playing until his hands were cramped and his voice had faded to a husky whisper. Then, amid cries of praise and adulation, the princess took his arm and led him from the room.

If she'd asked him, he would have pleaded exhaustion, but she didn't ask—only stripped them both, mounted, and rode him to climax after shuddering climax. Roland had no idea where he found the energy, but his body kept responding to her demands so he gave in and enjoyed it.

He woke amid pitch blackness, completely disoriented. Panicked, he thrashed about, then jerked up into a sitting position. Gradually, soft gray light filled the room. He saw the glimmering silver and red tapestries, the huge oval mirror, and the discarded clothes strewn about. Turning slightly, he saw a tangled mass of blue-black hair spilling over an ivory breast. He remembered and lay back smiling.

The light faded until the room was once again in total darkness.

He sat up.

The light returned.

He lay down.

The light faded.

Not bad, he thought. *I could grow to like this place. Good food, great clothes, a beautiful woman. And they appreciate music.* He dozed a little, images of life as a court favorite dancing through his head, and then he sat up again.

"Bathroom," he sighed. He considered waking the princess for directions but decided against it. Following his nose, he found the little room off the hall that served the purpose. When he returned, bright gold eyes peered up at him from the end of the bed.

"Where the hell did you come from?" he murmured, frowning.

Tom meowed imperiously, working his claws in and out of the mattress.

"Shhh!" Roland put his finger to his lips. "You'll wake her." He dropped the robe he'd found and looked thoughtful. "In fact, that might not be such a bad idea. Now that I'm rested I'm sure we can find something to do." Sliding back onto the bed, he bent his head over ruby lips.

"JESUS CHRIST!" He whirled around and glared at the cat. "You scratched me, you little shit!" He grabbed at his right cheek and his hand came away streaked with blood. "I'm going to skin you for a . . . a . . . Jesus Christ," he repeated, only this time it was more like a prayer. For the first time since he'd gazed at the princess, all jade and ebony and silver in the moonlight, he was thinking clearly.

A quick glance at said princess showed she still slept soundly. A quick glance around the room and he spotted his watch.

"Two forty-three," he muttered, strapping it on. It had to have been close to dawn when last night's party had finally broken up. That made it two forty-three in the afternoon. He looked at the princess again. The middle of the day. And she was sleeping *very* soundly. Gently at first, and then more violently, Roland shook her shoulder. Her chest still rose and fell, but that remained the only sign of life.

His heart beating painfully hard, he raced to the mirror and studied his neck. There were no puncture wounds.

Tom snorted.

"Well, she could've been," he hissed, feeling like a fool. "Where the hell *did* you come from?" he demanded again, bending down and staring at the cat. "Did Evan send you to find me?"

Tom twisted and began washing the base of his tail.

"Oh, that's very helpful." His tone was sarcastic, but it *was* helpful. Despair just couldn't be maintained in the face of such sublime indifference. He straightened and dragged both hands through his hair. *I've got to get away before she wakes up.* Because if he didn't, Roland knew, if she smiled at him again, he'd be unable to leave. So far, things had been pretty terrific, but he strongly suspected when Royal Interest in their new toy waned, the situation would be very different.

He dressed quickly in the black silk and velvet he'd worn to the feast—he had no idea where his jeans were—picked up Patience, and started for the door. Tom padded out ahead of him.

The cat certainly looked like he knew where he was going and as Roland certainly did not, he followed the cat. The hallways glowed, then faded as they passed. *Even if I'd been in my right mind on the way up last night, I'd never have remembered this.* The maze of corridors twisted and turned and doubled back on themselves with joyous abandon. *Fortunately, I'm too lost to be scared.* That didn't quite make sense but neither had life lately, so Roland let it stand. Nor was it entirely accurate. It sounded as if he and Tom were the last two creatures alive and that silence weighed on him. In spite of his best efforts to banish it, the phrase "the silence of the tomb" insisted on sitting in the forefront of his mind. He'd never understood it before; he did now.

Tom padded on, oblivious.

They passed a large open archway that Roland was sure he'd never seen before. Although Tom kept walking, Roland, for curiosity's sake, stuck his head into the room. In the dim light he could just barely make out a black rectangle flanked by two white triangles about five feet high. He took a step farther in and the two white triangles became two pyramids of skulls that stared back at him out of empty sockets.

All at once, the statement *"He expected thee to beg for thy life."* made sense.

Roland hurried to catch up with Tom.

As his footsteps faded away, the blackness above the altar began to thicken into more than just an absence of light.

* * *

"So you think it will be that easy, do you?" The Dark Adept smiled. "While your hosts sleep, you will slip back out into the light without even thanking them for their hospitality." The smile hardened and the ebony brows drew down. "I think not."

The small park was empty. He took steps to keep it that way. Leaning back on the bench, he stretched out long legs and lifted his face to the sun while his mind made a visit to the shadow realms.

When they reached the great feasting hall, Roland almost didn't recognize it. Empty of the court, it looked bleak and cold, the silvers dulled to gray and the blacks only to a reminder of who ruled in this realm. Roland shivered and moved closer to Tom as they began picking their way across to the door on the far side. They'd covered half the distance when a questioning note rang out. Roland paused, sighed, and turned. As he expected, the harp was leaning up against the great black throne.

"A fine way to treat a treasure," he said softly, squatting and stroking its graceful curve one last time, hating to leave an instrument he'd become so absurdly fond of. Sneaking out while everyone slept was one thing—with luck he'd be forgotten before breakfast ended—sneaking out with a national treasure was something else again. Regretfully, he stood and spread his hands. "I guess this is good-bye." The harp sounded again. "I wish I *could* take you with me." Very conscious of Tom's impatient stare, he turned to go. This time the note fairly vibrated throughout the room.

Roland winced and glanced around. "You're going to wake everyone up," he warned. He could feel the harp gathering itself together for another note and because it was what he wanted to do anyway, he scooped it up in his free hand.

"It was her idea," he explained sheepishly to Tom, who sat by the door, tail lashing the air. From within the case, Patience chimed an agreement.

Tom snorted, walked out the door and straight into what looked like a solid wall. There was a faint but audible thunk as his skull came in contact with something marginally harder than it was. Tom blinked, sat down, and began vigorously washing a front paw.

Nervously, Roland shifted his grip on the harp. "Yeah, okay. I believe you. You meant to do that." He glanced over his left shoulder, the hairs on his neck rising—he'd heard, or thought he'd heard a sound, metallic and recurrent, just beyond the point where the soft gray light dimmed and died. Forcing his gaze back down to the cat, he hissed, "If you know the way out, I suggest you take me to it."

Refusing to be hurried, Tom gave his paw a final polish, then used it to pat at the wall. His tail lashed. He dropped into a crouch, his head snaked from side to side, and he hissed.

The sound grew louder; identifiable. Metallic, yes. Footsteps. More than one set.

"Tom!"

The cat's ears flattened and he growled low in his throat, his attention still fixed on the wall.

"Yeah, okay. You're working on it." *I don't believe I'm depending on a cat.* Roland's armpits were wet, the black silk sticking to his skin. He could smell his own fear. Almost without willing it, he turned to face down the corridor.

"Oh, shit!"

A figure in a suit of black armor, similar to that worn by the riders but with more metal and less leather, stalked out of the shadows. A second followed a pace behind.

"I thought this lot slept all day," Roland protested to the universe at large. *It isn't fair! Maybe if I give back the harp* . . . Then he smelled the slightly sweet odor of rotting meat and knew these guardians were beyond reasoning with.

"No, not again." He backed up a step. The grinning, decaying faces in the giants' larder jostled for position in his memory. "I can't . . ." He swallowed and backed up another step. "I can't deal with that again." Another step and a half turn; turning to run. Something soft gave way under his foot.

He screamed, both in pain and terror as Tom yowled and dug sharp claws into the delicate skin behind his ankle. "I'm not a fighter!" he shrieked at the disinterested cat.

And then he didn't have a choice.

He dropped flat under the first swing, throwing Patience and the harp into what he hoped was safety at the base of the wall. The end of Patience's case dragged across the harp strings and they sang out, a discordant counterpoint to the clash of metal. Roland watched the great black sword arcing down toward him suddenly change direction and go skittering off point first against the stone floor.

The harp. The harp controlled the guardians. Or discouraged them. Or something. He scrambled out of the way of another blow, then felt himself slammed sideways as the second guardian brought a mace into play. *My shoulder! It broke my fucking shoulder!* But it hadn't, not quite, for fingers wiggled in a hurried experiment still worked. It hurt like hell, but he could use the arm. *The harp! I've got to get the harp.* He ducked a whistling blow that sprayed chips from the wall when it landed and in panicked desperation fell to the floor and rolled.

His knee crashed into the harp and the sword point descending toward his eye wavered, lightly kissed his cheek—leaving a searing line of pain behind—and vanished from sight. He pushed himself up with his good arm and collapsed against the polished wood as something pounded into his kidneys. Retching and blind with pain, he clawed at the silver strings.

The Dark Adept shifted slightly so that the sun fell directly on his face. The harp was barely more than an annoyance. Without the skill to play it, it would do this so-called Bard little good. He would finish this quickly. He was growing bored.

Breathing heavily, Roland forced his eyes back into focus. The random noise he was pulling from the harp appeared to be holding the guardians where they were. They stood swaying slightly, black armor creaking, arms moving in directionless jerks. As he watched, they turned and began making their way slowly toward him. He raked his fingers back and forth, filling the corridor with sound. They fought it and continued to advance.

"Hey, bubba, spare a buck?"

Jerked out of the shadow realm, the Dark Adept snarled and reached for power—and barely stopped himself in time. It would do his plans no good if he set a beacon for the Light. He spat a curse at the ragged old woman standing before him. He would remember her and deal with her later.

She clicked her tongue at him. "If you ain't got it, bubba, just say so. Ain't no call to be rude." Shaking her head and muttering about the ways of the young, she waddled away, dragging a protesting bundle buggy after her.

The Dark Adept ground his teeth. He did not rule in the shadow realm, though much of it called him Lord, and it would take time and effort he could not spare to reestablish contact. The guardians would have to finish alone.

"I should have flayed that old woman alive," he growled. It still wasn't too late. He sprang to his feet, whirled about, and . . .

There was no old woman in the park.

Tom howled suddenly and Roland's heart slammed up into his throat. "What!" he screamed spinning about. His jaw dropped as the cat disappeared into what seemed to be a solid wall. "Right. Sure."

Tom howled again, sounding barely farther away than he had an instant earlier.

One of the guardians jerked back and forth until it looked as if it had to fall and the other dragged along on a twitching leg but both kept coming.

"Right," Roland repeated. He only had seconds to

decide. *Well it can't be worse.* Snatching up Patience, he flung himself at the wall, closing his eyes at the last instant.

A metal hand closed about his ankle.

A jumbled impression of dark, then gray, then light, and the horrendous sound of something tearing that was never meant to tear.

He landed on grass, warm and dry and smelling slightly dusty in the warmth of the sun. For a moment, he did nothing but breathe and then, because it felt so good, he flopped over onto his back and did it some more. With one arm thrown up against the sun's glare, he took inventory.

His cheek. His shoulder. His back. His thigh. His ankle. His ankle?

"Oh, shit!" Metal fingers still dug into the bone.

He had to look, he knew it, but it took him a few minutes to gather the nerve. Finally, he sighed and sat up. The black gauntlet gleamed dully in the sunlight, the jagged edge where it had been torn from the rest of the armor a brighter black. Roland kicked his leg experimentally. The gauntlet hung on.

"GET IT OFF ME!"

During the wild thrashing that followed, the gauntlet brushed against the harp and fell free.

Roland took several deep breaths. "Nobody asked your opinion," he snarled at Tom, who'd sat quietly, tail curled around toes, watching the whole thing. Somehow, Roland managed to get to his feet. He glared down at the gauntlet. "Empty. The smell was a put-on. He was using my own fear against me. That lousy son of a . . ." He drew back his foot, thought better of it, and kicked viciously at a tuft of grass instead.

Tom stood, stretched, and slowly began pacing away.

"Yeah, all right. I'm coming." Carefully, Roland bent and picked up the two instruments. He hadn't felt this bad since peewee hockey, but he'd be damned if he'd fall over in front of a cat.

An hour and seven minutes later, they came to a

path. Fifty-six minutes after that, the path split, one route heading down into a pleasant valley and the other snaking up a rocky, barren mountain that had somehow managed to remain unseen until they actually got to the fork.

"Yeah, well, I've read *this* book," Roland sighed and collapsed on a convenient boulder. "And if you think I'm going to climb that mountain, you're out of your furry little mind." He shifted gingerly to ease the bruising across his back. "I'm going to be pissing blood as it is."

Tom yawned, pink tongue delicately curled.

"Same to you, hairball." Wincing, Roland stood. "So let's get going already . . ." He turned on to the treacherous path, made doubly so for him because he had no hands free to help him climb and he would not abandon the harp. Not now. Not after all they'd been through together.

Tom bounded ahead, pausing to wait for Roland at each new obstacle with a superior look on his face.

As darkness fell, the faint call of hunting horns sounded in the distance.

Roland tried to climb faster.

The horns grew louder.

Eventually, the path ended. So did the mountain.

Gasping for breath, Roland staggered to the edge of the cliff and looked off. All he could see, far below, were fuzzy white specks that had to be clouds.

Down at the base of the mountain, armored figures brushed with moon-silver highlights rose in their stirrups and shrieked their challenges.

"Now what?" Roland asked the night.

Purring loudly, Tom brushed against his legs, then leaped from the edge, his tail streaming behind him like a pennant.

"Oh, no," Roland took a step back, "I am not jumping off a cliff after a *cat*. Forget it. No way." He considered the alternatives. "I'll take my chances with the princess before I do something so damned stupid." And in his mind's eye he saw the jaw of the corpse move as the Darkness told him there was no way out save through him. He squared his shoulders. "Oh, hell, might as well make it *my* choice . . ." Like a swimmer entering cold water, he limped forward and threw himself into the air.

Patience and the harp played a harmony to his scream.

Chapter ELEVEN

"Please, let me help you with that."

The large-blonde-lady-from-down-the-hall positively preened as she allowed the handsome young man to haul her shopping cart up the stairs.

"A woman like you," he purred, "should be carrying urns, like a Cretan goddess, or flowers like a nymph of the spring. Not groceries."

She simpered as she dragged herself up the stairs behind him and, although she didn't usually have breath enough to talk and climb, managed to pant, "My brother-in-law says I've got the best bone structure of anyone he's ever seen."

The Dark Adept smiled. "Your brother-in-law is very perceptive." He waited patiently on the second floor for her to catch up. "But what could your husband be thinking of to allow you to walk about unescorted." His voice dropped. "There's a lot of strange people in this city, dangerous people. Especially for a lovely woman alone."

"Don't I know it." She rested a moment, one hand fluttering over her heart, like a pudgy hummingbird amid the purple flowers of her shirt. She lowered heavily mascaraed lashes. "Unfortunately, I don't have a husband."

"A wise decision not to limit yourself to just one man. A woman like you needs to be free."

She agreed with him all the way down the hall.

Selfish, vain, and stupid, he thought as they reached her door. *Mine for the taking.*

"Would you like to come in for a while? We could have tea. Or wine, maybe. I think I have a bottle of very nice wine." She smiled in the way she thought a woman of the world would smile.

"I'd love to come in. I have plans for you."

"Oh. My." She fumbled with her key in the lock, the almost forgotten sensation of being wanted making her clumsy.

By the time the glasses had been dug out of the clutter, he was no longer bothering to hide his aspect. She was his.

"Come on, bubba, open your eyes. I got better things to do than sit in an alley with you all night."

"Mrs Ruth?" Roland tried to focus on the bag lady, but her face kept slipping sideways and going misty around the edges. It didn't seem worth the effort to keep them open, so he let his eyes close. *I don't feel very good. In fact, I feel like shit.* His entire body ached, but pain seemed localized in his right shoulder, his left leg, across the small of his back, and his face. First the right cheek. Then the left. Then the right again. It took him a moment—his brain ached as much as everything else—but he finally figured out what was happening.

"Mrs. Ruth . . ." He wet his lips and tried again. "Mrs. Ruth, please stop hitting me."

"Not until you open your eyes, bubba."

Roland sighed. Why bother. Left cheek. Right cheek. Left . . . "Ow!" His eyes snapped open. "That hurt!"

Mrs. Ruth sat back on her heels and looked pleased with herself. "It was supposed to. Now get your ass in gear. You've got work to do tonight."

"Where am I?" He winced as she frowned. "Uh, never mind. I'll look." Teeth clenched, he heaved himself up on his elbows. Mrs. Ruth blocked the view to the front, so he carefully turned his head from side to side. In one direction, a rusty blue dumpster rose

up out of the evening gloom and the smell of rotting
foodstuffs suggested he was in back of a restaurant. In
the other direction, much farther away, traffic rolled
past the alley's mouth, the sound of engines muted by
distance. He could just barely see the edge of a sign:
Peking Gar . . .

"Chinatown." And then it sank in. "Chinatown.
I'm home." He looked at Mrs. Ruth, who nodded.
"Home," he repeated, struggling to sit up. He still
wore the black silk and velvet and just beyond his reach
the harp gleamed in the uncertain light. Images flooded
back; the giants, the child, the forest, the bears, the
sun, the prairie, the spears, the princess, the black
armor, and the final terrifying plunge off the cliff. . . .

"Shhh, bubba, shhh." Mrs. Ruth shoved a hand-
kerchief into Roland's hands and patted him comfortingly on a shaking shoulder.

Roland swallowed a sob, fought for control, and got
a fingernail's grip on it. He sucked in deep, shuddering
breaths and scrubbed at his face with the square of
cloth—which, surprisingly, smelled of fabric softener.
The memory of fear mixed with the mind-numbing
relief at being home, brought him as close to total loss
of self as anything that had happened in the shadow
realm.

"I know, bubba, I know." Not just meaningless
sounds of sympathy, she sounded as if she did know,
which steadied Roland further. "You've been through
horrors few men can imagine, but as bad as it seems
now, it'll make a better Bard of you in the end." The
sympathy left her voice and she returned to a brisk no-
nonsense tone, "You can have a wallow in it later. At
present there are those who need you."

"What happened to Tom? Did he get back?"

"Of course, he did. He's a cat, isn't he?"

Roland had no idea what being a cat had to do with
things, but he nodded anyway and began convincing
his battered body that it had to stand.

Two nights to Midsummer. Two nights. Only two.
The words ran through Evan's thoughts, a litany that

looped around and around. He sighed, wishing he
could take the time to enjoy this world. In so many
ways, it was so much closer to the Light than to the
Dark; both in its people and in the lives they had made
for themselves.

The day's rain had washed the sticky heat from the
air and the evening breezes were delicately scented
with the presence of green and growing life. Evan
didn't care for cities; they barricaded their inhabitants
away from the things that mattered. But as cities went,
this one wasn't bad; there were trees and open spaces
and evidence that it hadn't become more important
than the people who lived in it.

A group of children swirled around his legs and ran
off down the street, their laughter filling the evening
with Light. Evan smiled after them, a gentle benediction. One small girl stopped, turned, and stared back
at him, her expression puzzled, wondering why she
was drawn. Evan sketched a sign in the air between
them and the girl smiled as well, one hand reaching
out to touch the delicate lines of Light.

"Marian, come on!"

Their eyes met and Marian nodded solemnly, then
whirled and, whooping, ran off to join her friends.

This is why the Darkness must be stopped, Evan
thought, and bent his mind once more to the task at
hand.

He didn't exactly understand what had happened
yesterday between Rebecca and the Dark Adept. When
he'd arrived, freed from the glamour his enemy had
thrown about him, the struggle was over. Only the
power signatures and Rebecca remained.

"The watch in the pawnshop window was slow,
Evan," Rebecca had said, wide-eyed at his sudden appearance. But the power signatures told him that the
Darkness had attacked and something had stopped it,
something huge that had barely stirred and yet had still
slapped the Darkness down.

Today, he'd walked Rebecca to work and back,
spending the time between finding the faint path the
Dark Adept had left when he'd fled, too rattled to mask

properly. Tonight, he traced it, hopefully tracking the Darkness to its lair.

Two nights to Midsummer. Two nights. Only two.

"Where the hell have you been?"

Roland sighed and sagged against the wall of Daru's cubicle. "It's a long story," he said, shifting the weight of the harp on his shoulder.

"It had better be a good one. Rebecca's been worried sick." She looked him up and down and snorted. "You look like you've been to a costume party."

A shadow passed across his face. "No. It wasn't quite a party."

Daru's expression softened slightly. It looked to her like Roland had done a little growing up in the forty-eight hours he'd been away. He had a depth now that she hadn't seen before. "What happened to your face?"

"It's nothing." He touched his cheek where the point of the black sword had drawn a delicate line and ran his finger along the crimson beads of dried blood. "I don't want to talk about it."

"You tangled with the Dark Adept." She wasn't asking, but Roland nodded anyway. "You okay?"

Roland drew in a deep breath and exhaled slowly. Things seemed to stay together. "There was a time," he said, "when sanity hung by a hair. It's not a lot more secure now, but in comparison, yeah, I'm okay." He made the effort and straightened, ignoring the screaming pain in his kidneys. "Mrs. Ruth says we, you and me, have to get to Rebecca's right away."

"Mrs. Ruth says?"

"That's right."

"Rebecca's friend, the crazy old bag lady?"

"Right again."

Daru frowned and waved a hand at her buried desk. "I've still got stacks of paperwork to get done if I want to get out into the field tomorrow and you're telling me to just leave it because some crazy old bag lady says I should?"

Roland shrugged. His shoulders felt like they

weighed a hundred pounds. Each. "Look, I only know what Mrs. Ruth told me. She says Rebecca needs us, both of us, and that's good enough for me."

"You believe her?"

"Yes."

"Why?"

Roland's eyes narrowed. He didn't need this. "Because once you've become intimately acquainted with Darkness," he snarled, "it gets real easy to distinguish the Light."

Meeting his gaze, Daru had to believe him. She stood and snatched up her purse. "Let's go," she said, and led the way to the elevators.

Rebecca stared at the orange juice in the pitcher. There'd been more the last time, she was sure of it. She picked up the empty can and frowned at the label. Most of the big words made no sense but she could read, "Fill with three cans cold water." She looked into the pitcher again. Maybe they meant another, bigger can? Maybe the can was bigger last time. She thought she'd gotten the same kind. The picture was the same.

The sudden loud banging on the door startled her and she narrowly missed dumping the entire problem in the sink.

Maybe it's Roland, she thought, hurrying across the apartment. *Maybe he's come back!* She fumbled with the chain, twisted the lock off—Evan had insisted she use both anytime he wasn't with her—and threw open the door.

"Oh," she said.

The large-blonde-lady-from-down-the-hall filled the open doorway. Her hair, usually lacquered to a bouffant neatness, was in wild disarray. Her face, beneath the streaked remnants of thick makeup, was puffy and pale. Under the lilac muu-muu, her body shivered and shook, free of the restraint of girdle and bra, and, with a kind of horrified fascination, Rebecca watched the tips of her massive breasts swaying back and forth.

"It's all your fault!" she shrieked, lurching forward.

Rebecca tried to close the door, but the large-blonde-lady-from-down-the-hall had her weight against it and it wouldn't budge. She stumbled back as the woman staggered another step or two into the room. "What's all my fault?" she pleaded, growing more frightened by the second. "I didn't do anything."

Heavy arms spread and in one hand a carving knife gleamed dully in a white-knuckled grip. "This used to be a decent building until you moved in!" She lunged, the knife swooping down through the air in a murderous arc.

Rebecca stumbled away, whimpering. The blow missed, but she felt the cold air of its passage. "I don't understand!" she wailed. She wanted to run, but the large-blonde-lady-from-down-the-hall was between her and the open door.

Stagger. Slash. "You should all be locked up!" Stagger. Slash. "Away from normal people!" Stagger. Slash. "Why should we have to look at you?" Stagger. "DISEASED!" Slash. "CRAZY!"

The knife missed, but a flailing hand slammed Rebecca up against the wall. Her fingers touched the edge of something hard and metal. The empty orange juice can. Snatching it up, she threw it as hard as she could. It clanged off the far wall, distracting the large-blonde-lady-from-down-the-hall just long enough for Rebecca to grab the pitcher of orange juice and throw it in her face.

She screamed and clawed at her eyes, dropping the knife.

In her corner, Rebecca trembled. She couldn't go past to get to the door. She just couldn't.

Eyes streaming, the woman stared at Rebecca and smiled. "It doesn't really count, killing you," she said with terrible clarity, "because you're different." Leaving the knife where it had fallen, she advanced.

Rebecca scuttled along the wall, throwing everything she touched. The toaster from the top of her tiny refrigerator. Plants from the windowsill. Her plush dragon from the shelf over the TV. The rolled up towel . . .

The towel smacked the large-blonde-lady-from-down-the-hall on the chin and unrolled. The black dagger fell out at her feet. Swollen lips drew back off the great white slabs of her teeth and she bent to pick it up.

It looked absurdly tiny in her huge hand and not at all dangerous.

And then Darkness began to spill out of the blade.

A strange silence fell as the two women watched the shadow cloud spin once around the hand that held the dagger. Then it settled and began to grow.

When it reached the dimpled flesh of her elbow, the large-blonde-lady-from-down-the-hall began to shriek. "Get it off me! GET IT OFF ME!" She tried to drop the dagger, but her fingers wouldn't respond. The shadow slid across her shoulder and began to cover her chest, gaining speed. The shrieks became a wordless wail and then cut off as the shadow surged up and over her face. Hazel eyes stared for an instant out of the Darkness, their expression a mixture of pain and puzzlement.

As the body hit the floor, the shadow and the dagger disappeared.

From the back seat of the hatchback came a chord so doom invoking that Daru, listening to it, almost ran the car off the road.

"What was that?" she demanded, narrowly missing a cursing cyclist.

Roland swiveled around in his seat. "The harp," he said shortly.

"Why . . ."

"I didn't."

"Then wha . . ."

His lips thinned. "I think we'd better hurry."

Tires squealing, Daru pulled up under the no parking sign in front of Rebecca's building and she and Roland tumbled out. They could hear the screams from where they stood.

With Patience slamming against his legs and the harp tucked under his arm, Roland dashed up the path after Daru.

"The door," she cried, pounding on the glass. "It's locked!"

"What?" Roland skidded to a halt. "Don't you have a key?"

"Why would I have a key?" Daru protested. "I don't live here!"

"Oh, fucking great! There has to be a back . . ." From the guitar case came the muffled sound of a piercingly high note. The harp twisted in his grip and echoed it. Loudly.

But not quite loudly enough. A couple of cracks appeared, but the door held.

"Oh, yeah?" Roland set Patience carefully to one side and rested the harp on his hip. "Plug your ears," he told Daru, took a deep breath, and plucked the thinnest string, throwing himself into the single note as he'd thrown himself into the music.

The glass door trembled and shattered.

The sound still cutting through his head, Roland scooped up Patience and followed Daru into the building. He slipped on the broken glass and slammed his injured shoulder painfully into the wall. The world went away for a second and when it returned, the hall seemed to be heaving up and down and he couldn't hear a thing over the echoes ricocheting about the inside of his skull. *I should've known I'd pay for that,* he thought, somehow managing to get to the stairs and up them.

Daru pushed through the crowd of tenants gathered in front of Rebecca's door and stepped into the room.

"Oh dear god."

The apartment looked as if a major battle had taken place. Broken plants and shattered pots were scattered about and a fine layer of dirt covered everything. The couch had been shoved almost to the opposite wall and a large, bloated body in a purple gown lay beside it, the position too boneless for anything living. Rebecca crouched in the corner by the radiator, knees drawn up to her chin, eyes squeezed tightly shut, rocking back and forth.

Daru stepped over a toaster, and knelt by the body on the floor. Her fingers sinking deep into the rolls of fat, she probed the neck for a pulse. Nothing. Daru noted it without surprise. Over the years she'd seen a number of corpses, but none had looked as *dead* as this woman. She wiped her hand on her thigh, for the skin had been both cold and clammy, then reached out and tugged the purple fabric down over dimpled legs. "Death has little enough dignity," she thought, knowing full well what the police opinion of her action would be. Tampering with the evidence was not highly thought of.

Then she went to Rebecca.

"Ah. Ah. Ah." With every panted breath, Rebecca gave a little cry; a confused, wounded sort of sound.

"Rebecca? Rebecca, it's me, Daru. Open your eyes, honey. Everything's okay now, I'm here."

Rebecca gave no indication that she'd heard. Her cries began to grow louder and her rocking more violent. Suddenly, she threw herself sideways and Daru barely caught her before she slammed her head into the radiator.

"Hey, kiddo, relax, it's over now. It's all over." Roland reinforced Daru's grip and between them they held Rebecca immobile.

She fought to get away and her cries changed to shrieks of, "No! No! No! No!"

"What about slapping her?" Roland suggested, shouting to make himself heard.

"Too risky. It might frighten her more. We've got to calm her down. Reach her somehow."

Roland frowned and tried to remember why this all seemed so familiar. A long, long time ago—*No*, he corrected, *less than a week. It just felt like forever.*— Rebecca had panicked. He stood, dragging Rebecca and Daru with him. "We've got to get her outside."

"What?"

"Outside. Look, don't argue, trust me. This has happened before."

Daru shot a horrified glance at the body.

"Not that!" Roland snapped, giving Rebecca a little shake. "This!"

With no better ideas, Daru helped Roland maneuver Rebecca's almost dead weight out of the apartment, through the crowd of open-mouthed onlookers, and down the stairs. By the time they reached the first floor, they could hear sirens approaching.

"At least one of those lamebrains had the sense to call the police," Daru grunted as they struggled to get Rebecca past the shards of glass. "Now what?"

"Here." Roland moved off the concrete path and onto the grass. He turned and shoved Rebecca up against the trunk of the tree.

Her cry cut off in mid-wail. She took one great shuddering breath, collapsed against the rough bark, and started to sob, sinking slowly to the ground.

Roland knelt and gathered her up in his arms, murmuring all the comforting nonsense he could think of.

The first of the police cars pulled up. And then the second.

Daru went to meet them. *This* she would handle.

"Sastri? Daru Sastri? Of Social Services?" PC Patton couldn't believe her luck. Of all the people to be at the scene. "I'd like to have a few words with you about a friend of yours. A Mr. Evan Tarin."

"Now?" Rumor around the Department had it that Daru's eyebrows could slay with a movement. She used that movement now.

PC Patton felt herself flush. Beside her, she heard Jack fidgeting. "No, not *now*," she muttered.

By the time Daru allowed them to bother Rebecca, the body had been taken away, witnesses' statements had been recorded, and the carving knife had been removed as evidence.

"Rebecca," PC Patton kept her voice pitched low, the voice she used for small children. "Rebecca, I need to ask you some questions." Sastri had told her something of Rebecca's background and she'd promised to go carefully. *"I'm not an ogre!" she'd snarled. Sastri had apologized.*

Rebecca lifted her head from Roland's chest and scrubbed at her face with the palm of her hand. "You're the police," she said, sniffing. "The police are our friends."

"That's right. The police *are* your friends." *So-called normal people should be this cooperative.* "And I need to ask you, what happened in your apartment tonight?"

Rebecca's mouth twisted and her eyes filled again but she answered the question reasonably calmly although all in one breath. "She knocked on the door and I answered and she said I should be locked up and she had a knife so I threw the juice at her and now I don't have any and she dropped the knife but she still tried to hurt me then the Darkness ate her."

"The Darkness ate her?"

"Uh-huh." She buried her face again.

PC Patton stood. "You heard?" she asked her partner.

PC Brooks nodded. "It matches what the witnesses said pretty exactly. Except that last bit. Darkness ate her. I wonder what that means."

"Beats me." PC Patton turned to Daru. "You know?"

"I have no idea," Daru told her truthfully. She didn't add that she intended to find out.

"Well Homicide says it looks like a massive coronary." PC Patton nodded her head in the direction of the three shirt-sleeved men standing on the sidewalk. Without a murder to attend to, they were catching up on personal business. "So I guess we don't need to worry about it. Are you going to stay with her tonight."

"If she doesn't, I will," Roland spoke up.

PC Patton nodded down at him. *You can trust a man with eyes like that,* she thought as they walked back to the patrol car. *He looks like he's been through hell and survived. Dresses strangely, though.*

"She didn't recognize me," Roland said, wonder in his voice.

Daru snorted. "You don't look the same."

Roland shrugged and lifted Rebecca to her feet. "Come on, kiddo. Let's go inside."

Rebecca hicupped. "Darkness ate her, Roland."

"I wonder what she means," Daru murmured.

Over Rebecca's head, Roland's eyes met hers.

"*I* wonder where Evan is," he said.

"We still didn't talk to her."

PC Patton yanked the steering wheel around and the patrol car squealed onto Dundas Street. "I know."

"I think we should tell the sergeant."

"Tell the sergeant what? We don't have anything to tell him."

"Yeah, but . . ."

"We'll talk to him after we talk to her."

"I don't know, Mary Margaret."

"I do." She outmaneuvered a streetcar, the sudden acceleration pushing them both back in their seats. "Just leave it, Jack."

This was the place. Anyone who could See could have spotted it, for a pall hung over the three-story Victorian house. Evan had been very careful in following the Dark Adept's trail to this lair, using only a tiny fraction of his power, barely enough to do the job, not quite enough to give him away. Therefore, it had taken many hours to do a job he could've done in seconds, but he hoped that meant the Darkness remained unaware that it was discovered.

He sent a probe into the house and found only one life—dark but human—and ample evidence that he had come to the end of the trail. Pushing his hair back off his face, he strode up the walk and rang the bell. He heard it echo throughout the house, then heard footsteps approaching.

"Yes, can I help you?" Gray hair, pale blue eyes, and startlingly black brows. An assured voice, carefully modulated but devoid of emotion, even of curiosity.

It took all of Evan's control to not flare up and turn this man as far to the Light as he now was to the Dark. Instead, although his hand trembled with the need to hold himself in check, he reached out, touched the man on the chest and returned him to what he had been before the Dark Adept had begun to warp and destroy. He left him, however, the memories of the Darkness and of what he had nearly become.

Eyes wide, the man gagged and ran from the door.

Evan entered and closed it quietly behind him. Silently, he followed the path of Darkness up the stairs and into what had once been a large and attractive bedroom. It wasn't quite as bad as the hotel, but then the Darkness had been here a shorter time.

Suddenly the balance shifted and he nearly cried out, so intense was the shock. He did cry out a moment later when, projected from her now distant apartment, Rebecca's terror hit him. Tears streaming down his face, he stood rooted to the spot while his heart tore slowly in two.

I am sorry, my Lady, but if I must sacrifice you to destroy the Darkness, I will.

The Dark Adept whistled as he turned up the path to the house, the very picture of a successful young executive. He'd enjoyed himself this evening; as he saw it, he couldn't lose. Whether Rebecca lived or died, the Light would be more than occupied with the need to stop his tool. And what a tool, a lifetime of delusions and imagined slights honed into a weapon. Her virginity was an added bonus, taken only because she treasured it.

He pushed open the door and started up the stairs.

"Master, above you!"

The warning came barely in time. The Dark Adept threw himself below the blaze of glory, the very proximity twisting him in pain. He snarled up into the face of the Light, and vanished.

Evan came slowly down the stairs, his aspect shining out around him.

"Twice now," he said to the man who trembled and whimpered and hid his eyes, "you have freely chosen the Darkness. A second chance is not given to many. You will not get another." He clasped his hands together and the sword of Light rose up from their joining.

The only illumination in Rebecca's apartment spilled in through the windows, the ambient glow of a city night. Rebecca had been given a mug of warm milk and put to bed. Daru lay stretched out on the couch, her braid trailing on the floor. Roland sat in one of the kitchen chairs, picking out a lullaby on Patience. When Evan appeared he stood up slowly, and more slowly still put down the guitar.

"Welcome back," he said.

Evan's face lit up. He'd truly thought he'd never see Roland again. "You also," he said, joy wound about the words.

Roland refused to return the smile. "Where the hell were you?" he demanded. "Rebecca needed you."

"I know." The joy was gone. "I felt her fear."

"And you didn't care?"

"I couldn't come."

"I suppose you couldn't come when I needed you either?" Roland pushed past him and flipped on the light. Evan glowed too much in the darkness, became too unreal, too hard to accuse.

Daru muttered a complaint and sat up, rubbing her eyes. She saw Evan, saw the expression on Roland's face, and decided greetings could wait.

"Well?" Roland grabbed Evan's shoulder and yanked him around. "Where were you when I was . . . I was . . ." His voice broke and he dashed away a tear. "When I needed you . . ."

Evan spread his hands, the silver bracelets chiming softly. "Not even to save you could I leave my fight against the Darkness. I'm sorry."

"Sorry doesn't cut it!"

"The strongest steel," Daru said quietly, "goes through the hottest fire."

"Yeah?" Roland whirled on her. "Well, no one ever asks the steel how it fucking feels about it, do they?" He snapped his head back to face Evan, knowing that Evan was right, knowing he couldn't expect to count for more than every other life threatened by Darkness, but also knowing it hurt anyway. "Then what about Rebecca?" he asked.

"I understand, Roland." Rebecca's voice came tentatively from the door to the bed alcove.

Roland's anger deflated. "So do I, kiddo," he sighed. He met Evan's eyes. "Really." But he didn't try to hide the hurt.

Evan nodded, acknowledging the pain for that was all he could do, and turned to face Rebecca. "I would have come to you if I was able," he told her.

She smiled. "I know."

"Well," Daru tucked her legs up, making room on the couch, "you'd better sit down, Evan, and we'll fill you in on what you missed. Unless you already know the details . . ."

"No, I don't." He came and sat down, pulling Rebecca with him and tucking her in the circle of his arm close against his heart. One by one, beginning with Roland waking up in the alley—by unspoken agreement, no one asked him what had gone before—they told him about the events of the night.

"And then when the police people left," Rebecca finished, "we came upstairs and Daru made me wa . . ." She frowned in puzzlement toward the window. The others turned.

Tom sat on the window sill looking inordinately pleased with himself, a squirming piece of Darkness in his mouth. He leaped down, padded across the silent room, and dropped his burden at Evan's feet.

A cage of light appeared around it.

"Thank you," Evan said gravely to the cat.

Tom yawned.

"What is it?" Daru asked, peering down at the shifting black blob.

"Just what it looks like. A piece of Darkness broken off and given a limited life.''

"It's alive?''

"Oh, yes. And there's no more of it here than in the hearts of many people, an amount easily overlooked. I imagine the Dark Adept used it as his eyes and ears.''

"What are we supposed to do with it?'' Roland wanted to know, amazed that his voice remained so calm. He couldn't decide whether he wanted to stomp the disgusting little thing into the floor or run screaming from the room.

The Light Adept stretched out his hand, the cage became a sphere and rose about four and a half feet from the floor. "We are going to question it.''

The blob contracted in on itself with a terrified squeak. "Don't know anything!'' it shrieked.

Evan continued as though the interruption hadn't occurred. "And it is going to tell us of its master's plans.'' The cage glowed brighter.

It would be easy to feel sorry for it, Daru thought, squinting, *if it wasn't so symbolic of the whole problem. Darkness takes over a little piece at a time and we all shrug it off until it's too late.*

The Dark Adept's messenger twisted and writhed in the cage, staying as far from the sides as it could.

Evan waited and the others waited with him.

"He opens the gate on Midsummer Night,'' it whined at last.

"We know that. Where?''

Roland strongly suspected that Evan could get a concrete sidewalk to confess using that tone.

"He didn't speak of it. Truly. Truly. Truly. The sacrifice must set the gate!''

"Sacrifice?''

The piece of Darkness shifted as far away as it could get from the menace in Evan's voice. "Blood prepares the way,'' it whimpered.

The cage contracted and the Darkness keened as it came in contact with the Light. In a few seconds, only a dazzling mote of glory remained, then it, too, disappeared.

"Is it dead?" Rebecca asked.

Evan shook his head. "You can't kill Darkness," he told her, "merely banish it for a while."

Behind Evan's back, Roland rolled his eyes at Daru. She shrugged. In her experience, when the world occasionally reduced itself to platitudes, the only response was to go on. "What sacrifice?" she asked.

"The gate must have an anchor in this reality," Evan explained bleakly. "Tomorrow night an innocent will die to provide it." His fingers curled into fists. He spun about and slammed them against the wall. "And I can't stop him until I know where!"

Rebecca reached up and caught his hands in hers. "You'll find him," she said with absolute certainty. Daru and Roland nodded in agreement, less in absolute certainty than in hope.

Evan pulled Rebecca into his arms and rested his cheek on the top of her head. "I pray you are right, Lady," he answered wearily.

"Is there anything more we can do tonight?" Daru asked.

Evan shook his head without lifting it.

"Well, then," she stood, hanging her purse strap over her shoulder, "I think we'd better pack it in. You want a ride home, Roland?"

"I thought I'd stay. If nobody minds."

Rebecca turned in Evan's embrace and smiled brightly. "I don't mind, Roland. You've already slept on the couch."

"Evan?"

He looked up. "It's good to have friends around you."

Daru headed for the door, rummaging for her car keys. "Rebecca, you have my home number. If anything, and I mean anything, else unusual happens tonight I want you to call me."

"Okay, Daru."

The door closed behind her and Evan pushed Rebecca toward the bed alcove. "Return to sleep, Lady," he told her. "I will join you in a moment."

Rebecca nodded and stifled a yawn. "Should I make Tom get off the bed?"

"No. He has earned his place tonight."

"Okay. Night, Roland."

"Good night, kiddo."

Alone with Evan, Roland didn't know what to say, where to start.

The Adept spoke first. "Are you all right? I mean, physically? The shadow realms are . . ."

"Yeah, they are." Roland couldn't keep the anger out of his voice. *And I think I've earned the right to be royally pissed off.* He could hear a song in the anger, but Evan was waiting patiently for an answer so he took a quick inventory, opened his mouth to list damages, and stopped dead. Nothing hurt. Frowning, he thought back; he could remember pain as he knelt beside Daru in Rebecca's apartment and the effort of getting the nearly hysterical girl down the stairs and over to the tree had almost had him in tears but after that . . . He could remember no pain after Rebecca had calmed, accepting the sanctuary of his arms. "I'm fine," he said at last, because he was, even if he didn't understand why.

Evan nodded. "Daru is right, you have strengthened."

Roland spread his hands. "I survived."

"You came to terms with yourself." The blue-gray eyes pleaded for understanding as he added, "I would have come for you if I could." His voice had roughened and Roland suddenly realized that the decision had hurt Evan almost as much as it had hurt him. Maybe more; Evan was supposed to be the white knight, riding to the rescue was his job.

"Hey, don't worry. I do understand." And he did. Finally. He clasped Evan's shoulder lightly and the Adept looked at him in surprise, sensing the new lack of restraint.

"You've come to terms with that as well?" he asked, a small smile beginning to form.

Roland returned it. "Yes," he said. "I have." He

spun Evan lightly about and pushed him toward the bed alcove. "We'll talk in the morning."

"Good night, Roland."

"Good night, Evan."

"That piece goes there."

"This piece goes here."

"Is that the last of the dirt?"

"I think so."

"Bread cooker goes back on the cold box."

"Plant is busted."

"So fix."

"Can't fix plant!"

Roland wasn't entirely certain he was awake. He could feel the couch beneath him and the sheet draped across his legs, but the high-pitched voices drifting in and out of his head seemed more like a dream. He supposed he could open his eyes and find out one way or another, but it just didn't seem worth the bother.

"Brush floor."

"Polish bread cooker."

"Polish everything."

"Sparkly clean now."

He had a vision of a horde of tiny people all dressed like Errol Flynn in *Robin Hood*. ". . . but the shoemaker and his wife never saw the little folk again," he muttered.

"What is Bard muttering about?"

"Bard stuff. Get back to work."

Chapter TWELVE

"Roland? That you?"

"Yeah, it's me, Uncle Tony." Roland went up the four stairs from the door to the landing and rounded the corner into the kitchen. "What are you doing home? Shop closed today?"

"Nah. Your aunt's back went out again last night and I'm driving her to the doctor's at eleven. You got yourself a new girlfriend? I notice you haven't been home for a couple of nights."

Green eyes and ebony hair and a lithely muscled body wrapped in satin. "No. It's just that job I told you about."

Tony frowned and closed the paperback he'd been reading, tapping the ends of blunt fingers on the cover. "You aren't mixed up in anything illegal, are you?"

"Nothing illegal, Uncle Tony." Roland felt his lips curl up into something that was not quite a grin as, unable to resist, he added, "You can definitely say I'm on the side of the Light with this one."

"Side of the light," Tony snorted. He peered at his nephew through narrowed eyes. "Still, it seems to be doing you good, settling you down some."

Roland sighed. He couldn't see it. The tiny mirror in his bathroom had shown him the same face it always had, albeit with a new nick from paying more attention to his profile than to his shaving. He was also getting a little tired of people telling him how much he'd matured, not having considered himself particularly childish before. "I'd better be going. I just dropped by to change clothes."

"Wait a minute." Tony tilted his chair back and plucked an envelope off the counter. "This came for you yesterday. Looks like it's from that singer friend of yours." He held it out.

"Looks like," Roland agreed, glancing at the Tulsa, Oklahoma postmark as he shoved the narrow envelope in the back pocket of his jeans. "Tell Aunt Sylvia I hope her back feels better."

"You coming home tonight?"

"I don't know."

"Well, try to get some sleep. You look like hell."

Roland paused halfway down the stairs and leaned back around the corner. "I thought you said it looked like this job was doing me some good?"

"What's inside a man has nothing to do with the amount of sleep he's getting."

A platitude worthy of Evan, Roland thought, and said, "You sound like you've been talking to a friend of mine." He waved and headed for the door.

"Sounds like you're getting smarter friends," Tony called after him.

Roland laughed and was still smiling as he got on the subway and headed back downtown.

"Daru must be still out in the city somewhere." Roland hung up the phone and shook his head. "I talked to her answering machine this time instead of her secretary, but the message was the same. She'll call when she gets in. It's nine seventeen. I'm beginning to think that woman does nothing but work."

"Her work is important," Evan pointed out. "She fights the Darkness constantly, and today she can only be more successful than we were."

The day had brought them no closer to finding out where the Dark Adept intended to open the gate. It had been long and frustrating and they'd accomplished absolutely nothing.

"Well, maybe we can guard the sacrifice." Roland picked up one of the pineapple muffins Rebecca had brought home from work and then put it back down. He didn't really feel hungry and his mind kept playing word association games. Sacrifice. Victim. Corpse.

"How?" Evan demanded, both hands working through his hair because they wouldn't lie idle at his sides. "He can choose from a city full of people. His only criteria is innocence." Both men turned to look at Rebecca, who puttered around the tiny kitchen making tea. "She is the only one I *know* I can protect," he added in a softer voice.

"So all we can do is wait?"

"Wait until he begins and hope I can stop him before he finishes. Yes."

"Will you be able to save . . ." Roland's voice trailed off at the look of pain in Evan's eyes.

"I will do all I can, but . . ." Evan's voice trailed off in turn.

"There must be something else we can do!" Roland

smashed his fist down into the couch. Under the window, the harp buzzed faintly, an echo of his emotion.

Rebecca set the teapot down on the table. "We could ask Mrs. Ruth if there was something else we could do. Mrs. Ruth knows everything."

Somehow, Roland thought, remembering the bag lady bending over him when he woke in the alley, *I don't doubt that in the least.* He threw up his hands. "I'm willing to give her a shot at it. It beats sitting around here waiting."

"Very well," Evan agreed, forcing his hands to still with a visible effort. "You will go and speak to Mrs. Ruth, a wisewoman at the very least, it seems, and I will remain here in case the Darkness moves before you receive an answer." *For here, in this security, I can best guard my Lady. He will not have her even if I succeed at nothing else.* "Will you stay with me, Lady?"

Rebecca looked from Roland to Evan and frowned. She feared that Mrs. Ruth might not talk to Roland if he came alone. Mrs. Ruth could be very rude. But Evan wanted her to stay, needed her to stay even though she didn't quite understand why. "If Roland remembers the way," she decided at last.

"I remember, kiddo." He picked up Patience, told the harp he'd be back—it replied with a mournful sort of a chirp but seemed willing to let him go—and headed for the door.

"Wait!" Rebecca grabbed up a muffin, ran across the room, and pushed it into his hands. "Sometimes Mrs. Ruth is nicer if you bring her things."

"Thanks, kiddo." He winked at her, nodded at Evan, and left. There was no need for either of them to tell him to be careful.

Roland took the streetcar to Spadina and the Spadina bus north to Bloor. Three young women got on, laughing and talking, brightening the bus with their presence, and a chubby baby in a carrier smiled beatifically at him. He watched a teenager with a green mohawk give his seat to an old Oriental lady buried under packages and decided the world might be worth

saving after all. Humming a quiet tune to the motion
of the swaying bus, even the knowledge that tonight
Darkness might take another life couldn't completely
destroy his mood. He'd been in enough Darkness
lately. He was going to enjoy this little bit of Light.

What with traffic tie-ups, he enjoyed it for longer
than he'd intended. He could've walked the distance
just about as fast. *Well, now we know why heroes never
take public transit,* he thought as he joined the surging
crowd at the back door. The day had been hot, the
people reflected this, and one of the anonymous bodies had a parcel of fresh fish. *Next time, I walk.* The
exhaust fumes on Bloor Street seemed like country
breezes by comparison.

Only one bundle buggy stood guard by the lilacs and
Roland began to get a bad feeling when he dropped to
his knees and stuck his head into the leafy tunnel. It
smelled too good under there for Mrs. Ruth to be
home.

She wasn't.

But in the middle of the cleared area where the bag
lady usually sat, a peeled stick had been stabbed into
the ground and skewered on the tip of it was a trailing
gray banner. Roland reached out and plucked it free.

"A Dominion receipt?" he wondered. Then he
turned it over.

Written on the back, the pale pencil marks barely
visible against the limp and grimy paper, were the
words: "Who raised the barriers?"

Who indeed? Roland thought, frowning. He wondered if Mrs. Ruth always left cryptic messages when
she went out or if she meant this specifically as an
answer to the question he'd come to ask.

What do we do now?

Who raised the barriers?

Not that it was much of an answer, he concluded.

Shoving the paper in his pocket, he crawled out from
under the lilacs and stood, ignoring the curious stares
from passersby. The traffic crept by on Bloor Street in
a steady stream, giving him no reason to assume Spadina had miraculously cleared up since he'd gotten off

the bus. He checked his watch and sighed. Ten thirty-
three. Why weren't all these people at home with their
families?

*I'll do a quick search through the neighborhood. She
can't have gone far, she left half her worldly posses-
sions behind.*

Daru kept up appearances until the elevator door
closed behind her, then she sagged against the graffiti
covered wall. She couldn't remember the last time
she'd looked forward to a hot shower with such desperation. Tossing back her braid, she checked the time.
Eleven seventeen. Well, that explained it. She
shouldn't have let Mrs. Singh talk her into that third
cup of coffee.

As the elevator ground its weary way down the remaining nine floors, she worked out the time it would
take to get from where she was in the Jane/Finch corridor to Rebecca's apartment in the heart of the city.
There, at least, the hour would work for her; at this
time on a Thursday the parkway should be empty.
Though I'll probably arrive too late to be of any help.
Sometimes it seemed like that was her entire life, following behind the Darkness, picking up the pieces,
and trying to patch them together again.

She didn't regret her decision though, continuing
with her job rather than throwing all her time in with
Evan. People depended on her. Not faceless masses of
humanity, but individual people. They needed her and
she had no intention of letting them down. The little
battles often win the war, as her Uncle Devadas always
said.

The elevator wheezed to a stop in the lobby and the
door slid open in a series of quivering jerks, burying
the legend, ''Tony loves Shelley, and Anna, and Ra-
jete, and Grace.''

''Busy boy, that Tony''; Daru noted as she strode
across the dimly lit lobby. Half the lights had been
smashed again and she made a mental note to call the
building manager first thing in the morning. She picked
the electrical tape off the lock, restoring its function,

and it closed behind her with a satisfying click. All unarrived "boyfriends" could now sleep in the dumpster.

She'd parked her car under the one remaining street-light in the visitor's parking, half expecting, as she always did, never to see it again. The underground garage was moderately more secure—provided the door worked at all—but Daru had been staying out of underground garages lately.

After pumping the gas a few times, just to let the ancient car know she meant business, Daru turned the key in the ignition. Nothing happened.

"Don't be ridiculous," she snapped, trying it again with identical results. "The battery can't be dead." She popped the hood and got out to investigate, more because she hated inaction than because she knew what she was looking for.

The battery wasn't dead. It was missing.

Daru's father, who clung as tightly as he could to a traditional Hindu lifestyle, had always worried that the manners and morals of the people she worked with would rub off on his daughter. The manners and mor-als hadn't, but over the years she'd picked up an ex-tensive vocabulary he would not have approved of. She worked through it now, beginning in English and con-tinuing into French, Hindu, Portuguese, Korean, and the three words she knew in Vietnamese—which were biologically inappropriate to an automobile but made her feel a lot better.

She checked her watch again. Eleven twenty-seven. Transit ran until midnight. Throwing her purse over her shoulder, she locked the car and headed for the bus stop. Just before she reached it, a bus roared by.

She remembered a few words she'd forgotten back by the car and also repeated a few of her favorites under her breath. Then, with ill-grace, she settled down to wait the scheduled twenty minutes between buses.

The night seemed to grow darker.

A week ago Daru would have blamed it on her imag-ination. Now, she knew better. A warm breeze rubbed against her. Riding on it came a sweet familiar smell. She scanned the area and spotted the red glow at the edge of the shadow cast by the apartment building. The darkness was too deep to penetrate, but as she watched the glow moved two feet to the right, intensified briefly, then moved two feet again.

Three of them.

She could remain perfectly still and assume they hadn't seen her. But that would be a fool's assumption for the skin on the back of her neck crawled in response to the menace in their stares.

She could try to make it back to her car, locking the doors and hoping the light in the parking lot would make them wary. Hoping futilely.

If she hadn't fixed the lobby lock, she could've gone back to Mrs. Singh and called for help. But she didn't regret it for if the lock kept her out, it also kept out the three who watched.

Remaining in the bus shelter only meant she would be easily cornered.

Her back straight, she started down the sidewalk toward the distant lights of a major intersection. She supposed she was frightened, deep down, but anger was the only emotion she was really aware of. Anger that this was even happening. Anger that she couldn't stand and fight.

"Hey, pretty momma."

The voice came from just behind her left shoulder. How had they gotten so close? She didn't waste time wondering. She began to run.

The glow of the streetlights didn't seem to reach the ground and Daru ran in a kind of twilight zone, the slapping of her leather soles against the concrete almost, but not quite, drowning out the sounds of pursuit. She used all her breath for running; in this neighborhood a scream would bring no response.

Suddenly, almost directly in front of her, a young man held out both hands, his smile a humorless flash of white. "Let's party," he purred.

Too close to swerve, she dropped her shoulder, slammed him out of the way, then saw another two approaching out of the darkness. "More?" she panted and risked a quick glance back along her path. The original three seemed to be gaining. Daru knew she should stay on the main road, but she didn't see how she could. Taking in great lungfuls of the humid air, she put on a fresh burst of speed and darted up the dark alley between two buildings. Maybe she could lose them in the maze of high rises.

Behind her, she heard nasty laughter. "Why run, baby? You know you'll enjoy it."

She followed twists and turns and did everything she could, but the pack stayed on her. And grew larger. Echoes bounced about between the buildings and she knew that sooner or later, tired and confused, she'd take a wrong alley and end up . . .

Chest heaving, she leaned against a concrete wall and tried to catch her breath, ears straining to pick immediate danger out of the sounds of pursuit. That way; coming up the alley from her right. And . . .

Oh, blessed god, from the left as well!

She straightened and prepared to take a few down with her.

"Yo. Bubba."

Savagely, she bit back the scream and whirled around. Behind her, a pudgy little bag lady pointed at a bulging bundle buggy.

"Get in."

"What?"

"In. To the buggy."

"Mrs. Ruth?"

"Unless you'd like to be on the wrong end of a gang-bang?"

Daru got into the buggy. Somehow. The rags and bits of odds and ends that strained at the wire sides were only a thin layer of camouflage, the center was empty. Knees up by her cheeks, arms tight about her shins, Daru peered up at the bag lady's scowl.

"Why . . ." she began.

"Quiet, bubba," Mrs. Ruth said conversationally and piled an armload of rags on Daru's head.

Footsteps ran by going left.

Footsteps ran by going right.

Protesting shrilly, the bundle buggy began to move.

"Where . . ." Daru called.

Mrs. Ruth patted the top of the rags firmly. "Quiet, bubba," she said again.

Rebecca yawned and buried her face in the crook of her arm, squirming into a more comfortable position on the couch.

"Lady." Evan's voice seemed to come from very far away. "Why don't you go to bed."

" 'Cause I'm going to help you," Rebecca explained, yawning again. She pushed herself up into a sitting position and turned to face Evan who stood at the window. "We're going to fight the Darkness together."

He smiled at her and crossed the room to smooth tangled curls away from her face. "When the Darkness," he began, but Rebecca's fingers closing tightly around his wrist cut off the words.

"Look!" She pointed with her free hand at the white mist seeping in through the open window.

Evan frowned but held his power in check. Whatever else it was, this was not a thing of the Darkness.

The mist swirled into a column and took on the vague shape of a tall man with long curly hair and a workman's large hands.

"Ivan?" Rebecca's eyes widened. "What are you doing here?"

Evan recognized him now. This was the spirit that had guided him from the Light.

"Ivan? Why won't you talk to me?"

"I don't think he can, Lady. He has wandered far from the place he is tied to and has no strength for speech."

"But why? He never leaves the campus. Never. I didn't think he could."

"Lady, is there a large open area near where this spirit makes his home?" He knew he was right before Rebecca answered for Ivan lost all definition and the column of mist began to spin.

"Uh-huh. There's a big round field right in . . . Is that the place, Evan? Is Darkness *there?*"

"Yes, Lady, I think so." He bent and kissed her quickly, his eyes alight with the anticipation of battle. He would arrive before the sacrifice began, before the balance shifted. This time, Darkness would not escape!

"Evan, I want to go, too!"

"I'm sorry, Lady, the way I must travel, you couldn't keep up."

"I could," Rebecca protested scrambling off the couch. "I've got running shoes!" she wailed to the suddenly empty apartment.

The small body lay half its length above the grass, held in the air by bands of Darkness. Behind it stood a man who smiled as he raised his left hand above his head. From that hand arced the curved blade of a black dagger.

Evan wasted no time on subtlety. He gathered his power and shot a mighty bolt of pure white Light directly at the chest of the standing man, using over half of the strength he had available in a desperate attempt to stop the knife from falling.

The concussion knocked him backward and slammed him to the ground, leaving him momentarily blinded by the sudden explosion of energy that followed his blow.

The Dark Adept began to laugh. "Pretty fool," he said.

His voice, Evan realized, came from about twenty feet left of . . . "Illusion," he cried bitterly and struggled to clear his sight.

"No. A mirror. It showed you what you wanted to see and reflected your power back at you. Most of *my* power went into it and, were you able, you would find me an easy target now. But the Light is *so* predictable. You reacted exactly as I had anticipated, although I'd hoped you might throw everything and destroy yourself. It would have saved me the bother of dealing with you when I finish here."

Evan gained his feet and took two swaying steps toward the voice, barely able to see a shadowy outline through the starbursts of light that still blurred his vision.

The bells of the city began to ring midnight.

"Too late," the Dark Adept mocked.

At that instant, Evan's sight cleared.

He saw a curly haired child of no more than four stretched out in the exact center of the King's College Circle common. He saw the black knife touch her throat. He saw the blood on the grass.

And the balance shifted.

Evan cried out in pain and dropped to his knees, clutching at himself in a desperate attempt to hold together. He felt the Darkness approach and forced himself back on his feet to face it.

"Pretty fool," the Dark Adept repeated, his features sharply delineated by the amount of power he now carried.

The black whip sliced skin off the arm Evan threw up to shield his face. And then from his side. It cut lines of pain into his legs and slashed his defenses into pieces.

"I have won," the Darkness purred.

The black bolt hit Evan squarely in the chest and would have thrown him entirely off the common and onto the pavement of the Circle had he not slammed into the trunk of a young oak and slid down it to the ground. He lay limply for as long as he dared, calling up what little power remained to him. He was so tired and it hurt so much. When he thought he could do it without screaming, he took hold of the tree and, using it as a staff, struggled to his feet. Beneath his hand he felt the strength of the living wood rising from its roots deep in the earth, then, to his astonishment, he felt that strength flow through the contact and into him. Although no breeze moved them, above his head and down the whole line of oaks edging that arc of the Circle, leaves rustled as the trees entered the battle on the side of the Light.

Compared to what the Darkness could call on, now

that the sacrifice had so drastically shifted the balance, it wasn't much, but Evan welcomed it with his whole heart. He lifted his head, brought his hands together and from them blazed the Light.

"You really haven't got the sense to know when you're beaten, have you?" asked the Dark Adept, sauntering closer. "If you give up now, you'll still exist tomorrow and can watch this world fa . . . Damn you!" For an instant, but only an instant, he stared, face twisted with pain, at the stump of his arm. Then it was whole again and he was raising it to point at Evan.

Evan parried the first blow. And the second. The third snapped his head around and the bar of Light flickered. The fourth lifted him off his feet and the bar of Light died.

"We've got *what* going on at King's College Circle?" PC Patton asked, making a puzzled face at her partner.

"Fireworks," the dispatcher replied, the weariness in her voice clearly audible over the radio. The flu bug had put the whole force on extended shifts. "Two reports of fireworks and one of some nut-case with a light-saber."

PC Brooks mouthed, *Luke Skywalker?* and PC Patton shrugged.

"We're on it," she sighed.

The Dark Adept spread his fingers and looked down through the spaces at Evan, curled up and panting on the grass. "You should have run when you had the chance," he said, and flew backward as something hard rammed into his stomach, knocking him flat on his back and leaving him gasping for breath.

"Don't you hurt him anymore!" Rebecca screamed, standing over Evan, chin thrust forward and hands balled into fists. When she'd reached the Circle and found that Evan had fallen, she'd moved without thinking, lowering her head and launching herself at the Dark Adept.

A physical attack was the last thing he'd expected and so it had worked. "Oh, I'll hurt him," he gasped, sitting up and drawing his fury around him like a cloak, "but first, first, I'll hurt you."

He raised his hand to strike and suddenly found himself wrapped in mist. Mist that thickened and thinned, inexplicably blocking his sight and therefore his blow. Snarling with rage, he struck at it instead.

"You can't hurt me," the mist whispered, and two pale eyes met his. "I'm already dead."

"Oh, you're wrong," the Darkness warned. "You're very wrong. But destruction now is too good for the lot of you." Brushing a bit of grass off his jeans, he smiled. "Live. Live and know you failed when tomorrow I open the gate and the barrier falls. Why should I give you an easy out when you'll torture yourselves more exquisitely than I ever could for the next twenty-four hours." He vanished, his laughter merging with the sound of distant sirens.

Rebecca dropped to her knees and lightly touched the tip of one finger to the purpling curve of Evan's cheek. "Evan," she sobbed, "he's gone. What do I do now?"

Evan heard her as though from a very long way away. He couldn't find the strength to reply. And he couldn't face her with his failure.

"Evan?" She plucked at the torn sleeve of his T-shirt. There were wounds and massive bruising all over his body, but instead of blood each cut seeped Light. "Evan? You've got to get up!"

"He can't, Lady."

At the sound of the deep, slow voice, Rebecca whirled around and flung herself up and into the arms of the troll. "Oh, Lan, I don't know what to do," she cried.

Lan merely held her and silently stroked her back.

"He's hurt. Bad."

"I know, Lady. I felt his pain."

She sniffed and wiped her eyes on the hem of her tank top. "The police are coming," she said, turning her head to better hear the sirens.

"They will take him from you."

"They will?"

"He is not of this world. Let me take him to safety, Lady, for I owe him a debt."

"Yes. Yes." Rebecca pushed herself away and stared up at the troll, tears still spilling down over her cheeks. "You take him 'cause I can't carry him and I'll tell the police what happened. Daru says if I'm in trouble I'm to go to the police." As the patrol car roared up in a blaze of sound and light she whirled and started across the common to meet it.

Lan has Evan. Don't tell them about Evan. Rebecca tried to keep that separate from all the other bits and pieces, but car doors slammed and people started shouting and she felt everything beginning to get all mixed up. She stumbled over a tiny body, nearly invisible in the night, and the Darkness that rose up around it almost knocked her to her knees. The sacrifice. A number of the bits and pieces got away and she cried out.

PC Patton strained to see what was going on in the dark center of the common. "These things look pretty," she muttered, jerking her head at one of the old-fashioned street lamps, "but they give bugger all in the way of light."

PC Brooks shifted his grip on his nightstick. "Someone's coming. Sounds . . ." He paused. It sounded like a wild animal in pain, but the moving shadow looked like a person. "It's a girl," he added a few seconds later as the runner came closer to the light.

"Not just any girl." PC Patton stepped forward and Rebecca ran right into her arms, forcing her back a step to keep them both from going down.

"He killed her. He killed her," she sobbed, clutching at the policewoman with a desperate grip. "She was just a little girl and he killed her. It's too late now and he got away!" The last word rose to a wail.

By the second sentence, PC Brooks had radioed for backup. By the third, he'd snapped the searchlight on and flooded the Circle and the common it contained with light. By the fourth he was halfway to the small, pale shape lying crumpled on the grass.

PC Patton forced Rebecca's fingers to loose their grip on her shoulders, a little surprised that it took all her strength to do it, and she cradled the distraught girl in her arms. "Who killed her?" she demanded, shouting over the sirens of two arriving cars. "Who?"

Rebecca buried her head away from the noise and the confusion and whimpered. She wanted to go home.

"Rebecca? Rebecca!"

"Roland?" Rebecca's head snapped up and she wrenched free of PC Patton's hold, throwing herself across the space between them and into Roland's arms in the same desperate motion.

Somehow, Roland managed to keep his feet. "Shh, kiddo, shh. I'm here." He shuffled them both sideways until they stood on the grass, his hands running in soothing patterns up and down Rebecca's back. There were a million questions he wanted to ask, but he only whispered comforting words into her curls and provided an anchor for her to catch hold of. Soon they were the only island of quiet amidst the lights and the sirens and the men and women who had no idea of the real horror they'd stumbled upon.

No one noticed that the common had acquired another oak tree. Or that when the confusion died down the tree was no longer there.

Later, at the station:

"I've been staying with her, because of," Roland waved a hand, "last night." *Believe me,* said his voice, truth and sincerity behind every word. He hoped he wasn't laying it on too thick. He wasn't sure what he could do without Patience or the harp.

Heads nodded.

"I thought she was safe at the apartment." Which he had. "She suggested I go to Bloor to get some things." Which was true. "The Dominion there is open twenty-four hours." Which it was. Although he wasn't at it. "I was on my way back when I heard the sirens and saw the lights, so I went to investigate." And considering the scenarios he'd dreamed up on that wild run, seeing the "fireworks" for what they were and knowing what the Darkness was capable of, what he'd found had been almost a relief. "I have no idea what she was doing there."

"I followed him," Rebecca whispered, the first coherent words she'd spoken since Roland had appeared back at the Circle. "I have running shoes and I followed him."

"Followed who?" asked a homicide detective gently.

Rebecca butted her head into Roland's side and stared at the detective with wide, uncomprehending eyes.

"Did you follow your friend?"

She reached for Roland's hand. Evan was hurt. "Yes."

But because they didn't know about Evan, the detectives asked the wrong questions. And because Rebecca answered only what they actually asked and they heard her answers through the label they'd placed on her, they never found out what really happened.

"Did you see who killed the little girl?"

"Yes."

"Did you see him actually do it?"

"No."

"But you did see him?"

"Yes."

"What did he look like?"

When she described the suspect they were already looking for, they were happy and they believed and they stopped asking questions.

"You'll remain available," they said as Rebecca carefully printed her name at the bottom of her statement.

Roland said they would.

Not until they were in the cab on the way back to Rebecca's apartment, did he get a chance to ask about Evan and even then he could barely force the question past the sudden fear in his throat. *He couldn't be* . . .

"He got hurt, Roland," Rebecca sniffed. "And Lan the troll took him away."

"Took him where, kiddo?"

"Somewhere safe."

Where would a troll think was safe, Roland wondered. And then the cab pulled up in front of Rebecca's building and he knew.

"Roland, look!" Rebecca sprang out of the cab.

"I'm looking, kiddo." He paid the cabbie and exited only slightly more slowly. It was something to look at. Strange and wonderful creatures perched in every available nook and cranny. The old chestnut sagged under the weight of the littles in its branches.

Every eye was on Rebecca as she ran through the still broken door and pounded up the stairs.

By the time Roland reached the apartment she was kneeling by the bed, her hands running lightly up the length of Evan's naked body.

"I don't remember," she lamented in a voice so lost it pulled tears from Roland's eyes. "I don't remember what to do."

He touched her gently on the shoulder, not understanding but offering what support he could. He forced himself not to look away from the bruising and the half healed wounds. *If he can stand the pain of bearing them, I'll just have to stand knowing that he does.*

Tom stared up at them both from his position on the other pillow, his expression, Roland thought, vaguely accusatory. *You let this happen,* said the set of his whiskers.

"Lady?"

"I'm here, Evan." Rebecca pressed her face against his shoulder.

The Adept sighed and seemed to relax into her touch. When she moved away, he opened his eyes. The stormy gray had become bleak and leaden.

"Roland," he acknowledged the other man weakly. "I failed."

Roland licked away a tear that had reached his mouth. "There's still tomorrow," he said, fighting to keep his voice steady.

Evan let his eyes fall closed. "There may *only* be tomorrow."

Chapter THIRTEEN

"Roland?"

"Mmmph." He dragged himself up through flannel layers of sleep and managed to focus on Rebecca's face. "Wazzup, kiddo?"

"I'm going to work now."

"Work?" Twisting his brain into some semblance of rationality, Roland tried to sit up with a distinct lack of success. A large, furry cement block lay squarely in the middle of his chest. "Are you quite comfortable?" he demanded.

Tom yawned.

"Wonderful." Roland gagged. "Catfood breath. Just what I need first thing in the morning." The light that spilled through the curtains had an unused look. He checked his watch. Five thirteen. "Or last thing at night," he added. It had been barely four hours since they'd left the police station.

Rebecca lifted Tom to the floor.

He stalked off, pointedly ignoring them both.

"Now then." Roland got himself up onto his elbows. "Why are you going to work?"

"Because." Rebecca looked confused. "It's what I do."

She wore jeans and an old turquoise bowling shirt. Her hair clustered in damp tangles around her face. She'd obviously been up for a while and she certainly looked wide awake, but Roland noticed the dark circles under her eyes and the way she was worrying at her full lower lip.

"You're tired, kiddo," he said, swinging his legs off the couch and sitting up. "You didn't get much sleep last night. Why don't you take the day off."

"No." She shook her head, her hair fanning out with the motion. A drop of water hit Roland on the chin. "I'm not sick. Daru says you never take the day off unless you're sick."

Roland knew better than to argue against a "Daru says" so he tried a different tack. "But Evan . . ."

Rebecca's face softened. "Evan is mostly okay now, but he isn't finished yet. When he wakes up, he'll be better."

"And he'll want you here."

"Yes." Her expression became serious again. "But he said before I have to keep doing what I do so the Darkness doesn't," she hesitated over the word but got it out, "disrupt ordinary things." She sighed. "I think this is how *I* fight the Darkness. Don't you see, Roland? It isn't big or important, but it's what I do."

"I do see, kiddo." He reached out and took one of her hands, squeezing it gently. "And you're right. It's the ordinary things that are important. That's what we're all trying to save in our way."

Rebecca smiled and Roland felt the warmth of it wrap around him like two strong arms. "I knew you'd understand," she said. She freed her hand and headed for the door. As she slid the chain lock open, she paused and glanced back.

"It's Friday," she told him, as though she'd just realized a happy coincidence. "On Friday, I make blueberry muffins." And then she was gone.

Roland shook his head, slid the chain back on, and padded to the bathroom. When he came out, he paused beside the bed and stared down at Evan. In the dim light of the bed alcove, the Adept's skin seemed to glow faintly. His head was tossed back, multihued hair spread over the pillows, and the long delicate line of his throat exposed. Most of the bruising had faded to ugly gray smudges and the wounds were fine white scars. One long-fingered hand lay curled on his stomach. The other had been flung out, as though even in his sleep he'd tried to hold Rebecca as she left, and now it dangled off the bed. Roland eased it up and carefully laid it on the sheet.

He looks more fragile now, almost healed, than he did last night so badly hurt. Strong emotions surged

through him and Roland tried to put a name to what
he felt. It wasn't desire, although he could—would—
no longer deny that warmth was there. It wasn't pity,
although he felt that, too. A week ago, he would've
seen where this was leading and gone no further. A
week ago, he'd been a different man. He moved quietly out of the bed alcove.

It must be love.

Not for Evan, not really. But for what Evan was. For
what Evan had agreed to do. To suffer and perhaps be
destroyed so that a world not his own would not fall
to the Darkness.

Suddenly too restless to sleep, he lifted Patience
from her case, sat down on a kitchen chair, and began
to play, letting his emotions form the music. He sang
the words as they came to him, allowing them to
choose their own patterns. When he finished, the pale
light of dawn had long since been replaced by the
strong sunlight of a summer's day and he'd found a
song that would be a part of every piece of music he'd
ever play from now on.

> *"And I never can again be free*
> *For you are in my music*
> *And the music's all of me."*

It was the tag from one of his old songs, one of the
ones that Rebecca had said, "wasn't quite." It suddenly had a new relevance.

He stood, stretched, and realized he'd had an audience, for the movement sent them scurrying for cover.
They moved too fast for him to really See, but hover-
ing just on the edge of his awareness was the sense
they approved. He checked his watch. Nine forty-five?
He'd been playing for four hours?

*Christ. Time sure flies when you're having . . . hav-
ing . . . whatever it was I was having.*

Four hours without changing position should have
left him all but crippled. He seemed fine. Except that
his mouth was so dry it stuck to itself. Fortunately,
because he just wasn't up to making tea, herbal or

otherwise, he remembered he'd shoved half a package of sugarless gum in his pocket yesterday. But which pocket? Two guitar picks, a crumpled Dominion receipt, sixty-two cents in change, and the letter from Tulsa later, he found it and popped a piece into his mouth with a sigh of relief. It'd hold him until he could get to a cup of coffee.

He shoved the picks, the receipt, and the coins back into his jeans and took a closer look at the letter. It was unusually thin, their monthly correspondence tended more to bulk rates, and he hoped nothing had gone wrong. A quick glance into the bed alcove showed that Evan still slept, so he sat down again and tore open the envelope.

There were two sheets of paper. Scrawled across the first was a single sentence: *I don't know why, but I thought you could use this.* The second was a handwritten sheet of music with the notes sprawling sloppily up and down the staff, testimony to the speed in which they were written. Melody, harmony, chords; all there. And the lyrics . . .

Roland propped the paper up against Rebecca's teapot and again reached for Patience. Humming softly to give himself a reference, he slowly worked his way through the chording. It wasn't difficult—D, Dm, C, Dm—but it took him a while to put it together with the eerie tune. Finally he nodded and started again from the beginning, this time actually singing the words.

"Wind's four quarters, air and fire
Earth and water, hear my desire
Grant my plea who stands alone—
Ma . . ."

"Roland!"

The intensity of the cry jerked Roland to his feet and spun him around.

"Roland, where did you get that song?" The Adept was framed in the door to the bed alcove, panting slightly, hair wild, eyes bright.

"A friend sent it," Roland offered, keeping his

voice soothing, wondering if this was some sort of crazy reaction to the damages of the night before. "Why?"

"Because it's the answer! Don't you see? It's a goddess invocation!"

"A *goddess* invocation?" Roland began to protest, then paused. He didn't read much, Uncle Tony was right about that, but he seemed to remember from a comparative mythology course he'd once taken that back even before all the Olympus stuff people had worshiped a goddess of some kind. Or a couple of goddesses. "Okay, a goddess invocation." It still sounded strange, but then things hadn't been exactly normal lately anyway.

Then another memory surfaced. Mrs. Ruth's voice came out of the past. *This world is sort of a buffer zone between the Light and the Dark. When life indigenous to the world developed, barriers were raised around it.*

Roland pulled the Dominion receipt out of his pocket and turned it over.

Who raised the barriers?

Silently, he handed it to Evan, willing to bet he now knew the answer.

"I am such an idiot!" the Adept exclaimed, first reading Mrs. Ruth's message, then scanning through the lyrics of the song. He hadn't sounded happier since he'd arrived. "We can stop him! As late as it is, we can stop him!" Laughing with relief, he grabbed Roland by the shoulders and swept him up into an enthusiastic embrace.

After a few seconds of mutual back pounding, they pulled apart.

"Now," Evan punctuated the word with a wave of his arm, "we . . ."

"Uh, Evan . . ." Roland swallowed heavily. The imprint of warm flesh still clinging to him made it difficult to think. "Before we do anything, could you please put some clothes on."

Evan looked down the length of his body, then up at Roland.

"Sorry," he said, and dashed into the alcove to dress.

Not bloody likely you're sorry. Roland gave a mental snort, but he couldn't stop a stupid grin from taking up residence on his face. *First we save the world. Then we think about . . . whatever.*

When Evan came back out, the clothes that had been all but destroyed during the battle were clean and new. His bracelets and earring sparkled with light and even the happy face button was back on his T-shirt.

"Now," he began again, wrapping the third belt around his hips and buckling it, "we kick ass."

"How?" Roland asked, tucking Patience back in her case. "We use this song to call up some goddess and she sends the Darkness back where it belongs?"

Evan got an apple out of the fridge and bit into it. "Essentially," he said, wiping a dribble of juice off his chin with the back of his hand.

Roland sat back on his heels. "There's got to be more to it than that."

"There is," Evan agreed cheerfully.

"What?"

"I don't know."

"What!"

"Look, Roland, there's millions of people in this city. One of them has to be a witch."

"I think you got hit too hard on the head last night. Witches, as in ugly old ladies with warts and broomsticks, are not real." A sudden memory of a child baked crispy and brown left his lips pressed white. "At least not here."

"No, not here," Evan agreed, his voice soothing away the terror. "But witches, as in pagans, worshipers of the old ways, are real. And all we have to do is find them. They'll know how to use the song."

Roland sighed and stood. "Okay," he said and found himself smiling. Evan's mood was catching. "How do we find them? The Yellow Pages?"

Evan spread his arms, his eyes shining. "Why not? It's a place to start."

There were no witches in the Yellow Pages. Or the

white pages. Nor was there anything listed under wicca or its derivatives.

"Wicca?" Roland asked.

"Mmmm." Evan flipped to the Churches listing. "It's the old word. Unity, Wesleyan, damn. Maybe under temples." A moment later, he slammed the book shut. "I don't believe that in a city this size there's no listing for temples."

"Try occult," Roland suggested.

There was nothing listed under occult.

"Parachute," Evan murmured. "Parade supplies, Paralegal agents, Parapsychologists, see Astrologers, Psychic Consultants, Etc. Well, it'll give us a jumping off point."

"You really think this is going to work?"

"Yes. It feels right." The way Evan said *right*, left no room for doubt.

There were twenty-five listings under Astrologers, Psychic Consultants, Etc., in the Toronto Yellow Pages, from simple listings of personal names, to tea rooms, to companies that sounded more like slick investment firms. Roland pulled Rebecca's phone out from under the couch and plugged it in. He listened. Unplugged it. And plugged it back in again.

"I'm not getting a dial tone." He tapped the receiver gently against the floor. "Still nothing."

Evan took the receiver and held it to his ear. After a second his lips drew back and his brows drew down.

Roland assumed the Adept heard something he hadn't. He was sure of it a moment later when Evan slammed the phone down with enough force to crack the plastic. "We're cut off?" he asked tentatively.

"Yes," Evan agreed, and the anger in the word made Roland flinch. "He dares to detail to me what the Darkness will do to this world. Beginning with those who have helped me."

Roland backed out from under the lilacs and stood, dusting his knees off. "As far as I can tell, she hasn't come back yet."

Evan drummed his fingers on his uppermost belt and

looked distressed. "I hope she hasn't been taken by Darkness."

"Yeah." Roland relived a few moments of what that meant. "So do I." He took a deep breath. "Well, do we go get our future told. See if it lasts beyond to-night?"

Two of the listings in the Yellow Pages were in the Bloor/Spadina area. The first was almost directly across the street from Mrs. Ruth's cubbyhole. *Madame Alaina,* said the warped and fading sign in the second floor window, *Stars, cards, palms. No appointment necessary.*

A smaller and even more faded sign had been tacked to the door leading up and over an ancient drugstore; at least Roland thought it was a drugstore. The light was so bad and the windows so dirty he couldn't be sure. The stairwell smelled strongly of cooked cab-bage.

"This is nuts," Roland whispered as they reached the first landing and Evan raised his hand to knock.

"Trust me," Evan told him.

Roland sighed.

Evan knocked.

A few minutes later the door opened and a girl of about fifteen looked them up and down. She ignored Roland, her dark eyes fastening on Evan as if he was a present she'd like to unwrap. Without adjusting the volume of the cassette player she wore on her belt, she pushed a pair of headphones down around her neck and smiled broadly. The hit song of a popular new wave band came tinnily through the tiny speakers.

"Can I do something for you?" she asked, looking hopeful.

"We need to see Madame Alaina?"

"Oh." Her opinion of them dropped a few obvious notches. "You're not cops, are you?"

"No."

"Well, grandma's not seeing anyone today."

"It's important."

"Yeah, it always is." She shrugged lycra-covered shoulders. "Doesn't make any difference. She won't even get out of bed. Says it's the end of the world. Try coming back tomorrow.''

"Tomorrow will be too late.''

Her eyes grew shiny at the pain in Evan's voice.

Yeah, well, teenage girls are susceptible to that sort of thing, Roland thought, ignoring the moisture that had risen in his own. "Uh, wait a minute . . .'' he added aloud.

She half looked at him, most of her attention still on the Adept.

He took a deep breath and continued, feeling like a fool. "You, uh, wouldn't know any, uh, witches, would you?''

This time she really looked at him and didn't like what she saw. "Witches, yeah, right.'' She took a fluid step back and closed the door firmly in their faces.

Roland turned to Evan and shrugged. "Guess not.''

Evan sighed.

They clattered down the stairs and back out onto the street.

"I would have liked to have spoken to the grandmother,'' Evan said quietly as they walked west toward the neighborhood's other astrologer. "She would have had wisdom to pass on.''

"What? Evan, the woman was in bed because she thinks the world is going to end.''

Evan's silence spoke louder than words.

Roland felt himself flush. "Oh. Yeah.''

Child Slaughtered at King's College Circle! The headline stopped them both and they stared for a moment at the paper. Smaller headlines read: *Man Deliberately Strikes Four With Car.* and *Arsonist Torches Nursing Home, Seventeen Die.*

"It begins,'' Evan said, and walked on.

In the distance, sirens wailed.

The second address led them to a small frame house, bright blue and looking out of place among all the exposed brick and open concept renovations. Knee-high weeds filled the lawn, but upon closer inspection they turned out to be wild meadow flowers. Roland recognized the daisies and black-eyed susans although the rest still looked like weeds.

Evan rang the bell and they could faintly hear the first two bars of Beethoven's "Ninth Symphony" chime through the interior.

The woman who answered the door wore her long salt-and-pepper hair parted in the middle. Her flowered dress dropped yards of fabric from a square cut yoke to just above her ankles. On her feet, Roland noticed, were a pair of hundred dollar German sandals.

"Yes?" she said, smiling at them.

"We're looking for Sky Mackensie."

"I'm Sky. But you're looking for something else."

"That's right." Roland had always thought Astrologers, Psychic Consultants, Etc., were a group of loons and charlatans and here was the second one proving him wrong.

"You're looking for a past-life justification for why you turned your backs on society to pursue a forbidden love in this existence." Behind her, crystals strung all along the hall split the sunlight into rainbows.

"Uh, no." *Score one for the loons and charlatans.*
"No?"

"No," Evan told her firmly. "We're looking for witches. Wiccans?"

She touched one hand to her breast. "I went to university with a witch. She kept filling the bathtub with herbs and dripping candle wax all over the porcelain. We didn't stay in touch, though. I married Owen and I think she joined a lesbian terrorist group. I'm sorry. That's probably not much help."

"Not much," Roland admitted. The cuckoo clock in the entry said it was almost twelve. They had to get moving. "But thanks for your time."

"And if you ever do need to find a past life . . ."

"We'll keep you in mind."

"I take VISA and Mastercard," she said and closed the door.

On the walk to Chinatown, Roland could feel Evan's

mood hardening with every step. "Penny for your thoughts?" he offered at last.

"In a city of this size, someone must be following the old ways," Evan sighed. "After last night, the balance has shifted too far for me to stop him on my own."

"You're not on your own," Roland reminded him.

"Yes. I know." He tossed his hair back off his face and two middle-aged women dressed all in black fell silent to watch him pass. "But we have so little time."

The Chinese astrologer was, like Madame Alaira, up a flight of stairs and over a shop. But where Madame Alaina had worked from a crowded apartment—the glimpse they'd had of it through the open door had shown that it overflowed with embroidered pillows, beaded curtains, and fringe—this looked more like a small doctor's office, white and clean. Two padded chairs faced a large desk, the walls were hung with calligraphy, and interesting smells came from the large jars that filled a floor to ceiling wall unit.

"Can I help you?" A young Oriental man came through an interior doorway which led to a small kitchen.

"We're looking for," Roland pulled the piece of paper out of his pocket and ran down the list, "John Chin."

"I am he."

"Oh."

The young man smiled. "I know," he said, "you thought I'd be older."

"Well . . ."

"It's all right. I'm used to it. I . . ." His voice trailed off and he stared past Roland.

Roland turned. Evan was just Evan as far as he could see, all traces of aspect tidily tucked away, but the astrologer looked as if he were having a vision.

John took a step forward and bowed. "How may I help you, Holy One?"

Maybe he is *having a vision.* Vision or no, John Chin was undeniably aware of what Evan was. Roland tried not to feel jealous and for the most part succeeded.

Evan took the question at face value. "We need to find those who know the old rituals of the goddess."

"The Wiccans?" John asked, never taking his eyes off Evan. "They run a store called Arcane Knowledge up on Dupont. I can get you the exact address."

"Please."

He went to his desk and pulled out a brown leather address book. "Fourteen forty-six Dupont," he said after a moment.

"Fourteen forty-six," Evan repeated. "Thank you."

They were at the door when John's call stopped them.

"Holy one. The signs . . ."

Evan sounded weary as he answered. "Are all true."

"How can I help?"

Roland shielded his eyes as Light filled the small room, bouncing back off the white walls, and illuminating the astrologer.

"You help by being what you are." Evan spoke from the center of the glory. "The Light gains its strength from such as you."

Out on the sidewalk, swept along by the crowd, Roland rubbed his watering eyes and asked, "How did he know what you are, I mean before your little display of pyrotechnics? And you know," he frowned, "I don't think he even squinted when you lit up."

"In a simpler age, he would have been a saint."

"A saint? Oh." Roland tried for a nonchalance he didn't feel. "Oh, is that all."

"That attitude," Evan said, the weariness back in his voice, "is what allowed the Darkness to enter in such strength."

"I'm . . . I'm sorry."

"No, I am." Evan reached out as though to wipe the stricken look from Roland's face. "I'm tired, and I spoke without thinking. Please, forgive me."

Roland shrugged. "You're tired," he agreed, flagging down a cab. "Come on, let's go save the world."

Arcane Knowledge was a small store tucked between a Bank of Nova Scotia and a fish and chip shop. The display window, no more than two feet wide, held maybe a dozen pieces of silver jewelry scattered across a square of black velvet. Roland braced himself for major weirdness, but the bats and black cats motif he half expected turned out to be a number of normal looking displays of books, crystals, candles, and jewelry. Behind the counter were bags of dried plants and the whole place smelled much like John Chin's office with a faint overlay of hot oil and halibut.

He followed Evan to the counter and rolled his eyes as the young woman behind it began to hyperventilate. He might not recognize a saint when he saw one, but he sure as hell recognized hormones.

"We're looking for the Wiccan Church," Evan told her. "Can you help us?"

"Help you?" she repeated. "Oh, yes."

Evan waited for a moment and Roland hid a smile. "The Wiccan Church?" Evan prodded at last.

"Oh." She straightened and attempted to pull herself together. "Yes. They, uh, own this store. I mean the church part doesn't, but the same people do."

Bingo! Roland thought. *We've got you now, you son of a bitch.* He saw the tension go out of Evan's shoulders and knew the Adept had feared this would be another dead end.

And then the clerk continued, "But they've all gone out of town for some sort of," her hands windmilled, "thing. That's why I'm here all alone."

"They've gone out of town," Evan repeated slowly.

"Yes. They've got property in the country and they're there for the weekend."

"I have to speak to their Priestess." He leaned forward and she gulped as his face stopped inches from hers. "It's vitally important."

"There's no way to contact them. They don't even have a phone."

"No . . ."

"They'll be back on Monday." Her voice came out in an overwhelmed squeak.

"There may not be a world for them to come back to on Monday!" His voice had risen and the young woman cringed, her hands over her ears, her eyes squeezed shut against the vision he presented.

Although his own heart had turned to lead in his chest—there would be no help from the Goddess, any goddess, once again they faced the Darkness alone—Roland touched Evan lightly on the back. The muscles felt as if they'd been sculpted of stone.

"Hey," he said softly. "You're scaring her."

And then he was glad his heart was lead, for the look on Evan's face would have broken it.

"Roland, I . . ."

"I know." Not caring who saw, his fingers traced the curve of Evan's cheek. "I was counting on it, too. Come on." He jerked his head toward the door. "Let's go home and see if we can find another way."

Bit by bit the bleakness faded. Evan nodded. "Yes. There's always another way." His chin came up. "Thank you."

"Hey, things are never as black and white as you think they are." Evan's lips twitched and Roland felt himself flush. "Uh, forget I said that."

"No." Evan caught up the hand that still rested on his shoulder. "I will remember it for it is true and it is something that both the Dark and the Light too often forget." He leaned back over the counter and turned the brilliance of his smile on the cowering clerk. "Forgive me, I didn't mean to frighten you."

She rose hesitantly and tried a nervous smile of her own. "It's okay." And she really thought it was until she noticed, a few moments after the door closed behind the two young men, that every crystal in the store was glowing with a soft white light.

"All right, let's see what we've got." They walked up the path to Rebecca's building, having ridden the bus back in silence. It was past two. In less than ten hours, the world would end. Roland flicked the fingers of his free hand up to mark points. "We've got an Adept of the Light . . ."

"A slightly battered Adept of the Light," Evan corrected as they stepped through the still empty doorframe.

"If you like," Roland agreed. "A street musician everyone keeps calling a Bard although," his tone stopped Evan's protest, "I have it on good authority I'm not there yet. A magical harp said Bard can't play." In her case, Patience sounded a C, high and sharp. "A guitar that he can. A goddess invocation we don't know how to use. A social worker we can't find, and Rebecca. Hell," he stood aside while Evan dealt with the lock on Rebecca's apartment door, "with all that arrayed against him, the Darkness should be shaking in his shoes."

A small coffee colored shape scurried down the curtains and out the window as they entered.

Roland froze, but Evan didn't appear disturbed so he relaxed. On the other hand, Evan did appear to be communing with something Roland couldn't see. "Are you all right?" he asked nervously, wondering if he had time to get Patience free and if it would do him any good if he did.

"I'm an idiot!" Evan exclaimed for the second time that day. "I am an idiot."

Roland closed the door and slipped the chain on. "Why?" he asked.

"We know how to call the Goddess."

"We do?"

"Yes!" Evan threw out his arms and his bracelets emphasized the word like a silver percussion section. "The *song* is the invocation."

"Yeah. You said that this morning." Roland set Patience down and sat gingerly on the edge of the couch, keeping half his attention on the Adept and the other half on the window; just in case their visitor came back. "You also said this morning that we needed a witch. What's changed?"

"We needed the wiccans as a focus, needed their

rituals as a focus to guide the invocation to the goddess.''

"I repeat. What's changed?"

"Roland," Evan threw himself down on his knees and caught up both the other man's hands in his, "you will sing the song. Rebecca will focus it."

"Rebecca." Roland was very proud of the way his mind kept working. Given the circumstances.

"Rebecca. The gray folk watch over her. She has a simplicity, a clarity that is rare even amongst the Light. In the arms of the earth, she calms. Think of it, Roland, how it all fits together."

Roland thought of it. "They used to say that the simple people, people like Rebecca, had been touched by God, that they were his special children."

Evan's eyes were almost as silver as his jewelry. "Who raised the barriers?" he asked. "She watches over the world and She watches over Rebecca."

"Are you sure this will work?"

"No." Evan shook his head, his hair hissing across his shoulders like silk. "I'm not sure. But I have hope again and that *is* one of the biggest differences between the Dark and Light."

"Just hope?"

"Wars have been won and lost on it."

Twisting one arm in Evan's grasp, Roland looked at his watch. "Two forty-eight. She'll be starting home soon." Evan's fingers lit fires where they rested along his wrists. "What, uh, what shall we do in the meantime?"

Evan's grin was pure mischief as he answered. "I think you'd better rehearse your part a time or two."

Roland sighed, freed one hand and pulled the now much folded piece of music from his back pocket. "You know," he said, "you don't make it easy for people?"

"Rebecca!"

Rebecca paused, her hand on the kitchen door fairly trembling with her need to get home.

"Did you put your tins away neatly?"

"Yes, Lena."

"Have you got your uniform to wash?"

Rebecca chewed on her lip but otherwise remained frozen in the motion of leaving. Her food services uniform was folded, not as neatly as on other Fridays, in the bottom of her red bag. "Yes, Lena."

"Do you have your muffins for the weekend?"

"Yes, Lena." The muffins had been shoved on top of her soiled uniform. She waited impatiently for the next line of the litany.

"Now don't forget to eat while you're home."

Rebecca nodded for the motion was a part of it, too. "I'll remember, Lena." One more.

It never came.

Rebecca waited, unable to move until the last words were spoken. Unable to turn around to see what had stopped them. She could hear a strange gasping sound, a scuffling against the linoleum, and then a voice she knew, although she couldn't remember from where.

"You had been warned, Mrs. Pementel, that the smoking would probably kill you." The Dark Adept looked down at the cafeteria supervisor who writhed at his feet, one hand clutching at her chest, the other scrabbling against the floor. "A proportionately high number of women over fifty who smoke are taken by heart disease. What's that?" He bent slightly forward as the purpling lips formed silent words. "Help you? Oh, but I have helped you. Without my assistance you would surely have lived for another twenty-four hours." He smiled pleasantly. "And you wouldn't like the world in another twenty-four hours."

He watched the last moments of pain and he captured the last breath, drawing it into himself with deep enjoyment. Only then did he turn to study Rebecca.

He still hunted the other woman. She would fall in time, for there were a great many men who ran as hounds in this hunt. When he felt her taken, he would be there to observe the end. As for the other who assisted the Light, the so-called Bard had experienced the shadow lands and the Dark Adept anticipated showing him true Darkness. But this one . . .

"I don't know what came to your aid the last time,"
he said to Rebecca's back, noting with pleasure how
the muscles twitched visibly in their desire to move,
"but it can't help you now. You built this trap yourself. I merely used it." Stepping forward, he cupped
the curve of her waist in both hands.

Rebecca trembled but could no more twist out of his
grasp than she could continue out the door. The last
words had to be spoken.

"And the beauty of it is," he murmured into her
hair, his breath very hot on her scalp, "this afternoon's work has not affected the balance in any way.
I simply helped your late friend down a path she was
already well along and your problem is a natural con-
sequence of that. But perhaps you still don't understand." His hands glided upward, briefly caressed the
heavy swell of breasts, and came to rest about her
throat, the thumbs pressing painfully into the soft flesh
under her jaw.

"The Light will not be able to save you," he purred.
"For he will not know you are caught until it is too
late and by then he will be dealing with me. And he
will lose. And when I am finished destroying him, I
will come and claim you. I will enjoy that. You
won't."

And very suddenly she was alone with the pain his
hands and his words had left. Desperately, she grabbed
onto the quiet place the way Mrs. Ruth had taught her
to and while silent tears streamed down her face, she
fought the bindings that held her with a single-minded
determination. Evan needed her help. She had to get
to Evan.

At Evan's touch, Roland stopped muttering lyrics
and frowned up at the Adept. "I haven't much time to
learn this," he began and shut up as he caught sight
of Evan's face. "What is it?" he whispered, glancing
around nervously.

"Listen."

So he listened. Within the apartment: the rhythmic
rasp of Tom's tongue across a paw, the hum of the

refrigerator, the steady dripping of the bathtub tap. Outside the apartment: traffic, voices, and bells.

Bells? At least two sets of bells seemed to be clanging wildly, pealing out a discordant clamor. Roland looked at his watch. Three twenty-one.

"Rebecca's in danger," Evan said. And vanished.

"Mrs. Pementel? Mrs. Pementel!" The cafeteria door swung open and the accountant came face to face with Rebecca who was still standing with one arm outstretched to push open the door. "Oh," he said with a forced and uncomfortable smile, "it's you." When it became obvious she wasn't going to move, he inched around her, wondering nervously what all the eye rolling was about. He didn't care how good a worker she was, the girl should be in a home. "Have you seen Mrs. Pemen . . ." The question suddenly became redundant.

"Oh my God!"

Dropping to his knees beside the body, he groped frantically for a pulse. There didn't seem to be one although he wasn't entirely certain he was prodding the right places. *What if she's dead? Ohmygod! I've touched her!* He scrambled to his feet, took two steps away, then scurried back. *Help. I should go for help. But if she isn't dead, I should do something. Do what? Seconds count.* He cried out as a flash of brilliant light threatened to blind him.

"Rebecca? Lady? Are you all right?"

Rebecca? That was the retarded girl's name. The accountant scrubbed at his eyes until he could see a tall young man with a mane of strangely colored hair bending over the girl by the door. "Here now," he sputtered. "What? How?"

Evan ignored him. He could See the binding that held Rebecca in place, but he had no idea how to break it and Rebecca's voice was as bound as her body. He could feel the foul taint that said his enemy had been here, but Darkness hadn't set these bounds.

"You there. I need help!"

Reluctantly, Evan responded. He couldn't not re-

spond, not and remain as he was. He turned. He Saw
Rebecca's bindings stretching back to the body on the
floor.

"Who was this woman?" he asked, pushing past the
flabbergasted accountant who sputtered in indignation. The bindings looped around her, yes, but they
originated with Rebecca. *Oh, Lady, what have you
done to yourself?*

"I said, I need help!" The accountant waved an
ink-stained hand toward the floor, not knowing why
he expected this punky young man to be able to do
anything but sure that if he only exerted himself everything would be all right again. "She needs help!"

Evan had no time for finesse and it was Evantarin,
Adept of the Light, who raised his head and allowed
the mortal to meet his eyes. "She is beyond my help,"
he said.

*Ohmygod! A corpse. I'm in the room with a corpse!
I'm . . .* The thought became lost in shifting storms of
blue-gray and in a voice the seemed to echo inside his
head.

"I must help the living now. Who was this woman?"

"Pementel. Lena Pementel, the cafeteria supervisor." Incipient panic had been calmed; or delayed, for
he could still feel it, buried deep and straining to get
free.

"Did you know her well?"

"No. Yes. I don't know. We saw each other every
Friday to do the budget for the next week."

"Every Friday?" Evan stepped forward.

The accountant watched his reflection grow in the
strange gray eyes and squeaked, "Yes. She came up
to my office . . ."

"Your office? You never saw the ritual?"

"What ritual?"

Evan took a deep breath and forced his voice away
from Command. For the first time in his existence he
envied the Darkness' ability to cut to the heart and not
worry about the damage done. "The ritual that frees
my Lady," he said under tight control. Rebecca was

helpless, the Darkness could return at any time, and he wasn't strong enough to protect her.

"Well, uh, last week I was ready early and I, I came down here."

"And?"

"And they, uh, talked to each other."

"What did they say?"

"I don't remember." He spit the words out in a rush and ducked. When nothing happened he dared to glance up. What he saw made him squeeze his eyes shut again.

"Then you must relive the time . . ."

He sat in the office and waited while the cafeteria workers filed out calling their good-byes and exchanging sly looks about Lena's visitor. The retarded girl, Rebecca, was the last to leave. She'd barely reached the door when Lena called out to her.

"Rebecca!"

The girl paused, one hand on the door, and he wondered how long this was going to take. He'd figured coming down to the cafeteria would speed things up and he could get home early for a change.

"Did you put your tins away neatly?"

"Yes, Lena."

A pity she was retarded, he thought, she was actually kind of attractive in a lush sort of way.

"Have you got your uniform to wash?"

"Yes, Lena."

In fact, that combination of lushness and innocence was pretty erotic.

"Do you have your muffins for the weekend?"

"Yes, Lena."

Good god, it went on forever. No wonder it took Mrs. Pementel so long to reach his office every Friday.

"Don't forget to eat while you're home."

The girl nodded, her head bobbing up and down like one of those dogs you saw on dashboards of sixties cars. He snorted quietly to himself. The dogs probably had more in the way of brains.

"I'll remember, Lena."

"I'll see you Monday, puss."

"See you Monday, Lena."

The accountant started. He'd heard a voice. He knew he had. And the cafeteria door swung back and forth on its hinges. But there was no one down here. He'd come down to get Mrs. Pementel because it was after three and she still hadn't shown up in his office. And the cafeteria was empty. Of course, it was empty. There were no retarded muffin makers stuck in the doorway. No eyes that looked into his soul and found it wanting. That would be ridiculous. He was working too hard.

He took a step forward and the toe of his recently polished brown oxfords kicked into a yielding obstacle. He looked down.

"Mrs. Pementel? Mrs. Pementel!" Dropping to his knees beside the body, he groped for a pulse. "Oh my God! She's dead!"

Chapter FOURTEEN

The patrol car moved slowly around King's College Circle, its searchlight sweeping across the common. The police barricades had been taken down late in the afternoon, but the cars had been instructed to swing around the site when they could.

"You think he'll return to the scene of the crime?" PC Brooks asked as his partner stared fixedly out the window along the beam of the searchlight. He could see only grass and trees and maybe a faint chalk mark gleaming white in the sudden glare. He wondered what she saw.

"I hope he does." PC Patton ground the words out, her gaze locked on the center of the common. "I hope he comes back. I hope we're here. And I hope the son-of-a-bitch gives me the chance to blow him off the face of the earth." She saw a child's body lying discarded on the grass, although she knew the actual body had long since been taken away, and she knew she'd continue to see it until the child's murder was avenged.

They completed the circuit and PC Brooks switched off the light. On cue, the radio hissed and the dispatcher's emotionless tones called out: "Officer needs assistance, Bloor and Yonge, northeast corner. Repeat, officer needs assistance, Bloor and Yonge, northeast corner."

PC Patton thumbed the switch. "5234 responding." She settled back as Jack hit the siren and the gas simultaneously, one hand on her nightstick, her mouth a thin line. Right now, busting a few heads seemed a fine idea.

Behind them, Darkness thickened in the Circle.

Rebecca pulled her big orange sweater out of the closet and put it on. She wasn't cold and didn't expect to be cold. She wanted it for comfort. She'd bought it herself, no one had helped her and, although she couldn't have explained what she meant, it stood for independence. Strength. Besides, it was bright and Daru always said to wear bright colors at night so the cars could see you—the first Rebecca had heard that cars *could* see.

"Are you all right, Lady?"

She leaned back against Evan's chest, rubbing her head against his shoulder. "I'm a little bit scared, Evan. I still don't think I understand what you want me to do."

"I want you to listen to Roland sing. Really listen. And I want you to just be yourself."

"Is that all?"

"Yes. That's all."

"I think I can do that." She sighed. "I'm still a little bit scared, Evan."

"So am I, Lady." He laid his cheek against her curls and his arms tightened protectively around her. "So am I." He remembered the promise he'd made the troll and was ashamed he'd had to be asked. If they won, if they both still lived, and if she agreed, he would take her with him when he returned to the Light.

There, her innocence would be protected, her clarity would remain undimmed. He had realized, when he'd seen her trapped and touched by Darkness, just how much this meant to him. Such a life should be cherished and this world would not do it.

But first they had to win. And they both had to survive.

"It's past eleven," Roland called from the main room. "We'd better get moving."

Rebecca twisted in Evan's arms and hugged him hard, then took his hand and led him out of the alcove. "Did you call Daru while I was asleep, Roland?"

"I called, kiddo." He wouldn't meet her eyes. "She wasn't at the office all day. I left a message there and on her machine at home."

Rebecca frowned. "I wonder where she is."

Roland looked down at his guitar case, up at the ceiling, out the window, and over at Evan. Evan nodded.

"We fear the Darkness has taken her, Lady."

"Taken Daru?"

"Yes."

"Did *you* look?" she asked Evan.

He shook his head. "I don't have the power to spare," he explained sadly.

"Then you don't know the Darkness has her."

"She hasn't called, kiddo. Not us and not her office."

"That's okay." Rebecca pulled the sweater tighter around her shoulders. "Daru works very hard and is very busy. She can't always phone for every little thing."

Roland wasn't going to be the one to try to convince her. Although he personally believed that they'd never see Daru again, what would it hurt if Rebecca believed differently? *And after tonight it may be a moot point.*

From its place beneath the window, the harp sighed, rather as if a breeze had touched each string in sequence.

"I think it wants to go with us," Rebecca said.

"Not an it, kiddo, a she," Roland corrected, stroking a polished wooden curve. "And when this is over, I promise I'll learn to play her." *Provided I have fingers left to play with.*

The harp sighed again.

Rebecca echoed it. "I wish I'd heard your song," she sighed.

"You needed to sleep, Lady."

"I know."

"And you will hear the song in time."

"I know." They left the apartment and she carefully locked the door. "It gave me the neatest dreams though."

Behind her back Roland and Evan exchanged a speaking glance.

"What kind of dreams?" Roland asked.

"Like someone was telling me all kinds of things that I'd forgot. And it wasn't Roland telling me either, it was someone else though even in the dreams I knew it was Roland singing."

"What kinds of things did they tell you?"

"I don't know." She shook her head. "When I woke up, I forgot again. Maybe when I really hear you sing . . ."

"Maybe," Roland agreed.

A half a block from the apartment building they noticed they'd picked up a fourth companion.

"Rebecca. That damned cat is following us."

"No, he isn't."

Roland looked down at Tom and up at Rebecca. "Yes, he is. He's right here!"

"But he isn't following us," Rebecca pointed out. "He's walking beside us."

"I don't care where he's walking, tell him to go home."

"Cats go where they want to, Roland," Rebecca said. She thought everyone knew that.

Evan squatted down and Tom butted up against his legs. "It is a great battle we go to, small furred one, and while we do not doubt your courage, neither do we wish you to be hurt."

Tom placed one paw on the Adept's knee, his claws fully extended and just barely pricking into the denim.

Evan smiled. "You are a mighty warrior," he agreed, long fingers digging into the cat's thick ruff. "If you truly wish to join us, you may."

"I'll carry him across busy intersections," Rebecca offered.

Just great, Roland thought, as they continued walking. *As if we didn't have enough on our plate.* Although well aware that Tom had led him back to the real world, Roland's opinion of the cat, of cats in general, had not significantly changed. And as far as he could tell, Tom's opinion of him had not changed significantly either. The parallel scratches he'd acquired on his wrist that afternoon testified to that. He caught sight of their reflections in the glass doors of Maple Leaf Gardens and shook his head. *I wonder what the rest of the world thinks of this.*

The rest of the world didn't seem to notice. For eleven thirty on a Friday night in a major city, there was nothing strange enough about them to attract attention.

. . . except for one little boy, up long past his bedtime, who watched them go by with his mouth open and continued to stare after them until his mother shook him and told him to behave.

By the time they reached Yonge Street, with its traffic and its crowds, Roland felt as if they were walking through a movie. Everything seemed unreal, removed just a little bit from where they were; lights were too bright, shadows too sharp, sound too brittle, and the warm air slid over his skin without making contact. He had the impression that nothing existed until he looked at it, and it stopped existing when he turned his eyes away. The others felt it, too, for Evan held his hands away from his sides and he continuously swept the area around them with his gaze. Rebecca chewed on a lock of hair and watched only Evan, leaving her feet to find their own way without guidance. Even Tom lay quietly in Rebecca's arms, ears down, the tip of his tail snapping back and forth against her hip.

The light at the corner was red, and it stayed red for what seemed like a very long time. The crowd that stood with them shifted restlessly, constantly in motion, and it suddenly struck Roland just what kind of movie they were in. *It's a western. Just before the stampede, and when it starts you know the hero's best friend is going to get knocked off his horse and killed.*

"There's a storm coming," Rebecca said with absolute certainty.

"Yes," Evan agreed, "there is."

Roland wondered briefly if they were talking about the same thing and then decided it didn't matter. Sweat dribbled down his sides and his T-shirt stuck to the center of his back. He shifted his damp grip on the plastic handle of the guitar case and began reviewing the words to the invocation. It beat thinking.

The light changed. Finally. The traffic on College surged forward. A black Corvette speeding south on Yonge tried to beat the odds.

With a scream of tires and a slam of metal meeting metal, a brown Mazda plowed into the Corvette's side, throwing it into the path of an orange taxi. For the first few seconds, only the cars screamed. Then they came to rest in a twisted smoking heap and the people began to yell.

Evan threw himself forward and Roland yanked him back.

"It's eleven thirty-eight, Evan! We haven't got time to help!"

The taxi driver sprawled half out of the window. The blood dripping from his mouth pooled on the road below.

"Let me go!" Evan twisted free. "You don't understand. I *have* to help them!"

"I do understand." Roland tried not to see. Tried not to hear. Tried not to feel. "But you can help them best by defeating the Darkness!"

Evan took a step toward the wreck.

"Evan," Rebecca's quiet voice cut through the

noise, through the hysteria. Both men turned to look
at her. If he'd thought about it at all, Roland would
have assumed she'd be panicking, but to his surprise
she looked almost serene, an island of calm in the
midst of chaos. "If you stop here, Roland and I will
go on without you."

Evan jerked as though she'd hit him. He gave one
anguished cry and plunged through the gathering mob,
running toward the Circle.

Tom flowed out of Rebecca's arms and followed,
quickly disappearing amid the forest of legs and feet.

"Tom!" Roland called. "You stupid . . ."

Rebecca took his hand. Hers was cool and dry. His
was trembling.

"Tom can take care of himself," she said. "Come
on."

They began to run, pushing past the ghouls that always gathered to warm themselves around disaster and
pounding down College Street in pursuit of the Adept.

Not until King's College Road did they catch up with
Evan. He stood, staring up into the Circle, face bleak,
hands shoved into the pockets of his jeans.

He looks so absurdly young, Roland thought as he
let go of Rebecca's hand and stood gasping for breath.
The air didn't seem to have any substance in it and
running had burned a copper taste into the back of his
throat. He couldn't see Tom anywhere although a rustling in the bushes up ahead could've been the cat.

Slowly, Evan turned to face them, his eyelashes
clumped together in damp spikes, and his cheeks wet.
Rebecca moaned a quiet protest and threw herself into
his arms. Roland, jealous of the comfort being given,
being received, and hating himself for it, concentrated
on breathing. Then a strong arm pulled him into the
embrace and, for the moment it lasted, everything was
all right.

When they pulled apart, hands lingering for a final
touch, they *all* stood and stared up into the Circle.
The streetlights grew more sallow, more wan, the
closer they came to the Darkness until eventually the
Darkness devoured their light entirely. The great tur-

reted silhouette of University College that normally rose beyond the common was not black enough on this night to show against the starless sky.

Roland looked at his watch. Eleven forty-six. Fourteen minutes.

"Why," he'd asked Evan that afternoon, *"can't we go there early, like maybe before the sun sets, call up this goddess, explain the whole thing, go home, and let her handle it?"*

Evan's answer, as it often was, had been another question. "And will we ask a goddess to wait on our convenience?" This question he'd answered himself. "No. We will call her when we need her." He'd smiled at Roland's disgusted expression. "There is a maxim from the old ways that has carried over into the new; the gods help those who help themselves."

"Fortune cookie platitudes again," Roland had snorted.

Tipping his chair back, Evan had swung one booted foot up onto the kitchen table. "Some of those fortune cookies are pretty smart."

They walked toward the Circle; Rebecca holding Evan's hand, Roland holding Rebecca's. The contact helped, made it possible to keep putting one foot in front of the other, even knowing what waited at the end of the road. As they moved closer to the Darkness, the sounds of a busy city at night began to fade until they traveled in a silence unbroken except for the soft silver chime of Evan's bracelets. They didn't speak. It had all been said.

"So, uh, Evan, what's the Dark One going to be doing while I'm singing?"

"Trying to stop you."

Roland had suspected he knew the answer before he'd asked. He'd been right. "And you'll be?"

"Protecting you."

"I'm not doubting you or anything, but can you?"

Evan had smiled sadly. "I cannot defeat him, the balance has shifted too far for that, but I should be able to distract him long enough for you to finish the song. And then it will be out of our hands."

They walked around the Circle for a short distance, avoiding the actual area of the Dark Gate, and stepped onto the grass under the bordering arc of oaks.

Something rustled softly and Roland felt a gentle touch against his hair. He looked up. The tree branch above him was empty of littles and there wasn't a breath of air to move it. He shot a glance at his companions, but they seemed unaffected so he shrugged and let it be. Now didn't seem to be the time to start worrying about trees.

As they moved closer to the center of the common, the Darkness became almost a physical presence, oozing out from the place where blood had been spilled and swirling about their ankles, reaching misty tendrils toward their knees, climbing a little higher with every pass.

"Back," Evan growled. "This world is not yet yours." He spread his arms and except for the seething mass which marked the sacrifice, the common cleared.

"That's better," Roland said approvingly. Then he noticed that the rest of the world, the world outside the Circle, seemed separated from them by a barrier of smoked glass. He could see through it, but not well, and buildings were hazy and unreal.

Eleven fifty-seven.

"Uh, Evan," Roland put the guitar case on the grass and unsnapped the clasps, "as I never saw this song before this morning, what if I screw up?"

Evan clasped him lightly on the shoulder, his grip a reassurance, but all he said was, "Don't."

"Don't," Roland repeated. "Right." He lifted Patience out of the case and swung the strap around his shoulders as he stood. *Four verses, two choruses, and a Dm to a F change. Why me?*

Because you're all they have, said the little voice in his head.

Evan took Rebecca's face between his hands and looked deep into her eyes. "Thou hast my heart, Lady. Keep it safe."

Rebecca sighed, bit her lower lip to stop its quivering, and placed her hands over his. "I love you, too, Evan."

Roland waited for the clinch, but it never came, only a soft kiss and a parting. Moisture rose in his eyes and he blinked furiously to clear them. When he could see again, the Adept stood before him. Everything he wanted to say—good luck, be careful, kick ass—seemed too trite, so he only nodded once and hoped Evan would understand.

Evan nodded once in return.

"You have come to meet your destruction. How . . . noble."

He wore a black velvet robe that absorbed what little light remained. Behind him, the gate continued to grow.

As Evan turned to face the Dark Adept, his expression changed and he looked, just for that instant of turning, heartbreakingly sad. In the few seconds it took for Roland to understand, Evan had moved too far away for the Bard to stop him.

"He thinks he's going to die out there!" Roland whirled to face Rebecca who watched Evan with a kind of yearning desperation.

She sniffed. "I know."

"We can't just let him . . ."

"We have to let him."

"But there must be something we can do!"

"There is." She wiped her nose on her sleeve, never taking her eyes from Evan. "Sing."

The gate was taller than both the Adepts who stood before it, ten or twelve feet wide, and still growing.

His heart in his throat, Roland strummed the first chord, knowing as he did, he condemned Evan. The Dark Adept had no need to fight until the music gave him reason. Weighing Evan against the world, the world almost lost, but he forced his fingers to play on. Behind him, he could feel Rebecca listening with the single-minded intensity she brought to everything she did.

Then the Dark Adept looked past Evan, met Roland's eyes, and smiled. *You are mine,* said the smile.

*You know it, and I know it. And when this is all over,
I will claim you.*

Roland's fingers faltered. He forgot the chords. He
forgot the music. He forget everything but the Darkness. He began to tremble uncontrollably.

"Roland." Rebecca grabbed his shoulder, her fingers
digging deep into the muscles, forcing his awareness
away from the Dark Adept although he still heard her
words down the length of a long tunnel. "Evan won't
let him hurt you."

Evan.

*If he's willing to die for my world, I can damn well
sing for it.*

His fingers found the chords again. He began the
first chorus.

By the end of the second line, the Dark Adept's
complacent smile had slipped.

At the end of the third, he snarled and attacked.

The Light rose up to block him.

"Fireworks reported in the vicinity of King's College Circle. 5234, can you respond?"

PC Patton glared at the radio. "The streets have
gone crazy and they want us to check on fireworks?"
They'd spent the last hour clearing up a near riot at
Yonge and Bloor.

PC Brooks shrugged and reached for the micro-
phone. "Remember what happened the last time
someone reported fireworks in the Circle." He flipped
the switch. "5234 responding. We going in alone?"

"All other units are currently occupied, but backup
will be available if requested."

"Good. We're going in alone." PC Patton forced
the car, steering mechanism protesting, around a tight
U-turn and pushed the gas to the floor. "We've got
first shot at that bastard if he's back."

"And we'll deal with him by the book, Mary Margaret," her partner said mildly.

She bared her teeth in what might have been a smile.
"I'll make him eat the fucking book."

* * *

Evan staggered backward under a vicious strike but stopped the blow before it could get through to Roland. Roland did the only thing he could; he trusted in Evan's strength and kept singing. He didn't know if the Goddess was listening but he could feel the power building and every hair on his body stood on end. As Evan blocked another arc of black energy that left his right arm hanging useless at his side, Roland began the first verse.

> *"Eastern wind blow clear, blow clean,*
> *Cleanse my body of its pain,*
> *Cleanse my mind of what I've seen,*
> *Cleanse my honor of its stain."*

Although he'd been expecting something to happen, the touch of the wind on his left cheek almost made him miss a chord change. He turned slightly into it so he could watch what the last two lines would bring. Out of the corner of his eye, he saw the Dark Adept snarl, but neither the snarl nor the attack that followed could distract him now that the east wind had swept the tangles from his mind. He was still terrified but that didn't seem to matter anymore.

> *"Maid whose love has never ceased*
> *Bring me healing from the East."*

The Dark Adept howled.

Roland ignored him. For the east wind now brought an answer. Her hair streaming out about her, clad in a short white tunic, Daru stood just in front of Roland and slightly to the right. She faced the Darkness, her hands curled into fists at her sides. Even from the back, she didn't look like the Daru he'd known, for the power in the song was a pale copy of the power in her.

> *"Southern wind blow hot, blow hard,*
> *Fan my courage to a flame,*
> *Southern wind be guide and guard,*
> *Add your bravery to my name.*

Let my will and yours be twinned,
Warrior of the Southern wind.''

And the wind that came out of the south, smelling
of steel and blood, dressed Daru in golden armor and
hung a mighty sword at her side.

Evan collapsed to one knee, but just in time threw
his good arm up to tangle the black whip in his bracelets. Very faintly over the music came his cry of pain.

''Western wind blow stark, blow strong,
Grant me arm and mind of steel
On a road both hard and long.
Mother, hear me where I kneel.
Let no weakness on my quest
Hinder me, wind of the West.''

The wind now blew against his right cheek and Rebecca lifted her hand from his shoulder. As she walked
past him to stand beside Daru, Roland's mind worked
furiously, but no coherent thought managed to make
its way out of the shock.

Rebecca?

And the weirdest thing about it was that while Daru
had obviously taken on aspects of the Goddess, Rebecca looked just the same. Tangled curls, freckles,
big orange sweater.

So maybe the Goddess has been with her all along,
the small voice in Roland's head suggested.

Roland refused to deal with that.

Evan's head snapped back and his mouth hung open
as he fought for breath, but somehow he kept the
Darkness in its place. Light drained from a dozen
wounds.

Even before he began the last verse a chill traveled
the length of Roland's spine. Internal or external, he
wasn't sure. His back was to the north.

''Northern wind blow cruel, blow cold,
Sheathe my aching heart in ice,
Armor round my soul enfold.

Crone, I need not call you twice.
To my foes bring cold of death!
Chill me, North wind's frozen breath.''

Her black robes whipping about her in the freezing wind, Mrs. Ruth suddenly stood next to Rebecca. She no longer looked like a fat old lady, although she was still that. She no longer looked harmless.

The force of the blow lifted Evan into the air, where he writhed for an instant before falling to the ground.

And Darkness lost sight of the larger battle in its need to destroy what remained of this bit of Light.

Roland's chin came up and his eyes blazed as he gave the last chorus everything he had, throwing the song as a shield over Evan.

"Wind's four quarters, air and fire
Earth and water, hear my desire
Grant my plea who stands alone—
Maiden-warrior, Mother, and Crone.''

As the last note died away into silence, the Goddess spoke; one voice through the three mouths of her trinity.

"It is done.''

The Dark Adept, his hand still raised to deliver the final blow to the Light, laughed for the clocks had begun to ring midnight.

"Too late,'' he said.

And the Gate opened.

"Holy Mary Mother of God, Blessed Jesus, and all the saints, what the fuck is that?'' PC Patton slammed her foot down on the brake and the patrol car screamed sideways across King's College Circle until the tires of the passenger side snugged up against the curb.

She let the engine die and sat staring out the window, her knuckles white on the steering wheel.

The siren wailed for a second after the engine had quieted. PC Brooks leaned forward and switched it off. It was unlikely that anyone on the common heard.

A slab of Darkness twenty feet square stood in the center of the common, a slab so impermeable the mind insisted it was solid even when confronted with the evidence that it was not. From out of it, formed of Darkness and shaped by it, came a creature out of an addict's nightmare. As it stepped free, it rose up on powerful hind legs, its scaled body gleaming dully black, and raked the air with massive furred paws. Great curved talons shredded the night and each of its seven heads opened a fanged mouth and roared.

"They're shooting a movie here tonight, right?"

"I don't think so, Mary Margaret."

Beside it stood a man in black; at his feet lay a crumpled figure.

"That's him! The guy in the sketch! The bastard who's been carving up the city!"

"Are you sure?"

"Of course, I'm sure!"

Facing it were three women; one in golden armor, one in long black robes, and one in a big orange sweater. They looked familiar, although the eye refused to See them as individuals. They also looked at least as dangerous as the creature they faced. Behind them stood a man with a guitar.

More afraid than she'd ever been in her life, PC Patton stepped out of the car and walked around it to stand by her partner's door. Slowly he got out to join her.

"Do we call for backup?" he asked, his hand plucking at his holster.

"No."

"Then what do we do?"

She looked from the beast to the man to the women and frowned. Something big was going down, something . . . She looked at the women again and chewed her lip. "We wait," she said at last.

"Oh, shit!" Roland took an involuntary step back as the seven heads shrieked.

Mrs. Ruth muttered speculatively, Rebecca sighed, and Daru loosened her sword in its sheath.

The Dark Adept shook his head, stroking the beast lightly on one obsidian flank. "Kill it," he taunted the Maiden. "Destroy it. But the Darkness will continue to come and sooner or later you will fall and the body you wear will be killed. Without you, the rest of the One in Three is nothing." His smile was satiated as he rubbed himself up against an enormous haunch. "And you cannot close the gate, for blood was spilled to open it."

"What?" Roland so far forgot himself that he stepped forward again. "What does he mean, you can't close the gate? That's what you're here for!"

The three bodies of the Goddess turned and again three spoke as one.

"Blood is needed to cancel blood."

The Crone continued alone. "An unwilling sacrifice opened this gate, Bard. It will take a willing one to close it."

The seven heads of the beast roared again.

And Roland understood.

He was all they had.

I don't want to die.

He wet his lips and very, very carefully laid Patience on the grass.

I don't want to die.

The first step was the hardest thing he'd ever done in his life. The second and third were no easier.

You'll probably never know this, Uncle Tony, but I'm seeing a job through to the end.

He moved between Rebecca and Mrs. Ruth. Between the Mother and the Crone.

Please, don't let it hurt too much.

Then something small and heavy darted through his legs. He staggered, recovered, and saw Tom launch himself into the air, hissing and spitting.

The great front paws of the beast dragged Tom off a head that now glared from only one eye and with a single, easy motion ripped the cat in two.

As the blood splashed on the ground, the Goddess cried, "Done!"

And the Dark Gate disappeared.

"No!" screamed the Dark Adept. "It was just a cat!"

The Goddess smiled and the Dark Adept quailed before her. "There's no such thing," she said, "as just a cat."

In one fluid motion, Daru unsheathed her sword and charged, the great golden blade whistling around her head in a glittering arc.

The battle happened too quickly for Roland to follow and very little of the noise and confusion of actual blows struck by either side penetrated past the knowledge that he still lived. He picked up Patience and held her tightly, as if the familiar feel of the guitar could convince him of his continuing reality.

The beast had only two heads remaining when it finally fell. It thrashed once and faded from sight, leaving behind a stain on the grass and a stench that lingered until the east wind blew it away. The Maiden stood in the center of the stain, leaning on her sword, the golden armor dripping with dark fluids. Her teeth were bared and her eyes blazed. She threw back her head and laughed.

The Dark Adept began to back away, his entire body twisted with panic. With his eyes locked on the Goddess, he couldn't watch the ground and when his heels slammed into Evan's side, he fell. For an instant they lay face to face, the Dark Adept and the Light, then Evan, who had lain there conserving the very little strength he had left, drove a small dagger of Light into the heart of Darkness.

The Dark Adept wailed, and died.

Roland never saw Rebecca move. One moment she stood by the Crone, the next she knelt by Evan, his broken body gathered up in her arms.

His head lolled against her shoulder and although he tried, he couldn't raise his hand to touch her cheek. "Forgive me, Lady." His velvet voice had been broken as well. "I was blind."

She stroked his hair. "There is nothing to forgive."

He sighed, fighting the pain for a few seconds more

of life. "I'm glad," his eyes found hers, "you're here at the end."

"What end?" She leaned forward and kissed a pain line from his brow. "There are no ends, only beginnings. The Circle always comes around."

He managed a weak grin. "Fortune cookie platitudes," he whispered.

The Mother smiled and the world sang in response. "Perhaps," she said.

Tears streaming unheeded down his cheeks, Roland felt his heart start beating again. *I should have known she wouldn't let him die.* And when a moment later Evan stood before him, holding open his arms, Roland went to him and held him with everything he had left.

"I thought you were dead," he sobbed into the warmth of Evan's shoulder.

"I thought I was, too," Evan answered into his hair. "And then I thought you were."

"He didn't even like me."

Evan understood. "Who can say with cats. We will honor his memory, for he was a mighty warrior against the Darkness. But it's over now. We won."

"Over?" Roland pulled back a little to look into Evan's eyes. "Over?"

The Adept nodded.

"Over," Roland said yet again. Then reaction set in and his knees gave out.

Evan held him until he steadied.

"We won."

Smiling, Evan nodded.

"Then the world is balanced again?"

"No." The Crone stood before them. "The world will not be balanced until the Light returns to his place."

Evan gave Roland's shoulders one last squeeze then released him and moved to Rebecca where he dropped to one knee and bowed his head. "I would not presume to ask this, Lady, save that I gave my word to another. Would you come with me when I go?"

Roland felt as flummoxed as Evan looked when the

Goddess answered, the mouths of all three women moving with the words.

"Yes. For it will right a grievous wrong."

The Crone actually laughed at their expressions and, as Rebecca pulled Evan to his feet, said, "I suppose you want an explanation."

Evan seemed incapable of speech, so Roland forced out a single word. "Please." And, with a shudder, he hoped that it would not draw the Goddess' attention to him.

To his relief, the Crone alone began to speak. Bad enough in itself but the parts were not nearly as overwhelming as the whole.

"Only the Goddess is eternal. These bodies we wear are as mortal as any born of woman. When they die, the aspect they contain moves on. When the body of the Mother dies, the aspect moves instantly to a vessel that has just begun to menstruate. The last time this happened, it coincided with the accident that killed Rebecca's parents. The trauma brought on Rebecca's blood, the Mother needed a vessel . . . At the instant of possession the aspect is operant and the Mother is a healer. So she healed.

"Had the accident happened a week earlier, Rebecca would have died, never knowing the touch of the Goddess. Had the accident happened a week later, Rebecca would have died and the Mother would have moved to the next vessel in line. Because the accident happened at the exact moment it did," the Crone spread her arms and the sleeves of her robe flapped in the sudden chill wind like the wings of a great black crow, "Rebecca lived and the Mother was trapped in a flawed vessel, one that could neither properly contain her nor release her."

"We were drawn to her," the Maiden spoke for the first time, "to protect her."

Again the three gave voice as one.

"I am the fulcrum on which the balance depends."

Roland made a triangle with his hands, then crumpled one corner.

"That's it exactly," agreed the Crone. She turned

to Evan. "If you take the vessel with you, the Mother will be free to move on and it will not be so easy for the balance to be disturbed again."

And if the Mother moves on, Roland thought, *how much of Rebecca will be left?*

Evan didn't seem to have any doubts. "Will you come, Lady?" he asked again, but this time for himself, not for a promise.

Rebecca nodded, eyes shining. "Yes."

"Done!" said the Goddess and a shimmering curtain appeared in the air. "Return to the Light with our blessing."

"Wait!" Rebecca pulled out of Evan's grasp and spread her arms. The mangled bits that were Tom came together until a pale gray tabby with a proud white tip to his tail lay on the grass. She knelt by his side and stroked the length of his body. "Good-bye, dear friend, I'll never forget you." A silver tear splashed against the soft fur, then she held out her hands and the cat sank into the earth. "Journey safely until you find fat mice and thick cream and a loving hand always willing to scratch behind your ears."

Roland wiped his eyes and sniffed. *You don't even like cats,* he reminded himself, but the old argument had lost its force.

Rebecca took his head between her hands and pulled it down to kiss his brow. "My mark is on you," she said, "my protection and my love."

This is a Goddess, said the small voice in Roland's head.

This is Rebecca, Roland told it.

He hugged her tightly. "Be happy, kiddo."

"You, too, Roland. I think you've found your music now."

"I think so, too, kiddo."

She pulled the key to her apartment out of the front pocket of her jeans and handed it to him. "Will you take care of my plants?"

"Sure thing."

"And see the littles get their milk?"

"A bowl every night," he swore.

She smiled at him then and the whole wretched week was suddenly worth every bit of pain and terror.

She moved away and Evan took her place, gently adding his blessing to hers.

Roland took a long look—it would have to last him— and said, "I'm sorry we didn't . . ."

The silence grew as the Adept took a long look in return. Then he winked. "Maybe next time."

Next time! screamed the little voice in Roland's head. *Next time!*

Shut up, Roland told it.

Arms about each other, Evan and Rebecca stepped into the Gate and for a moment Roland thought he saw a warrior in blue and silver with a jeweled sword at his hip, a being of glory whose great white wings brushed the top of the Gate, and the Evan he had come to know, all three together in one. Then the glowing images formed over Rebecca, too, although instead of a sword she cradled a bound sheaf of wheat.

Then, just for a second, the shimmer cleared and he could see past them into the Light. He took a step and then another and then the Gate faded and Mrs. Ruth stopped him with a hand on his chest.

"Bards can See, but they can't ever go through," she explained though not unkindly. "It's one of the things that makes them Bards."

"But . . ."

"Forget it, bubba."

He looked at her, really looked at her, and saw just a fat old bag lady bulging out of an old black dress. Daru wore white shorts and a shirt, the only sign of the Maiden-warrior the cast mark on her forehead.

"It's really over," he sighed.

Mrs. Ruth snorted. "Don't you ever listen, bubba? Nothing ends. The Circle always comes around." She reached up and slapped him lightly on the cheek with one pudgy hand. "Go home. Get some sleep. Learn to play that fancy harp you've acquired. Stay out of trouble. Don't be a stranger. And you," she waved the hand at Daru, "eat more. You're too skinny."

Then she turned and waddled away.

Roland knelt to put Patience in the case and looked up to see Daru staring down at him.

"What are you going to do now?" she asked.

Roland shrugged and stood. "What she told me to do, I guess."

Daru nodded. "That's always wisest."

"So are you . . ."

"I'm just myself. By tomorrow I won't remember that I was ever anything else."

"But her?" Roland jerked his head in the direction Mrs. Ruth had taken.

"The Crone Remembers. It's part of her job." Daru sighed and stretched. "I don't know about you, but I could use some coffee."

Roland thought about it for a minute. "Yeah," he said, "me, too."

They walked across the common toward the lights of College Street and the normal sorts of strangeness found in twenty-four hour doughnut shops.

"So this, uh, Maiden thing, you don't . . ."

"No."

"Oh."

On the other side of the common, Police Constables Patton and Brooks shook themselves free of the stupor they'd been wrapped in and got back into their car. The person—or thing, they were no longer sure—responsible for at least two deaths would never be brought to trial, but Justice of a sort had been done and they were satisfied.

"We, uh, going to report this?" PC Brooks asked, tapping his fingers against the dash. His partner raised a sarcastic eyebrow and he flushed.

PC Patton thumbed the microphone switch.

"Go ahead, 5234."

"We're just leaving the Circle."

"And the fireworks?"

"The situation took care of itself. 5234, out."

She put the car into gear, and they drove away into

the darkness that was nothing more than the darkness of a summer's night.

Overhead, a creature that was not quite a squirrel ran along the hydro wires on its way to spread the news.